You're Enough, June Nelson

JESSI HANSEN

Copyright © 2024 Jessi Hansen
ISBN: 9798330439768

To anyone whose story needs a rewrite

CHAPTER ONE
The Weight of a Name

When I first started writing, everyone said I should use a pen name. "Trust us, June," they'd advise, their voices dripping with concern, maybe a tinge of condescension. "It'll hurt less when the bad reviews start rolling in, easier to keep your real self out of it."

But I never imagined my words would go anywhere. So, I sent out queries for my debut novel and put my full name on every submission, feeling a strange combination of pride and defiance. *June Nelson*. It's who I am, and I wasn't going to hide behind an alias.

Turns out, that wasn't the smartest decision.

I couldn't believe my luck with my first novel—an agent, a publisher, and real-life readers holding my book. I felt like I was walking on cloud nine. I wrote more stories, each one carrying the name June Nelson across the cover, each one making its way into the world like a piece of my heart gift wrapped between the pages of the book.

Then the bad reviews started trickling in, slowly at first, then like thick drops of rain before a storm. Words like *mediocre* and *mundane* seemed to latch onto my name. June Nelson became synonymous with disappointment.

No matter what I wrote, it wasn't enough. I wasn't enough.

Every new story felt like a ticking time bomb, each word a reminder that I have to do better, be better. I so badly wanted—*want*—to be someone extraordinary, someone whose books are talked about in coffee shops and lobbies and book clubs.

But I'm not extraordinary. I'm just June. Plain June.

"How do I look?" I ask, my voice quivering with hope, possibly a little insecurity, as I turn to Sutton Turnpot, the sandy-haired model standing at my bedroom door.

Sutton. *Sigh*. He's the whole package—an aspiring singer, a smile that could light up any room, and currently, my boyfriend. We met six months ago, and after just two dates, he moved in. I guess that's what happens when you're 34 and feeling like the clock's ticking faster than it should. I want the whole deal—marriage, kids, a family. And I'm running out of time.

"Listen, June," Sutton begins, running his hand through his artfully tousled hair, his tone already hinting at words I don't want to hear. "This has been fun, but I met someone. Two days ago, on Broadway. We collided like two stars, and I just knew—she's the one. We're in love. This is over."

"What?" The word falls out of my mouth, my brain struggling to catch up.

"I already moved my stuff out of the drawer you let me use," he says, like he's talking about something as casual as sorting socks.

He what? When?

"But... What about my book launch party tonight?" The words leak desperation as they leave my mouth. "Sissy said if this book flops, I'll need to find a new agent. I need you, Sutton. I need you tonight."

"June, didn't you hear me?" Sutton's frown deepens, his eyes narrowing as my stomach twists. "I'm in love with someone else."

I blink, trying to piece together the remnants of my shattered thoughts. "I let you live here rent-free." It comes out small, barely a whisper. "You... You owe me."

"I promised Horn I'd meet her for dinner," he says as if it's the most reasonable thing in the world.

"Horn?" My head snaps up. "What kind of name is that?"

"She's one-of-a-kind, like a unicorn," he proclaims with a dreamy smile.

"If she's one-of-a-kind, shouldn't she go by Unicorn?" I mumble, more to myself than to him.

"A unicorn is the only creature to traipse this barren land with a single horn," Sutton replies, utterly serious.

I roll my eyes at his absurdity. "Pretty sure narwhals also have a single horn. Maybe she should go by *Two-of-a-Kind*."

"June," Sutton chides, exasperation coloring his face. "I'm going to have to ask you not to talk about the love of my life that way."

"Get out," I demand, pointing to the door.

He gives me one last tight smile, the kind reserved for someone who's just handed you the wrong coffee order. "It was fun. Best of luck with your latest novel. I know you're going to need it."

As I watch him walk out, it feels like I've been hit by another wave of one-star reviews. You're dull and uninteresting, June. You're never going to write anything dazzling and brilliant. You're not a unicorn. You're not even one-of-a-kind. You're a nobody, June Nelson. A freaking nobody.

I swipe at the tears threatening to spill over and smooth down the front of my black dress. Why can't I hold onto anyone? Why does the love I write about in my books feel so impossible in real life?

Because they're stories, June. Fantasy. Not real, no matter how badly you wish they were. There's no such thing as true love. There's just... *heartache*.

My phone dings, snapping me back to reality. I don't have time to cry. My career is hanging by a thread, and I need to focus. In true June Nelson fashion, I'll save the tears for later.

News Alert: June Nelson's latest novel, *Retrospective*, misses the mark, says popular book blogger, C.R. Draper.

My heart sinks as I click on the link.

C.R. Draper. Ugh. The blogger who has been my personal nemesis since Sissy sent her a copy of my second book. She's practically made it her mission to annihilate every word I've written since.

"June Nelson professes to be a romance novelist," The Draper Diaries begins, "but her stories always seem to miss the mark, especially when it comes to executing believable love connections. Her latest novel, *Retrospective*, while decently written, is a snooze fest. The story follows a middle-aged woman reliving her life through old journals. As she reflects on fifty years of regrets, Giselle wonders what would have happened if she hadn't let the love of her life go. The story alternates between reality and redundant dream sequences, leaving the reader questioning why her agent, Sissy Barnes, is calling this a romance for the ages. Someone should tell Sissy to put it in the Horace and Morgan bargain bin where all Nelson's books inevitably end up."

"The bargain bin?" I whisper, horror and disbelief flooding me. She didn't just say that.

It's over. All of it. Once Sissy reads this review, she'll be done with me. My writing career, the one I've poured every ounce of my soul into, is officially dead. Killed by a single review.

One review.

I'm crushed. *Retrospective* was my last chance, and Draper just called it a snooze fest.

And she called out Sissy for hyping it up. That's not going to end well—for Draper.

Maybe *Retrospective* could have been a romance for the ages if I were a better storyteller. But I'm not. I'm mediocre. Mundane. Just like they all say.

I close out of the review, my career's death sentence, and dial Mom's number. I know she won't answer. She hasn't answered in years.

The phone rings, each unanswered chime a reminder of how alone I really am. Finally, her voicemail picks up, as if she's too busy to even let me down directly.

"It's Veronica!" The sound echoes through the line, bubbly as seltzer. "If it's Friday, I'm playing Bingo at the Senior Center. If it's any other day, I'm either napping by the pool or out with the gals. Leave a message after the beep, but don't hold your breath for a call back!"

The forced cheeriness of her message grates on me while I wait for the impending beep.

"Hi, Mom. It's me, June," I start, wishing she could hear the pain in my voice. "Your daughter. I know you forget sometimes. I'm calling to let you know I'm done. No more writing. It's over."

I swallow hard, forcing myself to keep going. "A big-name book blogger tore *Retrospective* apart before it even hit the shelves. I sent you an advance copy last week, but I'm sure it's collecting dust somewhere." I try to laugh, but it comes out as a broken sigh. "She called it a snooze fest,

Mom. Two stars. TWO. Now it's going to end up in the bargain bin like everything else I've ever written."

I pause, the weight of my own words heavy on my shoulders. "I don't know what to do. I thought maybe this one would be different, but it's not. It's just more proof that I'm never going to be enough for anyone."

The silence on the other end is deafening, a void where I used to wish for comfort and understanding. But Veronica Nelson left when I was ten, and I've been filling that void with words ever since. Maybe I've been trying to rewrite the story, to create a happy ending where there never was one.

It's hard to believe in fairy tales when the heroine is always left behind.

I can still see Dad, falling to his knees when we came home from soccer practice and found her goodbye note on the counter. She'd run off to Florida with some French guy named François, leaving us in a cloud of expensive vanilla perfume and broken promises. I was sure it was my fault. How could it have been Dad's? He was perfect. He was the kind of man who believed in me, who made me feel like I could be anything.

But now, standing here in my empty apartment, I feel like nothing.

"Pull it together, June," I murmur to myself, brushing away a tear. "There's a launch party to get to."

Even if Draper did call *Retrospective* a snooze fest, I owe it to myself to celebrate one last time. One last night to pretend that I'm not just a plain, mediocre writer destined for the discount bin.

I grab my purse and glance at the pile of overdue bills on the counter. I'll deal with them tomorrow, along with mourning the death of my writing career. For now, the cold, empty apartment seems to breathe a sigh of relief as I step out into the hallway. Even the walls are tired of me.

The frigid New York City air hits me like a slap to the face, and I wrap my arms around myself as the chill seeps into my bones. There have been so many times in my life when I've had to smile through the pain. Tonight is just another one of those times.

I raise my arm to hail a taxi, and to my surprise, one pulls up immediately. Maybe my luck is finally turning around. Or maybe it's just a fluke. Either way, I'm not getting my hopes up.

"5th Avenue," I tell the driver as I buckle my seatbelt and clutch my purse like a lifeline.

As we drive away, I can feel my phone vibrating incessantly in my bag. It's probably Sissy, either panicking about the Draper review or fuming because I'm late. Any other day, I'd answer. But tonight, I can't. Not yet.

"They're diverting traffic," the driver says, glancing at me in the rearview mirror.

"Why?" I ask, sitting up a little straighter.

"Beats me." He shrugs. "You might be better off walking from here."

I sigh as I pay the fare and step out into the drifting snowflakes. The city is alive around me, but I feel like I'm moving in slow motion, my heels clicking against the pavement as I weave through the gridlocked cars.

I'm already late, so what's the rush? Maybe I'll find something else to do with my life. Maybe there's a job out there that pays better and doesn't crush your soul.

But that's not what I want. I wanted to be a writer. I wanted that to be enough.

I stop in the middle of the sidewalk, staring up at the snow-filled sky. "Why?"

People walk around me, barely noticing as I stand there, questioning the universe. "What do you want from me? I never asked for much. Just one good thing. Why couldn't I have that?"

As I'm yelling at the sky, it hits me—I'm not really mad about the writing. It's Sutton. No, it's more than that. It's the loneliness, the feeling of being untethered ever since Dad died.

"Am I heading in the wrong direction?" I mutter softly. "Should I keep going?"

No answer. Just the sound of snow crunching underfoot and the distant hum of city life.

"Am I going too fast? Too slow?" I try again, feeling ridiculous for asking questions to a sky that I know can't answer.

And then, as if on cue, something flies through the air and hits me straight in the face. The word STOP looms large, inches from me as I stagger backward, arms flailing.

Stop.

I asked for a sign. Is this it?

Before I can make sense of it, I lose my balance, falling, falling, falling into the cold night air. I brace myself for the impact, for the pain that's sure to follow when I hit the ground.

But instead, I land on something unexpectedly soft and warm.

Wait. Why is it soft and warm?

CHAPTER TWO
Back in Time

Birch. Cedar. Oak. The familiar scent of wood lingers in the air, but I'm searching for something more, something sweeter. When the faintest trace of rose hits my nostrils, my eyes snap wide open.

Bright pink walls. Boy band posters. The scratchy feel of flannel beneath me.

I must be dreaming. I have to be.

The radio clicks on, blaring an obnoxious jingle that pulls me further into the dream I've found myself in. "The station with the best pop-rock music in the morning. It's DJ Sonny with Carp and Holly, coming to you live from the studio—let's get looooooooud!"

Yep. Definitely dreaming.

I reach over and instinctively slam my hand on the gray OFF button.

My eyes widen as I pull my arm back. Muscle memory kicks in. I knew exactly where to find the button, as if I've done this a thousand times.

"Pinch yourself, June," I mutter. "If it doesn't hurt, then you'll know you're dreaming."

But I won't pinch myself. Because if this is some kind of twisted dream, I'm not ready to wake up just yet. I haven't drifted back into the past and landed in my teenage bedroom. That's impossible.

Time-travel isn't real.

It can't be.

Nope.

Nope, nope, nope.

This is just a dream. One I'll wake up from any second now.

I close my eyes tight, willing myself to return to the cold, dark New York City sidewalk. But when I crack an eyelid open after what feels like forever, I'm still here.

Well, this is... unexpected.

Not sure what else to do, I roll out of bed and shuffle over to the mirror above my dresser. The girl staring back at me is someone I haven't seen in years—mousy brown hair, chocolate eyes, and a splatter of freckles across her nose.

"Hello, old friend," I whisper, running my fingers over my face, reacquainting myself with Teenage June. No forehead wrinkles. No crow's feet. No lifeless brown eyes. I'm young again—young, naive, and innocent.

Gosh, I've missed this.

Though, let's be honest, Teenage June could really use a skincare routine. Why don't I remember having so many zits?

"Focus, June," I scold myself. "We need to figure out what year it is."

I start rifling through papers, searching for a calendar or a homework assignment. But when nothing with a date turns up, I remember something important—Teenage June used to have a flip phone.

"Now, where did I keep it plugged in?"

My feet carry me around the room as I check every electrical outlet, coming up empty-handed. Then, with a sigh, I remember. Teenage June slept with her phone, just in case Dina called in the middle of the night with one of her debilitating panic attacks. I spent countless nights lying awake, listening to my best friend breathe deeply on the other end of the line, waiting for the tiniest shred of morning light to break through.

I wonder if Dina still has those panic attacks. We haven't talked since our big fight 13 years ago.

Dina Noble was my childhood best friend, and the reason 34-year-old June steers clear of friendships. People always talk about romantic relationship breakdowns, but they never tell you how hard it is to lose your best friend.

I yank the blankets off the bed, searching until I find the pale pink flip phone tangled in the flannel sheets. With a small victory cheer, I flip it open and squint. Wait—Teenage June had 20/20 vision. I don't need to squint.

There, on the screen, is today's date: December 5, 2007. I've traveled 17 years back in time.

17 years. It feels like a lifetime.

I stare at the phone in my hand, emotions rushing through me. Why this date? Why did I fall back in time to December 5th?

"You're dreaming, June," I remind myself.

But what if I'm not? What if this is my chance to do things differently? What if the universe is giving me a do-over? A chance to make better decisions, to right a few wrongs?

I wasn't so insecure until Mom left. I didn't constantly fear scaring people off until she disappeared. Until I started tearing myself down in the mirror every day, numbing myself to the guilt. Until that day in my twenties when I decided to stop filling my head with negative thoughts and started burying the pain of Mom's abandonment with avoidance.

But now, I'm here. What if I came back to help myself? What if I'm supposed to help Teenage June figure out who she is so we don't have to struggle so much in college—in our early-twenties? I could show her how to push forward. I could make sure she spends more time with Dad before his car accident. I could help her chase her dream of becoming President of the Bloomford High Book Club.

I could do things differently.

I could change our destiny here and now.

I could—

"June!" A shrill voice cuts through my thoughts. It's Lily, my stepmom. The woman whose rose spray replaced my mother's expensive vanilla perfume when she and Dad got married when I was 14.

"Coming!" I yell back, apprehensive. I can't remember the last time I saw Lily. Was it at Dad's funeral when I was 23?

If I'm being honest, I haven't thought about her much since that explosive fight we had when she sold the house four months after Dad's death. She got rid of all his belongings without even asking me if I wanted anything.

Lily Nelson made my teenage years hard and unbearable. She made my twenties hard and unstable. And I didn't let her make it to my thirties.

I smooth down my reindeer pajamas before reaching for the door. There's a lot of June Nelson history in these thin, papery walls. History I'm not sure I'm ready to deal with just yet. But I have to. If I'm going to help Teenage June, I have to face the one person who made it impossible to love my younger self.

My bare feet sink into the tan carpet as I walk down the hallway, passing Dad and Lily's wedding photos on the wall. I'm either absent from the pictures or hidden behind something. Lily never liked that I was mousy and timid. She was always embarrassed by me, embarrassed that I didn't put as much time and effort into my appearance as she did.

I shouldered a lot of hurt from her snide remarks over the years. Sometimes, I think I still do.

Looking back, I think she believed that if people were laughing at me, they weren't looking at her. Lily carried around a lot of shame. For what, I couldn't possibly guess.

"Breakfast is on the table," Lily calls out as she hears my feet pad across the yellow-and-cream checkered linoleum.

I glance down at half a pomegranate sitting alone on a white plate and roll my eyes. "I'm not eating that."

Lily pauses, her long blond hair swishing against her back as she turns to face me. She's wearing a bright pink velour tracksuit, sudsy plate still in hand.

"What did you say?" Her blue eyes widen in surprise.

I clear my throat, standing a little straighter. "I'm not going to eat that."

"Is this some ploy to get money from your dad so you can grab fast food on your way to school?" she asks, as if she's caught me in some elaborate scheme.

"If it was," I say, crossing my arms over my chest, "I don't see how that's any of your business."

"June," she narrows her eyes, her tone slipping into that all-too-familiar warning. "Watch your attitude."

"Or what?" I tap my foot impatiently on the floor, feeling a surge of confidence that I haven't felt in years.

I can't believe I'm arguing with Lily. I can't believe I'm letting her get under my skin like she used to.

"Or you'll lose your phone," she threatens, as if that's supposed to scare me.

I tilt my head, curiosity getting the better of me. "In what universe is half a pomegranate considered a sensible breakfast for a teenage girl?"

"It's what I eat for breakfast," Lily replies, raising her pencil-thin blond eyebrows.

"It's 72 calories. That's practically starvation." I scoff, watching as Lily's mouth drops open in shock.

"I'm just trying to help you, June," her tone softens, but the sting of her words remains. "You could be so pretty if you'd just lose ten pounds."

I nod slowly, feeling the strain of her words settle in my chest. "I've never heard of anyone losing weight because someone tried starving them. I know I'm not as skinny as you, Lily, but you don't have to rub it in my face every day. And stop pretending that half a pomegranate is going to fix me. Stop trying to make me look like you. I'm not you, Lily. I never will be."

Lily's face crumples and I can hear someone clear their throat behind me.

"June Gloom." His deep voice fills the kitchen, and I freeze. It's been over a decade since I heard it, a decade of feeling lost, orphaned, and alone.

I turn slowly, my heart pounding in my chest. "Dad."

Tears well up in my eyes as I take in the sight of him standing there, alive and well, right in front of me. It's like a dream I never dared to hope for.

"What's going on?" He tilts his head, concern etched on his face.

My pulse races and my hands tremble. One tear slips out, then another. I don't even think—I just run to him, throwing my arms around his neck and inhaling the familiar scent of wood.

"Daddy," I whisper, the words cracking with emotion. I can't believe he's really here. I've missed him so much.

"June," Dad exhales, hugging me tight. "What's wrong?"

"It's my fault," Lily speaks up. "I'm sorry, Bud. I upset her. I didn't mean to. I was just trying to help."

Dad gently pulls away from me, his hands resting on my shoulders. "Go get ready for school, June. Dina will be here soon."

I swallow hard, trying to keep my emotions in check. "Okay."

"I'm... s-sorry, June," Lily stammers, stepping forward. "I'll get you some money for breakfast."

I nod, wiping away the tears staining my cheeks, and head down the hall. Once I'm safe inside my room, I shut the door and lean against it, overwhelmed by everything that just happened.

A waterfall of tears spills down my face as I cover my mouth with my hand, trying to stifle the sobs. I didn't realize how much I missed Dad until now. Losing Mom was heartbreaking, but losing Dad? That was earth-shattering.

There's a quiet knock. "June?"

I take a deep breath and wipe away the remnants of my tears.

When I open the door, Dad is standing there, looking worried. "Are you okay?"

"I'll be fine," I manage to say, forcing a small smile.

Dad hands me a twenty-dollar bill. "I'm sorry about what happened back there. Lily feels bad."

I shrug, taking the money. "I just want to get ready for school."

"I know the two of you butt heads," Dad says, "but she loves you."

The lump in my throat burns as I force myself to nod. "Dina will be here soon."

"And June," Dad sticks his head into my room, his eyes shining with pride, "you're perfect the way you are. You know that, right?"

My heart swells as he runs a hand over my head, and I blink back fresh tears. Teenage June needed to hear that. 34-year-old June needs to hear it even more. "I know, Dad."

"You're enough, June Nelson," he declares with conviction. "You're enough."

My lower lip trembles as his words sink in. "I love you, Dad."

"I love you, too." He smiles, then brightens as he remembers something. "Is today the big vote for President of the Book Club?"

I inhale sharply, the memory crashing over me. December 5, 2007. The day I lost the presidency to Cheyenne Radcliff.

"Yeah," I reply hoarsely. "I think so."

"You're going to get it," Dad says with a confident grin. "I can feel it."

But I didn't get it. I lost to Cheyenne by three votes.

Unless… Unless I can change those three votes.

"I have to get ready," I tell Dad, taking a moment to memorize the laugh lines around his brown eyes. I've missed the sound of his voice. I've missed everything about him.

"Right." He backs out of the doorway, giving me a triumphant grin. "You're going to win, June. I just know it."

"I hope so," I reply, shutting the door and searching for an outfit.

A horn blares in the driveway just as I find my favorite sweater.

Dina Noble is officially here to pick me up.

Gulp.

CHAPTER THREE
Ghosts of Friendships Past

I nervously stare out the window at the boxy green van parked in the driveway. My heart beats like a drum, each thud adding to the anxiety I'm feeling. The last time Dina and I spoke, it ended so badly that I've never really recovered.

In the present, I don't have friends—other than my agent, Sissy Barnes. I tell myself it's because I'm too busy, but, deep down, I know the truth. I'm still not over losing my best friend.

It was my fault. Of course, it was my fault. Dina didn't do anything wrong. She always did the right thing, which is one of the many reasons we were so close. But it's also the reason why our friendship ended. Dina always does the right thing. No exceptions.

Taking a deep breath, I head outside, excitement and unease battling for space in my chest. My heart pounds harder with each step, each one bringing me closer to the one person who used to know me better than I knew myself.

Just when I think I can't handle the tension anymore, the driver's side window rolls down, and Dina sticks her blond head out. "Why are you walking so freaking slow?"

My face breaks into a wide smile. "I'm having a moment."

Dina points an accusatory finger at me, her eyes narrowing in mock annoyance. "You're going to make us late!"

The tension drains out of me as I grab the car door handle, a laugh floating up from somewhere deep inside.

"Are you ready for the history test third period?" she asks, raising a curious eyebrow as I slide into the van.

"Um..." I trail off, just realizing how unprepared I am. "No."

"What about our presentation in psych?" she presses, her voice full of Dina Noble determination.

I shake my head, feeling a bit like I'm drowning.

"Your acceptance speech for when you win Book Club President?" She looks at me expectantly.

I scratch the side of my face, worry coursing through me like a deer caught in headlights. "I'm prepared for none of it."

Dina's eyes widen as she reaches over to touch the back of her hand to my forehead. "Are you sick?"

"Nope." I click my tongue as I buckle my seatbelt. "I'm perfectly fine."

"Did you get hit in the head by one of Lily's pomegranates and get a concussion?" Dina asks, half-joking but fully concerned.

"I didn't." I chuckle, appreciating her effort to make light of the situation.

"Then what's wrong with you?" she implores, each word laced with worry. Her ocean-blue eyes search mine, trying to read the thoughts I'm not saying out loud.

I take a deep breath. Should I tell her? I mean, I have to, right? She's going to figure it out. This is Dina we're talking about—nothing gets past her.

"I need to tell you something." I clear my throat, trying to steady my trembling fingers. "But you can't freak out."

"I'm freaking out, June," she says, her eyes widening with anticipation.

"Uh..." How am I supposed to convince my best friend that I'm 34 years old and somehow ended up in the past after a freak accident involving a traffic sign?

"Are you dying?" Dina blurts out, her face paling.

"No." I lick my lips nervously. "I'm from the future."

"The future?" She raises her eyebrows in curious disbelief.

"Yes." I nod. My heart races as I wait for her reaction.

Dina studies me carefully, her eyes narrowing. "What's my favorite food?"

"That's a trick question," I exhale, relieved that she's testing me. "You love coffee, which you claim is a main food group."

"Dang it." She snaps her fingers, a grin tugging at the corners of her mouth. "That's correct."

"Anything else?" I ask, hoping to reassure her.

"Who was my crush in 5th grade?" she quizzes, leaning forward, her eyes locked on mine.

"You mean your celebrity crush or your weird crush on Linc Hunt's older brother, Jed?"

She tilts her head, her expression shifting to surprise. "I never told you about Jed. How did you know?"

"Because I'm your best friend, Dina Noble. I know everything about you. You could ask me anything, and I'd know the answer," I reply with a small smile. "You also drank a little too much at a frat party in college and told me about Jed."

"He's not that weird," she mumbles, looking a bit defensive.

"He brought his pet pigeon to school in his backpack when we were in elementary school," I remind her with a grimace. "He was weird."

I watch as Dina tries to process everything I'm saying, her mind working through the impossible. For some reason, I think she believes me.

"My 17th birthday is tomorrow," she says, tapping her chin with her finger. "What do my parents get me?"

"A baby blue Volkswagen Beetle," I reply without hesitation.

"Ken and Alicia would never." She waves me off with a flick of her wrist.

"They do," I insist, knowing what's coming. "You'll see first thing tomorrow morning."

"They can't afford it." Dina shrugs as if that settles it.

"Your dad got a huge bonus a few weeks ago after closing a big deal," I explain, pursing my lips. "He buys you the car with it."

Dina's eyes narrow, and I can see the gears turning in her mind. "What am I like in the future?" she asks.

I swallow hard, not sure how to answer. "Um... I don't know."

"Do I die?" she gasps dramatically.

"No." I hold up a hand to calm her down. "You're alive. It's just that we're not that close in the future."

"Why not?" Dina frowns, her voice filled with hurt. "Why aren't we glued at the hip, June?"

I bite my lower lip, the memories of our fallout flashing in my mind. "We... drifted apart in college," I say, the lie heavy on my tongue. I'm not ready to tell her the real reason. I'm not sure I'll ever be ready.

Tears fill Dina's eyes, and I can see the heartbreak written all over her face. "I can't even right now."

"You're a teacher," I reveal, trying to shift the conversation to something positive.

"Am I married?" she sniffles, wiping away a tear.

"Yeah, but I've never met your husband. We lost touch before then"

"Do I have children?" she continues her interrogation.

"Last I heard," I smile, "you were expecting number five."

"FIVE KIDS?!" she nearly yells, her eyes wide with shock.

"Five," I confirm with a nod.

"That's crazy, June. I just... I can't imagine a future without you in it." She reaches for my hand and squeezes it tight, her touch grounding me in the moment. "We've been best friends since preschool."

"We're both happy." I force a smile, the lie burning in my throat. "Really happy." But the truth is, I'm not happy in the future. Not even close. I can't bring myself to tell her that, though. Not now. Not when she's looking at me with so much hope.

Dina wipes another tear off her cheek. "Are you married? Do you have a job? Kids?"

"I'm not married," I say, pressing my lips together. "But I am a published author."

"Shut up!" she squeals, her face lighting up. "An author? June, that's always been your dream!"

"I'm not a great one, though," I admit, chewing on the inside of my cheek.

"I doubt that." Dina beams, her eyes shining with pride. "You've always wanted your books in Horace and Morgan bookstores. They're there, right?"

In the bargain bin.

"They are, but there's this book blogger who's trying to end my career," I confess. "I think they might be right about the kind of writer I am."

"Why?" Dina shakes her head, not understanding. "What kind of writer are you?"

"I write romance stories, but I'm pretty unlucky in love," I divulge with a shrug. "I'm a fraud."

"June," Dina says firmly, "you are the most amazing writer I've ever known, and I know Future Dina has bought every book you've ever written."

I want to believe her. I want to believe that somewhere in the present, Dina Noble-Peterman has all my books on a bookshelf, reading each one with delight. But the memory of our last conversation—the hurt in her voice, the finality of her words—makes it hard to breathe.

I don't ever want to see you again, June Nelson! How could you? How could you do that to him? How could you break his heart so carelessly? He... He's loved you for years. He loved you when no one else knew you existed. He loved you when you didn't even like yourself. No one, I mean no one, is ever going to love you the way he did. I can't believe you're being so selfish. Go back there and fix this. I don't even know you anymore. I don't think I can be friends with someone like you. Someone who chooses substance over heart. You always said you'd never turn into Lily, but you have. You have, June.

The painful memory makes it hard to breathe. Even harder to watch as Teenage Dina blindly cheers me on.

I've done a lot of horrible things in my life, but that night, *that night* takes the cake.

"How did you get here?" Dina's question pulls me from the tangled web of memories.

I smile sadly. "I asked the universe for a sign. The last thing I remember is getting hit in the head by a stop sign."

Dina bursts into laughter. "A literal sign sent you back?"

"It would appear so," I say, trying to match her lighthearted tone.

"Your life must be so glamorous," Dina gushes, her eyes sparkling with admiration. "Your words in print, read by people all over the world."

"Glamorous isn't the word I would use," I admit, swallowing the lump in my throat. "It's more late-night editing sessions in my robe and endless emails."

"Sounds glamorous to me," Dina grins. "You write meaningful, thoughtful words that people actually read, June. They read them."

Well, when she puts it that way, it almost sounds magical.

I clear my throat, needing to shift the conversation. "What are we going to do about my speech?" I ask, steering us away from the too-bright picture Dina has painted of my life.

"If you're from the future," Dina shrugs, "then you already know if you won."

"I didn't win," I admit, the memory still stinging. "I lost by three votes. Kira Campbell, Johnny Williams, and Jose Martinez were the swing votes. We have to convince them to vote for me instead."

Dina gnaws on her lower lip, thinking it over. "We can talk to Kira in psych and Jose at lunch. Johnny's going to be tough, though. He seriously hates your guts."

Ah, Johnny Williams. He asked me to the homecoming dance two years ago, and I said no. Ever since, he's decided we're mortal enemies.

"I know." I sigh, already dreading that conversation.

"We'll figure it out," Dina declares with a determined nod. She reaches behind her for her backpack, rummages through it, and tosses her notebook at me. "Start studying.

You focus on history, and I'll get us through our psych presentation. We'll work on your speech during lunch."

"Sounds like a plan."

"Oh, and June," Dina scrunches her nose, "can I ask you one more question about the future?"

"Anything," I say, bracing myself.

"Does Patrick's band make it?"

Patrick Noble. Dina's older brother and my first love. Except she doesn't know that last part yet.

"I don't know," I answer truthfully as my palms begin sweating.

"Why not?" Dina frowns, clearly puzzled.

"After graduation, I moved to New York," I explain, my voice surprisingly steady. "I heard through the grapevine that Patrick went back to school for architecture, but I don't know if anything came of it."

"But, like," Dina persists, "you'd know if he made it. He'd be selling out stadiums and gracing the covers of magazines."

"In the future," I shake my head, "there are lots of different ways to make it. People don't have to land record deals for their music to be heard. There are all kinds of social media platforms that let artists deliver their art directly to fans without a middleman. So, there's still a chance he's a big deal out there somewhere."

"The future sounds so..." Dina trails off, her tone full of wonder.

"Scary?" I offer.

"Great." Dina sighs dreamily. "You're a writer. I'm a teacher, and apparently, I'm very happily married with five kids. Are you sure?"

"I'm positive."

Dina puts the van in reverse and looks over her shoulder as she backs out of the driveway. "I wonder if I still have panic attacks in the future. Maybe I've outgrown them."

"Maybe," I say softly, hoping it's true.

"Maybe I've healed from that trauma, you know?" she muses wistfully. "Maybe I've figured out how to deal with what happened to me."

Four years ago, Dina was riding her bike home from my house when a stray dog chased her. It eventually caught up to her and bit her leg. She had to get three stitches, a tetanus shot, and two weeks of antibiotics. It was super traumatic for her.

After that, Dina's anxiety skyrocketed. Even driving alone terrifies her now. That's why she picks me up every day—we're in this together.

"It gets better in college," I encourage her, trying to offer some comfort. "You start seeing a different therapist."

"I don't want to talk about it anymore." She purses her lips as she drives through the neighborhood. "I want to focus on how awesome my life turns out."

"It does," I assure her, my heart aching as I say the words. "It really does turn out awesome."

Dina sits beside me, full of hope, and I can't help but feel that hope suffocating me. I don't know if her anxiety is better in the future, but I have faith that she's figured it out. Dina has always been strong—she survived a vicious dog attack and came out the other side. I should tell her that.

Instead, I bite my tongue as we approach Bloomford High. The place that tore me down and left me a shell of who I once was.

When we pull into the parking lot, I take a moment to breathe. This place was a nightmare for me, but Dina made it bearable. At the end of the day, isn't that what we all need? One friend—one person—who reminds us who we are when we've forgotten.

I unbuckle my seatbelt just as someone opens the passenger door. When I glance up, I'm met with a pair of large navy eyes staring back at me.

Patrick Noble.

In the flesh.

CHAPTER FOUR
The Overtones of First Love

"Hi," he says, and suddenly, years of memories flood my mind, crashing over me in nostalgic waves. Moments. Sweet snippets in time. Reminders that once upon a time, June Nelson's life was a lot like a romance novel.

But instead of choosing happily ever after, I chose me. I became the villain in my story. In Patrick's. And in Dina's.

"Hi," I manage to reply, my breath catching in my throat. I don't remember him being this... breathtaking. I can't recall the sun ever dancing across his face like it is now, casting brilliant rays of golden light. Or the way his dark, black hair falls effortlessly across his forehead. His piercing navy eyes are as deep as the jeans I'm wearing. The soft dimple on his left cheek as he tries—and fails—to hide a smile. My heart aches, an old wound reopening.

"Careful," Patrick licks his lips, his voice teasing, "or Dina might catch you drooling."

Heat rushes to my cheeks, and I quickly glance down at the blacktop as I step out of the van.

Did an 18-year-old just make me blush?

Not just any 18-year-old, June. *18-year-old Patrick.*

I force myself to look at him again, trying hard not to give myself away. But his words, those words from so long ago, rush back like a favorite song I can't forget.

You are the most beautiful person I've ever met, June. I love your laugh.

Patrick loved me—really loved me. The kind of love I can't stop writing about. The kind of love I've spent the last

13 years searching for in every passing face, every heartbeat, every half-hearted connection.

And now, standing here in front of him, I know exactly why I haven't found it yet. I already did.

"Go away!" Dina groans as she rounds the van, finding her brother standing way too close to me.

"You parked next to me." Patrick shrugs casually, closing my door with a thud.

"Literally everyone in this school drives a silver sedan," Dina chuffs. "How was I supposed to know I parked next to yours?"

Patrick's sweatshirt-covered arm grazes mine, and I feel a shiver run down my spine. Goosebumps irritatingly erupt across my skin.

"You wear contacts," he retorts, pointing to the *Crowing At Midnight* band logo on his back window. "And this? This is hard to miss."

Patrick has a point—the blocky letters and the image of a black crow in flight cover most of the glass.

"Isn't that, like, a traffic violation?" Dina crosses her arms over her chest, narrowing her eyes at her older brother.

"Nope," Patrick says, standing firm.

"Can you even see out the back?" Dina continues. "How are people supposed to feel comfortable in the backseat when they can't even look out the back window?"

"What happens in the back seat of my car is none of your business," he replies with a grin.

Dina rolls her eyes dramatically. "You're disgusting."

"So are you." Patrick flashes his eyebrows at her.

"Am not."

"Are too," Patrick quips. "I read your diary. Jed Hunt? Really?"

"You did not!" Dina stomps her foot, her face flushing with embarrassment.

"Oh, but I did." Patrick laughs, clearly enjoying her reaction.

"Well, at least I didn't kiss Cheyenne Radcliff," Dina huffs, crossing her arms even tighter.

"It was Spin the Bottle," Patrick defends himself. "Not like I had much of a choice."

"Anyway," I interrupt, trying to diffuse the sibling tension, "we have to get going, Dina. Remember? Our history test? Our psych presentation?"

Dina growls lowly at her brother. "I'll see you at dinner."

"Not if I see you first," Patrick rasps, making eye contact with me before he steps around us and heads toward campus.

Siblings. I always wanted at least one.

"Can you believe him?" Dina grumbles as we start walking.

I sigh. "Yeah, he's... totally lame."

"Lame?" Dina scrunches her face in disbelief. "I hope they're still not saying that in the future."

"Not really," I admit, nudging her with my shoulder. She smiles, and I feel a little better. "But on occasion, I accidentally blurt out 'Oh, snap!' and I get a few eye rolls."

"I wonder why you're here, June," Dina frowns, her expression thoughtful.

Me too, Dina. Me too.

"Maybe it has something to do with the Book Club President vote today?" I offer, grasping at straws.

Dina exhales heavily. "But are you supposed to change things for yourself while you're here? Or are you supposed to re-learn some monumental teenage lesson and keep everything the same?"

"I have no idea," I admit, scratching the side of my face.

"What's being in love like?" Dina blurts out, then covers her mouth, as if she didn't mean to say it out loud. "I didn't mean to… that just came right out."

"You'll find out in two years," I tease.

Dina smacks her lips. "I do? Who do I fall in love with?"

I hesitate. What if the purpose of my return is to re-learn a monumental teenage lesson? What if I tell Dina something and it alters the future?

"I don't know." I side-eye her, trying to be careful. "What if I'm not supposed to tell you?"

"You already told me I'm an elementary school teacher expecting my fifth child in the future," she points out, her logic unassailable. "What's one more piece of information?"

I clear my throat. "You fall in love with a hot football player in college. Except he's not like a regular football player. He likes to read and write poetry. You win him over with your wit and charm, and he charms you with the written word."

"That sounds so romantic," Dina says, doing a happy dance beside me. "What's his name?"

"Beau Blaze," I reply.

"Oh, he has a super hot name."

"The hottest," I agree, smiling at her excitement.

"You said you don't know the guy I'm married to." Dina's eyebrows knit themselves together. She never misses a thing. "So that means I'm not married to Beau Blaze. Why don't we work out?"

I shrug, trying to play it off. "I have no idea. You were still dating him when we stopped talking."

"Are you planning on telling me why we stop talking?" Dina presses, her eyes narrowing slightly.

"Nope."

"I can't keep us from breaking up, June, if you don't give me anything to go on," she argues. "I need to salvage our friendship, and you're making it very difficult not to."

"Listen, Deen," I raise my eyebrows, trying to sound wise, "sometimes things don't work out. It's not anyone's fault; it's just... life."

"You have 34 years of life experience, and that's the answer you're giving me?" she asks, incredulous.

I shake my head. "This is going to sound backward, but the older I get, the less I feel I know about the world. Everything gets more confusing with each passing year."

Dina lets out a defeated groan. "There's nothing you could do that would make me want to stop being friends with you."

"Let's focus on getting through today," I suggest, trying to keep us on track. "Then, we'll figure out our friendship, okay?"

"Fine," Dina grunts, clearly frustrated.

"That's the spirit." I give her a thumbs-up, and she rolls her eyes.

Dina loops her arm through mine and pulls me in the direction of the library. As we walk through the halls, old fears start bubbling up, fears I thought I'd left behind. The name-calling, the insults, the endless bullying.

You're enough, June Nelson. You're enough.

Dad's words from earlier this morning play on a loop in my head, a broken record of reassurance. Words I desperately needed when I was 17. Words I need even more now at 34.

We find an empty oval table near the stacks of books and settle in, pulling out our binders. As I flip through pages of notes, my fingers trace over the little doodles I'd drawn in the margins—flowers, trees, tiny houses. I used to spend so much time lost in my head, daydreaming in class because my real life felt too sad, too heartbreaking to face.

I wanted my mom, but she wasn't interested in being a mother. I wanted my family to stay together, even though I knew that was never going to happen. I wanted Lily to stop reminding me how much she didn't like me. I wanted to feel worthy of good things. But I didn't. I never felt worthy of anything good, especially not a relationship with someone who saw my worth. I self-sabotaged back then, and I'm still doing it now, 17 years later.

Why?

Maybe that book blogger, C.R. Draper, was onto something. Maybe I struggle to write believable love connections because I'm afraid to write something real and raw. I'm afraid to tell the world that we mess up in love. We mess up big time, especially when we're young and wounded.

Why didn't I write that in *Retrospective*? Why didn't I write something honest, something that could be considered a romance for the ages?

I spend so many hours agonizing over character choices and growth, but I haven't changed in years. I haven't made wise decisions or grown myself. I'm still the same fraud I was the night I told Patrick it was over.

"Are you okay?" Dina's eyes soften as she notices the tear slipping down my cheek.

I shake my head, wiping it away. "No."

"Do you want to talk about it?" Her eyes are wide with concern, watching me closely.

There are things a 17-year-old can't understand. It's not that Dina isn't smart or capable, but she hasn't lived through what I have. She hasn't spent decades hurting herself internally the way I have.

"The presentation is in 45 minutes," I say, checking the time on my pink flip phone. "We need to use this free period to figure out how I'm going to pull this off."

"How *we're* going to pull this off," Dina corrects me, her determination shining through.

I read through my history notes while Dina jots down bullet points on index cards for our presentation.

History has always been a tough subject for me. I know it's important—of course, it's important. But I'd much rather be reading *The Great Gatsby* than memorizing analytical data on the Prohibition era. I remember stories—beautifully transcribed words on a page—better than I do a list of dates.

Focus, June. You have to focus!

The minutes tick by agonizingly slowly until Dina interrupts my thoughts. "How's it going?"

I blow out a tired breath. "Not great."

"It's one test," she says, giving me a tight smile. "If you flunk, you flunk."

"Thank you for that," I exhale, tilting my head. "But I pride myself on my B average GPA. I'd like to maintain it, even if I am from the future."

Dina props her elbow on the table and rests her chin on her hand. "Do grades really matter that much?"

"In the grand scheme of things?" I ask, echoing her thoughts.

She nods.

"I guess it depends on how you look at it," I continue. "I have an English degree, but my certificate doesn't say Harvard on it. It lacks prestige."

"Look at you, though." Dina inhales sharply. "You didn't need Harvard to be a successful writer."

I shake my head. "I guess not."

"You made your own way in the world, June."

"Success," I begin, but then I trail off.

"Success what?" Dina prompts, her curiosity piqued.

"Success can have lots of different meanings," I say as I close my notebook, knowing I won't be memorizing anything else this morning.

"What does it mean to you?" Dina challenges, her eyes locked on mine.

I chew on the inside of my cheek, thinking it over. "I used to think success was being pretty and getting a publishing deal. Now, I think it looks more like liking the person you see in the mirror first thing in the morning."

Dina's face lights up. "No wonder you're famous in the future, June. You're so smart."

I blink slowly, a small smile tugging at my lips. "You have to stop going on and on about how great you think I am in the future, or I will lose it."

"Fine." Dina sits up straight and hands me the index cards. "You'll be talking about Pavlov's theory."

"Excellent," I say, high fiving the air. "I'm practically an expert on the concept of associative learning. I did a ton of research on it when I wrote my second novel, *Midnight Crown*."

"Huh." Dina purses her lips, a thoughtful expression crossing her face.

"What?"

"Oh, nothing." She brushes off, but then hesitates. "It's just that... No, I... No."

"What?" I ask again, more curious this time.

"*Midnight Crown* kind of sounds like Patrick's band *Crowing At Midnight*."

I nervously tuck a strand of hair behind my ear. "And?"

"And if I didn't know any better, June Nelson, I might think they're connected somehow."

"*Midnight* is a popular word," I snap, a little too quickly. "Patrick and his band don't own it."

"Okay," Dina caves, hiding a smile with a smirk.

"What now?"

"You're just a little defensive, that's all."

"Sorry," I apologize, feeling a bit sheepish. "It's been a weird day for me. My boyfriend broke up with me in the future, and I got a bad review on my latest release. Then, I ended up here. In the past."

"Your boyfriend broke up with you?" Dina gasps. "Why?"

Sutton Turnpot, you slick, greasy weasel.

"He fell in love with someone else," I explain, trying to keep my voice from breaking.

"I'm so sorry, June."

"It's alright." I hitch a shoulder, chewing on the inside of my cheek. "It wasn't meant to be."

The bell rings, signaling the start of what's sure to be an interesting day.

"You ready for this?" Dina asks, pushing her chair back and standing up.

"I'm ready to kick this presentation in the—er, butt. Let's kick it in the butt."

Dina laughs, her eyes sparkling. "I like you, 34-year-old June. You're everything I hoped you'd be when you were old."

Old?

Did Dina just call me old?

CHAPTER FIVE
The Price of Being President

"And that's why associative learning is a prime example of how behavior can be conditioned over time," I conclude as I glance out at a classroom full of peers who look less than interested in Pavlov's Theory of Classical Conditioning.

Mrs. Steiner rises to her feet, clapping enthusiastically. "Excellent, June. Just excellent."

"Thank you." I nod, feeling a small surge of pride as Dina gives me a wink.

"Any questions?" Dina asks the class, her tone light.

"Yeah, I've got one," a voice calls from the back, and I instantly recognize the buzz-cut, jersey-wearing footballer smirking at the cheerleader beside him. My skin crawls at the sight.

What's his name again? I should know it, but I can't remember.

"What's the question, Connor?" Dina rolls her eyes, clearly unimpressed.

Connor! The quarterback of the high school football team. I should have guessed.

"Could June use some of that conditioning on herself and lose a few pounds?" Connor cracks, his words laced with malice.

Always at my expense.

The cheerleader beside him snickers, and half the class joins in.

Blood rushes to my ears, pounding like a drum as I bite down on the inside of my cheek. I didn't come back here to be the target of insults *again*. I came back for... for...

Well, I still don't know why I'm here. But I'm not going to stand here and take this like I used to.

"Why don't we test it out on you first?" I shoot back, steady and confident. "Maybe we can condition you to be a decent human being. At the very least, you might learn some manners."

Connor's eyes narrow into slits. "You look like a giant blob."

Memories of my junior year flood back—the varsity football team was the worst in Bloomford High's history.

"Ouch," I reply with a cruel smile. "That really hurt coming from someone on the lowest-ranking football team in the state."

A dramatic yawn echoes through the room, and my eyes land on Cheyenne Radcliff. With her luminous gold hair, she looks like a picture of sweetness, but I know better. She's more like a snake in sheep's clothing.

"Are you two done yet?" Cheyenne's tone drips with disdain. "We're supposed to watch a movie now that presentations are over. Isn't that right, Mrs. Steiner?"

Mrs. Steiner pushes her oval spectacles up the bridge of her nose. "Yes, yes we are. Can you get the lights, Cheyenne?"

Dina and I exchange a look before we trudge back to our seats. No matter how the presentation went, the real focus of this class period is convincing Kira Campbell to vote for me for President of the Bloomford High Book Club.

"Switch seats with me," I whisper-yell at Dina, who happily complies.

I plop down at Dina's desk, conveniently located right next to Kira's.

"Hi, Kira," I say, waving awkwardly.

Kira shushes me, pointing to the front of the darkened room where Mrs. Steiner is struggling to get a VHS tape to play.

"Listen." I clear my throat, trying to sound casual, "I wanted to talk to you about the vote today in Book Club."

"I'm voting for Cheyenne," Kira responds with a click of her tongue.

"Is there any way I can convince you to vote for me instead?" I press, feeling a twinge of desperation. "Anything."

"Anything?" Kira's eyes light up with interest.

"Yes, anything."

"I want to go on a date with Patrick Noble," Kira confesses lowly.

"Oh." I tilt my head, caught off guard. "Well—"

"You said anything," Kira reminds me, her eyes narrowing slightly.

"I did say that," I admit. "I didn't realize you liked him."

Kira scoffs. "Who doesn't?"

Oh. Right.

"I'll, um, talk to Patrick."

"Awesome." Kira clasps her hands together, clearly pleased.

I gulp nervously. Teenage June didn't interact much with Patrick until *after* he graduated.

This is for Book Club President, June. You have to talk to him.

Fine.

"What did she say?" Dina pokes me with her pencil.

I give her a thumbs up, though I have no idea how I'm going to get Patrick to take Kira Campbell on a date. But if I want to win that vote, I'll have to figure it out.

History class drags on as I watch the seconds tick slowly by on the analog clock. Mr. Garcia passed out the test ten minutes ago, but he won't stop talking. No wonder so many people struggle in his class—he always goes off on tangents that have nothing to do with the material. Someone should really tell him.

A lightbulb clicks on in my head, and I raise my hand. "Mr. Garcia? While your tale of encountering an extraterrestrial spaceship is, uh, terrifyingly awe-inspiring, can we please start the test?"

Mr. Garcia pauses mid-sentence, looking a bit flustered. "Um... Yes. Go ahead and begin."

Johnny shoots me a death glare from across the room. I guess he was enjoying Mr. Garcia's story. Oh well.

Somehow, I manage to finish the history test with a few minutes to spare. But instead of reviewing my answers, my thoughts drift to one person—Johnny Williams.

Here are the facts: Johnny Williams asked me to the homecoming dance our freshman year. I turned him down because I thought it was a joke. Ever since, Johnny has hated me.

But something doesn't add up. Johnny was indifferent when he asked me, almost like he didn't care. It wasn't until after I turned him down that he became... well, barbaric.

Think, June. In all your stories, why does the antagonist loathe the protagonist?

There has to be an inciting incident. A moment when they become enemies. In my stories, it's usually jealousy, disappointment, or rejection.

What if... No. Johnny Williams couldn't have actually liked me, right?

But what if he did? What if I rejected him, not because he's a terrible person, but because I thought it was a pity ask? I never considered that he might have genuinely wanted to take me to the dance. That he might have liked me.

The bell rings just as Dina drops her pencil onto her desk, looking a bit defeated.

"How'd you do?" I ask, hoping for a glimmer of positivity.

"Not great," she admits, gathering her test and stuffing it into her backpack.

"Really?"

"I couldn't stop thinking about how we're going to win over Johnny," she says, her brow furrowed in concentration.

I let out a frustrated breath, my eyes locking on my former arch-nemesis—no, wait, is he still my arch-nemesis? I can't keep track anymore.

"I have an idea." I snap my fingers together. "You turn in your test, and I'll deal with Johnny."

Johnny is quick on his feet, but I manage to catch up with him outside the Language Arts building, panting heavily.

"Johnny!" I call out, bending over to catch my breath. Teenage June doesn't have much more stamina than 34-year-old June.

"What?" he groans, not even bothering to hide his annoyance as he tugs on his backpack straps.

"I need," I gasp for air, "to talk to you," another gulp, "about Book Club President."

"No, June." He shakes his curly blond head firmly. "No."

"Can you just hear me out?" I plead, desperate.

He turns to walk away, but something in my voice must get through to him because he stops, sighs, and turns back to face me. "You have one minute."

"I'm sorry," I begin, trying to gather my thoughts. "I'm sorry that you asked me to the homecoming dance, and I turned you down."

"You're not seriously—"

"I'm talking," I interrupt, raising a hand. "I only have one minute, so let me say this." Johnny falls silent, and I continue. "I'm sorry. I didn't say yes because I was afraid you were messing with me. I thought you were only asking me because you pitied me. I'm... I'm awkward. Everyone knows that. It's a constant topic of conversation in these halls. I didn't think someone might actually like me. Like me enough to take me to a dance, anyway."

Johnny exhales heavily, his expression softening just a fraction.

"I would have said yes, but I was scared," I continue, my voice trembling slightly. "My answer had nothing to do with you. It was how I felt about myself. I... I struggle to see in myself all the things my friends and family see in me. I am so sorry that I thought you were kidding. I didn't think someone like you might like someone like me. If I had known you were being genuine, I would have said yes. Saying no to you is something I have regretted for many years."

"You thought that I pitied you?" Johnny tilts his head, looking genuinely puzzled.

"Yeah," I answer, feeling small under his gaze. "I did."

I watch as Johnny shakes his head in disbelief. "You're only saying this because you want me to vote for you."

I mean...

"When I started that impassioned speech," I admit, biting my lower lip, "yes, I did want you to vote for me. But I do understand why you might not want to. Still, it felt good to get that off my chest. It felt good being honest."

Johnny shifts uncomfortably, scratching the side of his face. "My friends teased me for weeks after you turned me down. They couldn't believe I wanted to go with you. And then they couldn't believe you said no."

"I am truly very sorry," I say, my tone softening. "I never meant to cause any harm. I never meant to make you feel bad."

Johnny studies me for a long moment before speaking. "I see people try to make you feel bad every day. You act like it doesn't bother you."

"It bothers me," I spill. "I'm just really good at pretending it doesn't."

Johnny sighs, running a hand through his hair. "Now that I know why you said no, I get it, June. I really do. But I already told Cheyenne I'd vote for her."

My throat tightens as I nod. "Okay."

"But..." Johnny pauses, shifting his weight from one foot to the other as if he's torn between making a decision. "I'll think about it."

A spark of hope lights inside me. "Really?"

"Yeah."

"Thanks, Johnny," I exhale, relieved.

He gives me a small smile before heading off toward his next class, leaving me standing there, hand on my chest, trying to steady my racing heart.

"How'd it go?" Dina startles me as she appears beside me. I jump, and she bursts into laughter. "Oh, Old June, you're so funny."

I am not old.

"He's going to think about it," I tell her, grinning triumphantly.

"You convinced him?" Dina stares at me in awe.

"I convinced him to give me a chance," I say, smacking my lips. "I just need a few people to take a chance on me. That's how I win the vote."

"Come on." Dina grabs my arm, pulling me along. "We're going to be late for P.E."

"I, uh, need to do something." I swallow hard. "Can we meet up for lunch?"

Dina nods. "Yeah, I'll tell Mr. Teller you have your period, and your cramps sent you to the nurse's office."

I laugh, shaking my head. "You're a genius, Dina Noble."

"I am." She bows dramatically before scurrying off.

I watch her go, feeling lighter. I spent all my high school years yearning to feel worthy in the eyes of so many people. But I didn't need all of them. I just needed a few to take a chance on me.

Just a few.

My heart dips in my chest as I turn down the hall and head toward the culinary building. Patrick has a free period, but I know he hangs out in the quad by culinary, writing song lyrics.

When I see him, he's sitting on a green picnic table, strumming his guitar. He looks like a dream that's just out of reach.

"Hey." I wave as I approach slowly, my heart pounding.

"June." Patrick jumps off the picnic table, his eyes lighting up when he sees me. "What are you doing here?"

"I have a huge favor to ask of you," I say, trying not to smile as he fails to hide his own.

"You need me for this favor?" Patrick asks, sinking his teeth into his lip, the playful glint in his eyes unmistakable.

"You're Patrick Noble, right?" I tease, surprising myself with my boldness.

Patrick looks taken aback, clearly not expecting me to flirt with him. 17 years ago, I would have been terrified to even speak to him like this. But I spent three years madly in love with him. I know he's not that scary. He's... perfect, really.

"I am," he remarks, tilting his head as if to study me.

"I want to win Book Club President," I confess. "I've never wanted to win something this badly before. It's important to me."

"Okay." He nods, his navy eyes lingering on my lips a little too long.

"I need you to take Kira Campbell on a date," I say, the words coming out hoarser and more muddled than I'd intended.

Patrick rubs the back of his neck—a clear sign he's uncomfortable. "I don't think I can do that, June."

I shift my weight from one foot to the other, trying to hide my disappointment. "It was worth a shot."

"She put you up to this?" Patrick asks, raising an eyebrow.

I shrug, feeling a little embarrassed. "Yeah. She said she'd vote for me if you took her out on a date."

Patrick fiddles with his guitar, his eyes never leaving mine. "Why did she think you could convince me?"

I shake my head, feeling the sting of his question. "I don't know, Patrick. Maybe she thinks we're friends."

"Are we?" he asks, his voice softening.

"I've always been your friend," I reveal, fighting back the burn of tears. "I always will be. Even when you hate me, I'll still be your friend."

"I could never hate you, June." He clicks his tongue, his eyes searching mine. "Never."

There are so many things I want to say to him. I want to tell him that no one has ever loved me like he did. No one ever saw me—all of me—and loved every inch the way he did. No one's ever been as kind and gentle with me. No one's ever measured up. No one's ever seen straight through the mounds of insecurities and made me believe in myself the way he did. If it wasn't for Patrick, I never would have found Sissy Barnes.

He's the reason 34-year-old June is a writer.

"Same," is all I manage to say in response.

"I'll do it," he agrees, biting his lower lip. "But I'm going to need something in return."

"Whatever you want, Patrick," I reply.

"Spend an entire day with me," he proposes, his tone playful but his eyes serious.

My heart lodges in my throat. "I-I don't think that's a good idea."

"The choice is yours."

One day. It's just one day, June. Put on your big girl panties and spend the day with your first love.

"One whole day?" I clarify, needing to be sure.

"One whole day," Patrick repeats, his face lighting up with a familiar, heart-stopping grin.

I take a deep breath, steadying myself, and hold out my hand. "You have a deal, then."

The moment his fingers slip into mine, everything else fades away. The bustling sounds of students hurrying to their next class, the chatter, and the footsteps fade into the background. All I can focus on is the warmth of his hand in mine, the way his touch sends a jolt of electricity through my entire body. For a second, I forget how to breathe.

Patrick's gaze locks onto mine, and for a moment, it feels like we're the only two people in the world. The years melt away, and suddenly, I'm that girl again—heart racing, butterflies in my stomach, completely and utterly captivated by him.

"I'll talk to Kira," he says softly, not breaking eye contact.

"Thank you, Patrick," I sigh wistfully.

He nods, his thumb brushing lightly over the back of my hand before he reluctantly lets go. The warmth of his touch lingers even after his hand pulls away. I'm left standing there, trying to remember how to function.

"One whole day," he reaffirms, a playful smirk tugging at his lips as he picks up his guitar.

"One whole day." My heart dips in my chest.

He grins before turning back to his spot on the picnic table, strumming a few chords as if nothing monumental just passed between us. But as I walk away, I know it did. Something shifted—something big.

I can't help but smile to myself. Maybe this trip back in time isn't just about winning a vote or fixing old mistakes. Maybe it's about rediscovering something I'd lost along the way. Something I wasn't even sure I could find again.

CHAPTER SIX
Play the Game

Kira Campbell ✓

Johnny Williams ✓

All that's left is to talk to Jose Martinez. But I know he won't vote for me. How could he? He's secretly dating Cheyenne Radcliff. No one knows—not yet anyway. Cheyenne's reputation couldn't handle the scandal of dating a Glee Club member. Not when she's at the top of the social food chain.

The whole school will find out next year when Jose breaks up with her in the culinary quad, making front-page news in the *Bloomford Bulletin*. Cheyenne won't just be embarrassed—she'll be dethroned.

Do I risk it? Should I ask him to vote for me instead?

I can't tell him I know about his clandestine affair with Cheyenne. Blackmailing a teenager is beneath me, and I'm not interested in ruining their relationship. Relationships are hard enough without external noise. It's the internal noise that does them in. Just like it did with Sutton and me.

For a moment, I let myself feel the lingering sorrow from Sutton's breakup speech—the one where he told me he was in love with some chick named Horn.

Does it hurt, June? Yes.

If it does, then why aren't you lying on the floor, a bawling, sobbing mess?

Six months isn't a lifetime with someone, but it's long enough to dream about a future. Sutton wasn't forever. He was just a moment. Moments pass. He will pass. These emotions will pass.

I know when people aren't just moments. I know when they're forever. Grieving a moment is heartbreaking. Grieving a lifetime without someone is life-altering. Earth-shattering. I've had to do it more times than I can count. It never gets easier.

"Well?" Dina's tapping her foot restlessly against the concrete outside the Language Arts building. "What have you decided?"

I don't need Jose to win. I just need Kira and Johnny. But if Johnny decides not to vote for me, I'm going to regret not talking to Jose.

"We'll corner him by the band room," I decide, my voice firm.

"What are you going to say to him?" Dina asks, her eyes wide with anticipation.

I shake my head, giving her a nervous smile. "I have no idea. We'll figure it out when we get there."

"We're really doing this!" Dina squeals, linking her arm through mine as we walk down the hallway. The crowd thickens as students spill out of classrooms, eager to eat lunch.

Dina's grip on my arm tightens, and something tugs at my heart. Dina was never just a moment. She was a lifetime—a forever friend.

Why did I make so many bad choices? Why did I let my pride—my ego—get in the way of our friendship? Why did I walk away from this? Why did I think I could find something better?

Because, June, you didn't know this was forever until it was too late.

A lesson learned. To date, the hardest one learned.

"There he is!" Dina points toward a tall figure leaning against a brick wall. 17-year-old Jose is chatting with one of the Glee Club members as we approach.

"What do you think Jose is up to in the future?" Dina whispers, her curiosity piqued.

He went on to star on Broadway and has had several small TV roles. I shouldn't second-guess every tidbit of information I'm feeding her, but this feels harmless.

"Broadway," I say with a grin. "He won a Tony award in 2018."

"Shut up." Dina's eyes widen as she jumps up and down. "Should I get his autograph now? You think it'll be worth anything in 20 years?"

I shrug, trying to suppress a smile. "Who knows."

Dina smooths down her blonde hair as we approach, and I can't help but roll my eyes playfully. "Act cool."

"I can do that," she lies through her teeth.

"Hi, Jose." Dina waves awkwardly, trying to act casual.

Jose glances at us, his expression bored, like he'd rather be talking to anyone else.

"I was hoping to talk to you about Book Club," I start, clearing my throat. Why am I so nervous? Jose is a 17-year-old kid. I have 34 years of life experience and a slew of semi-successful books under my belt. I can do this.

Jose runs a hand through his short brown hair. "What about it?"

The few drama students congregating nearby glance at me before turning to whisper among themselves.

"The vote for president is today, and I'd like to take a moment to tell you why I'd be the right person for the job." I give him my most hopeful smile, awkwardly adjusting my sweater.

"I'm voting for Cheyenne," he says flatly, flashing me a look before returning to his conversation.

"Um," I start again, feeling Dina's supportive nudge. "I know you think she's the right person to lead Book Club, but I think I am. I think I love books more than she does. I know I understand why books are so important, especially to people like me and people like you."

"People like me?" Jose raises an eyebrow, skeptical.

"Cheyenne is popular and pretty and poised. She has no idea what it's like to have to fight to fit in. To have her voice heard. To be seen. The only place I feel seen is in stories—in the books I read."

Jose shifts uncomfortably and crosses his arms over his chest.

"Sometimes," I continue, my voice softening, "I read a book, and someone like me—someone timid, shy, and reserved—gets to be the heroine. The ordinary girl gets to save the day. It... It changes how I see myself. Doesn't it do that for you, too?"

He exhales, his gaze flickering with uncertainty. "I don't know."

"Not everyone gets to lead the life they want—the life they crave. Books... well, they give us the chance to, you know?"

Jose tilts his head, studying me. "June, right?"

I nod, feeling a flicker of hope. "Yeah."

"I think you're forgetting something."

"Am I?"

"When I step onto a stage, everyone sees and hears me." He smirks, his confidence reasserting itself.

I gnaw on my lower lip, realizing I might be losing the fight. "Right."

No wonder he and Cheyenne get along so well. They're both full of themselves.

"No offense," he says, holding up his hands, "but you're never going to win. Cheyenne is at the top of the food chain for a reason."

"She won't always be," I say quietly, knowing full well that it'll be Jose who takes her down in the end. He'll be the one who single-handedly destroys her reputation.

"Shoo." Jose swats at me dismissively as if I'm an annoying gnat.

"You shoo!" Dina snaps, coming to my defense.

I rest a hand on her shoulder, gently pulling her back. "Come on. We're done here."

"Yeah, we are." Dina glares at Jose before turning away.

The rejection doesn't sting as much as I thought it would. Honestly, it feels... freeing. I put myself out there. I'm fighting for what I want. Maybe not in the way everyone else would, but I'm doing it the June Nelson way.

"I don't get it," Dina grumbles, shaking her head as we sit on a bench outside the library.

"Don't get what?" I ask, trying to push away the swirling thoughts in my mind.

"You..." she trails off, her brow furrowing as she searches for the right words. "You're so fearless. How could you ever think you're timid or shy?"

I lean back on the bench, feeling the cold steel grate pressing into my legs. "Because I was. I am."

"You're anything but." Dina sighs, her voice full of conviction. "You figured out a way to get Kira to vote for you. Johnny 'I-hate-June's-guts' Williams is actually considering voting for you. And just now, you gave that bold speech to Jose."

"I'm not the same person I was in high school," I admit softly. "I've changed a little." But even with all that change, there's still a part of me that's hesitant, that holds back, that can't quite figure out how to stand up for myself in the present.

"I'm wondering if that's why we're no longer friends in the future," Dina says, clicking her tongue in thought. "Maybe you outgrew me."

I shake my head firmly. "Never. I messed up, Dina. Me. Not you."

"But it's not like me to just give up," Dina argues, a stubborn edge to her voice. "I'm tenacious and loyal. You know that."

"You are those things," I agree, my heart aching with the truth. "But you also know when something has run its course. You're smart, Dina. You don't force things."

"I'm sorry for going on and on about this," Dina apologizes. "I'm just gutted, June. I don't want to lose you."

"If I could make things right, I would," I tell her, wishing with everything in me that I could change the past. "But I didn't fall back in time to the night our friendship ended."

"Why didn't you go there instead?"

"I don't know." I shrug, uncertain. "I guess it was more important that I came here."

"The vote is in," Dina checks her phone, her face scrunching up in anticipation, "13 minutes."

"What if I lose again?"

"What if you win?" Dina counters, a glimmer of hope in her eyes.

I smile at her, my best friend, my forever friend. "Then I go back to the future?"

"I hope not," Dina says, with a thoughtful look, pursing her lips. "Hey, how did you get Kira to vote for you?"

I hesitate, knowing she'll figure it out soon enough. "She wanted me to ask Patrick if he'd take her on a date."

"Why would she ask you to do that?" Dina scoffs, her nose wrinkling in disbelief.

Because he's in love with me. Because he'd do anything I asked him to. And everyone knows it except for you, Dina.

"No idea," I say, hitching my shoulder in a casual shrug.

"Huh." Dina stares up at the blue sky, her thoughts drifting.

"Your birthday is tomorrow." I change the subject to something lighter, something happier.

"The big 1-7," she says, wiggling excitedly beside me. "Can you believe it?"

"I can't wait for you to wake up to that Volkswagen Beetle tomorrow morning." I stretch my legs out in front of me, trying to get comfortable.

"It'll be a miracle if that actually happens."

"It will," I promise, knowing the future holds that small, perfect moment for her.

"You should spend the night tomorrow," Dina suggests. "We can have a sleepover and watch movies."

"Sounds like the perfect Friday night," I tut, feeling a warmth spread through me at the thought. "We should start heading toward class." I raise an eyebrow at her, knowing she's as anxious as I am.

"You nervous?" Dina asks as we stand up.

"Yes." I don't want to lose this time.

"Will it change anything?" Dina wonders, walking beside me, her voice quiet.

It might be the thing that changes everything. What if I had won Book Club President? What if people had rallied behind me and helped me see my worth sooner? What if I hadn't cared what Cheyenne thought? What if I had just loved myself as I was?

So many what-ifs.

Everyone arrives at AP English a few minutes early. Cheyenne is already making the rounds, thanking students in advance for voting for her. Her confidence radiates off her like she's already won.

I want that confidence. I want that drive. I want to know I'm going to win before I win.

"Everyone," Mrs. Bliss announces, silencing the chatter, "please take your seats. We'll be voting for the new Book Club President today. This person will shadow Cleetus until May, and then take over next year. How exciting!"

"Can I say—" Cheyenne begins, but Mrs. Bliss cuts her off with a firm look.

"I'd like Cheyenne and June to come to the front of the class," Mrs. Bliss commands. "They gave their speeches last week, and you've had a week to think about who you feel would best represent our club. We'll vote by a show of hands. If you'd like June to be our president, please raise your hand now."

I survey the room, my heart pounding. Out of the 22 students sitting in front of me, nearly half shoot their arms into the air. I see Kira's hand up, but it's hard to tell if Johnny's is, too. He's sitting in the back, and as quickly as the hands go up, Mrs. Bliss counts and tells everyone to lower them.

"Those who would like Cheyenne to be our president, raise your hand," Mrs. Bliss instructs.

The vote looks about even as my eyes scan the room, landing on each person voting for Cheyenne. It's not until my gaze settles on Johnny in the back, his arm raised high, that I feel my heart sink.

I'm not going to win. The only person I could get to vote for me did it for a favor. For a shot with Patrick.

"10 to 12." Mrs. Bliss clasps her hands under her chin. "Cheyenne will be our president."

Dina's face falls—hard.

I'm not sure what happens after that. Everything feels distant, like I'm watching it all unfold from outside my body. English passes in a blur, and Algebra II doesn't fare much better.

It's not until I'm standing next to Dina's green boxy van after school that I realize I've been stuck in my head for the past two hours.

"Did you win?" Patrick asks, appearing beside his car as he unlocks the door.

I swallow hard, my throat dry. "No."

He lets out a heavy breath and turns to face me, his expression gentle.

"Hang in there, June," Patrick says softly, tucking a stray strand of my mousy brown hair behind my ear. "Not every loss is a loss."

"What do you mean?" I furrow my brow, confused.

"I mean," he says, biting his lower lip as he tries—and fails—to hide a smile, "a closed door doesn't mean you lost. It just means it's not your door."

When he says things like that, my insides turn to mush.

"Thank you," I whisper.

"Saturday," he says, his voice teasing as he flashes his eyebrows at me.

"Saturday?"

"Our day together." He winks, making my heart flutter. "I'll pick you up at nine."

"In the morning?" I clarify, my pulse quickening.

"Yes." He grins, and my heart aches in the best possible way.

Patrick was never just a moment for me. He was the lifetime—forever.

He's the earth-shattering, life-altering event I'm still not over.

CHAPTER SEVEN
Unfinished Business

I close the front door quietly behind me, hoping to slip down the hall unnoticed. But as soon as the soft click echoes through the entryway, the bolt latching in place, Dad's head pops out of the kitchen.

"So?" His eyes are bright with excitement, too much excitement. "Did you win?"

My breath catches, and I clutch my history book a little tighter to my chest. "No."

"Ah, June Gloom." Dad's shoulders slump, and he hangs his head. "I'm so sorry, kiddo."

"There will be other votes," I say, trying to brush off the disappointment with a casual shrug. But even I can hear the strain in my voice.

"I made my famous chocolate chip cookies," Dad discloses, trying to cheer me up as he smacks his lips together like a kid with a secret stash of candy. "Want one?"

"Yeah." I nod, managing a small smile as I drop my backpack onto the little wooden bench Lily insisted Dad build for the entryway.

When I wander into the kitchen, Dad is tossing the store-bought chocolate chip cookie dough wrapper into the trash just as the oven timer blares. I slide into one of the chairs at the kitchen table and watch as he pulls the cookie sheet from the oven, the smell of melted chocolate filling the room.

"How many, June Gloom?" he asks, looking over his shoulder at me.

I sigh, the heaviness of the day wearing down on me. "Two."

"Only two?" Dad tosses a skeptical look my way.

"Only two," I confirm in a tone that lacks any real enthusiasm. "You want me to get the milk?"

"What else are we going to dip our cookies in?" Dad's eyes widen in mock horror, and I can't help but smile a little at his antics.

I push myself out of the chair and open the fridge. Inside, everything is a reminder of Lily's obsessive need for health and fitness—leafy greens, berries, and green drinks that look anything but appetizing. I spot the half gallon of skim milk hidden in the back, behind a bin of apples. The milk is always hidden, tucked away as if it's something to be ashamed of.

Sometimes, I feel like I'm that half gallon of milk. Pushed to the back, out of sight, while the prettier, healthier things get all the attention.

Dad sets two glasses on the counter, and I fill them both before shoving the milk back into its hiding spot.

"Tell me what happened," Dad says as he places a plate of warm cookies in the center of the table.

I sit down across from him, picking up a cookie and staring at it, the edges still gooey. "I lost. Cheyenne won."

"There's got to be more to the story," Dad presses, always looking for the silver lining.

"I'm not popular, Dad. I'm not well-liked. I'm..." I trail off, frowning at the cookie in my hand as if it holds the answers.

"You're what?"

I glance up at him, feeling small and insignificant. "I'm just June."

"I know high school can be rough," he notes gently, the words thick with the kind of understanding that only comes from experience. "And I know it's even harder without..."

He doesn't say her name. He never does. It's just as painful for him to speak it as it is for me to hear it.

Mom.

"Doesn't help that I like cookies more than carrots," I joke, trying to lighten the mood.

"That's not funny, June," Dad chides, leaning back in his chair, his expression serious. "You're..."

"I'm what?" I ask softly, wanting to hear him say something, anything, that makes me feel less like a failure.

Dad's brown eyes fill with tears, and he blinks them away quickly. "Is it my fault?"

"Is what your fault?" I ask, confused.

"That you're..."

"Weird," I finish for him, a small, bitter smile tugging at my lips.

Dad groans, shaking his head. "You're not weird. You're perfect just the way you are."

I smile at him, my heart aching as I realize just how hard it must be for him to watch me be so hard on myself. It's not about my looks; it's about how I see myself, and I never realized how much that hurt him.

"It's not your fault," I tell him, shaking my head. "It's hard to explain, but it's not your fault."

"Can you try?" he asks softly, almost pleading.

I set the cookie down and place a hand over my heart. "There's a void in here that I haven't figured out how to fill yet."

Dad's face falls, and I know he understands what I mean. "Your mom."

"It's going to take time for me to figure out how to live with the pain of her leaving," I admit, feeling the truth settle over me like a thick, unyielding fog.

"I just hate seeing you miserable, June Gloom," he says, his bushy eyebrows drawing together in concern.

"I hate seeing you miserable, too," I counter.

Dad takes a bite of his cookie, chewing thoughtfully before replying. "I'm not miserable."

"You're not happy, either," I acknowledge, tilting my head to the side, challenging him to be honest.

"Nothing gets by you," he sighs, forcing a smile that doesn't quite reach his eyes.

"Dad," I say, swallowing hard against the lump in my throat, "you can't spend the rest of your life trying to fix something Mom broke. She did the breaking, not you."

"I didn't help," he remarks. "Besides, she might have broken it, but I know I can fix it."

"You can't mend what someone else broke," I say firmly, needing him to understand. "Not when it comes to broken hearts. The only person who can do the mending is the one who tore this family apart. And she's not going to. She's not going to fix a thing. Not now, not ever."

The words hang in the air between us, heavy and final. But they're true, and they're honest, and they're real. And as much as they're for Dad, I know I needed to hear them, too.

"I know," Dad mumbles quietly, resigned.

"You're not responsible for fixing me," I state. "I am. I'm responsible for my peace, just like you're responsible for yours."

Dad chuckles lightly, the sound more of a release than a sign of amusement. "Where did all this newfound wisdom come from?"

"Self-reflection." I grin, trying to lighten the mood.

"I'm sorry you lost today." Dad frowns. "I wish you had won."

I break off a piece of cookie and pop it into my mouth, chewing slowly. I didn't win again. I tried to change the past, but nothing changed. I'm still no closer to figuring out why I'm here than I was this morning.

"I wish I had, too." I shrug. "But sitting here eating cookies with you... this feels better than winning."

Dad laughs, the sound warm and comforting. "Yeah?"

My heart clenches as I watch him dip his half-eaten cookie into his glass of milk, the simple motion so familiar, so precious. Through a curtain of unshed tears, I commit the moment to memory. These are the moments that make up a life, ones that stay with you when everything else fades.

"I love you, Dad," I whisper, a tear slipping down my cheek.

He reaches across the table and takes my hand, squeezing it gently. "You'll never love me, June Gloom, as much as I love you."

I know he's right. I know he gave me everything he had, hoping it would make up for all that we had lost. But the thing about loss is that sometimes it's not about what you lost; it's about what you gain afterward.

Maybe the vote for Book Club President is a reminder of that. Of all the things I've lost, there's always been something better gained in the end.

"Well," I sniffle, wiping away a tear, "I should get started on my homework."

Dad nods, his eyes soft with understanding. "You should."

I leave the cookies behind and grab my backpack, the day weighing heavy on my shoulders, but somehow, a little lighter now.

Thankfully, I make it to my room before Lily gets home from teaching aerobics classes at the YMCA. She'd fly off the handle if she found out Dad made cookies.

In the sanctuary of my teenage bedroom, I take a deep, sobering breath before plopping onto the tan carpet.

I still don't understand why I'm here. I don't understand why that stop sign sent me back to this part of my life. Nothing even remotely interesting or exciting happens between now and college.

Patrick.

I push the thought away as quickly as it comes. I didn't come back for Patrick. I walked away from him later on. If I needed to make things right with him, I would have fallen back in time to the night I left him. To the night my friendship with Dina ended.

But being back here, I can't help but wonder. Why did I think I'd be okay without him? Why did I convince myself that Patrick possibly being married to someone else—having kids with someone else—was what I wanted?

Come on, June. First loves never last. Maybe they do in your books, but not in real life.

This isn't a romance book.

And that leads me to the next logical conclusion: I came back to fix things with Dina. But how does this period of my life connect to the breaking of our friendship?

A soft knock interrupts my thoughts.

"Yeah?"

The doorknob twists, and Lily's face appears as the door swings open. "Hey."

"Hey," I reply, clicking my tongue.

"Can I come in?"

"Sure, Lily."

She shuts the door behind her and sits down in front of me, crossing her legs under her. The sight of her so close, in this room that feels frozen in time, sends an unexpected wave of emotion through me.

"What's up?" I ask, trying to keep my voice neutral.

Lily gnaws on the inside of her cheek, a nervous habit I've seen countless times. "I'm sorry about this morning."

Honestly, I'd completely forgotten about it.

"It's fine," I say, waving it off, hoping to end the conversation before it even begins.

Lily blows out a tired breath, the kind that comes from deep inside. "No, it's not. I'm sorry, June. I'm sorry if I made you feel bad or small. I... I know how hard it is to be a teenage girl, and I don't want to add to the pressure of high school."

I huff in disbelief. "How hard could it have been to be popular?"

She shakes her head, and my eyes land on her black bike shorts. She's so thin, the elastic hem doesn't even dig into her toned thighs. "I struggled with my self-image. I was made fun of."

"You were?" I laugh, the sound harsh and unkind.

Lily licks her lips nervously. "I was. And I was never popular, June."

"I've seen your senior yearbook," I disagree, rolling my eyes. "You ran track and field, and you were the captain of the varsity volleyball team. You were popular."

"There's a difference between popularity and visibility."

"Is there?" I challenge, raising an eyebrow.

"I'm trying to relate to you in the only way I know how," she says softly, her voice filled with something I don't expect—vulnerability.

"I don't need you to relate to me or to mother me," I assure her, the words coming out sharper than I intend. "I have a mom, and let's be honest, she left a sour taste in my mouth when it comes to nurturing female roles in my life."

Lily flinches as if I've slapped her. "Okay, June." She stands slowly, the hurt evident in her eyes. When she reaches the door, she turns back to look at me. "If you ever do need someone to talk to, I hope you know that I'm always here to listen."

"Okay, Lily," I respond mechanically, watching as she leaves, the door clicking shut behind her.

For a split second, I forget that she sold the house without telling me and that she got rid of all Dad's things without asking if I wanted anything. I forget that she's made me feel insecure and unworthy since the day she walked into Dad's life.

For a split second, I remember that she's human. That she never had the one thing she craved more than anything in the world: a child of her own.

I open my mouth to say something—anything—but she's gone, and the moment passes.

I let my head fall back onto the soft carpet and cover my face with my hands. I didn't expect this to be so complicated. I didn't expect Teenage June's life to be this messy.

Maybe I didn't come back to win Book Club President, or to see what I missed out on with Patrick, or to fix my friendship with Dina.

Maybe I came back to the past to make sense of my present.

To make sense of my future.

CHAPTER EIGHT
A Birthday to Remember

My phone rings bright and early, pulling me from a deep, glorious sleep. I groan, rolling over in bed, my hand fumbling through the sheets to find the source of the noise. Finally, my fingers close around my phone, and I flip it open, pressing it to my ear with a sleepy, "H-hullo?"

"JUNE!" Dina's voice blares through the speaker, so loud and excited that it makes me wince. "I got it! I got the car!"

"What time is it?" I mumble, still half-asleep as I try to sit up.

"WHO CARES, JUNE?!" Dina screeches, her excitement contagious even through the phone. "You were right! I got the baby blue Beetle! You really are from the future!"

"Told you," I manage, rubbing a hand over my face. My room is still dark, with just a faint glow creeping around the edges of the curtains. How early is it?

"I'll pick you up in 30 minutes, and then we can grab lattes at the coffee shop!" Dina is so full of energy it makes me feel guilty for wanting to crawl back under the covers.

"What time is it?" I ask again, trying to process everything through the fog of sleep.

"6:30," she chirps like it's the most normal thing in the world to be this awake at such an ungodly hour.

"I need to shower," I tell her, stifling a yawn.

"Then, hurry up!" she insists, her excitement unwavering.

"Ugh," I grunt, hanging up and falling back onto the mattress. I wish I could sleep longer, but I have my best friend back. Even if it's just for the moment, I don't want to miss out on a single second with her.

Half-asleep, I manage to roll out of bed, my feet barely catching the carpet as I fumble toward the door.

***

"It's comfy, isn't it?" Dina flashes her eyebrows at me as we sit in her brand-new car, the smell of fresh leather filling the air.

I nod, grinning. "Super comfy and absolutely gorgeous."

"It's brand new, June!" She claps her hands together like a little kid on Christmas morning. "Patrick is so going to be jealous."

I smile to myself. I know Patrick. He loves his little sister, and he never had a problem with her getting a brand-new car. In fact, he was the one who suggested it to their parents as the perfect birthday gift.

"Your birthday present," I say, handing her a small wrapped gift I had stashed in my bag.

Dina's eyes widen with surprise. "You didn't have to, June."

"I know," I shrug beside her, "but Teenage June picked it out a few weeks ago, and it was already wrapped."

"Teenage June," Dina repeats with a chuckle. "You're funny."

"Open it," I urge, my excitement bubbling over.

Dina carefully peels back the gold wrapping paper, her curiosity growing. "What did you get me?"

I just smile, watching as she slides the small square box out of the wrapping.

When she pops open the top, her face lights up. "You didn't."

"I did," I confirm, my grin widening.

Dina gently lifts the gold, circular pendant necklace out of the box, twirling it between her fingers as the first rays of daylight dance across the car's interior.

"My birth flower," she whispers, her voice full of awe as she takes in the delicate etching on the pendant.

"A narcissus," I say, remembering the hours I spent picking out the perfect design.

"It's beautiful, June," she sighs, quickly fastening it around her neck. When the clasp is secure, she places her hand over it, right on her chest, and says, "I'm never taking it off."

The last time I saw her, Dina was still wearing it. I wonder if... No, never mind. Don't go there, June.

"I saved up all my allowance money to buy it," I reveal, my heart swelling with pride at how much she loves it.

Dina chews on the inside of her cheek, her eyes serious as she looks at me. "Can I ask you a question?"

"Sure," I reply, stifling another yawn.

"Are you in love with Patrick?"

Her question hits me like a bucket of cold water. "Why are you asking me that?"

"Because... Well, I was thinking about it last night," she says quietly. "Why would we stop being friends? There's nothing you could do to make me stop being your friend except hurt my brother."

"I'm not in love with Patrick," I say, and it's the truth. 34-year-old June isn't in love with Patrick. I might be in love with the idea of what could have been, but I don't know who Patrick is now. I barely know who I am.

There's a part of me that loves Patrick. I think I might always love him. But being in love with him? No, I haven't felt that in a long time.

"But is Teenage June?" Dina presses softly, like she's afraid of the answer.

I glance out the passenger window, avoiding her gaze. "I don't know."

"Why don't you know?"

I should have lied. I should have told her that Teenage June isn't in love with him. But Dina's too smart for her own good. And she can read me like a book.

"Because he's Patrick." I clear my throat, struggling to find the right words. "And my feelings for him have always been complicated."

"I..." Dina starts, but trails off, her words lost somewhere between us.

"I'm sorry," I apologize for the interruption. "Can we get coffee? I—it's still early, and I don't want to have this conversation without some caffeine in me."

"Okay," Dina agrees, though I can see the hurt in her eyes.

The drive to the coffee shop on Willow Way is quiet. My mind, however, is anything but. Dina figured it out. Of course, she did. She's insightful and observant. She's also incredibly intelligent. She noticed how my book *Midnight Crown* was too similar to Patrick's band *Crowing at Midnight*. She figured out that the only reason she'd never speak to me again was if I hurt someone she loved.

Maybe this time I can find a way to make it right.

"What can I get you?" the barista asks, snapping me out of my thoughts. I blink slowly, trying to piece together how I ended up here when it felt like I was just sitting in Dina's driveway, handing her a birthday present.

"Skinny vanilla latte," I rattle off my order, the words tumbling out on autopilot.

"You're not getting your usual?" Dina mumbles beside me.

I rub my tired eyes. "Um... This is my usual."

"Your *teenage* usual?" she prods gently, nudging me with her elbow like she always used to.

I shake my head. "I'm good with this."

After we pay, we find a small table tucked away in the corner of the café. As we settle in, I adjust my sweatshirt, still trying to get used to the way this version of my body feels, the way it takes up space. Everything about it feels like it belongs to someone else—a girl I thought I'd left behind years ago.

When I was a teenager, I used to tear myself apart in the mirror every morning. I'd stare at my freckles, round cheeks, and mousy hair, wishing I could trade them in for flawless skin and glossy locks like Cheyenne Radcliffe's. I'd promise myself that today would be different—I'd eat better, skip breakfast, survive lunch, and then lose control when I got home from school. It was a vicious cycle, one I felt trapped in, unable to escape.

But somewhere along the way, I did escape. I found a way to stop numbing the pain and start leaning into it, using it to fuel something bigger.

Patrick.

Or maybe I didn't escape at all. Maybe I just found another way to hide.

I squeeze my eyes shut tight, pushing away the scratchy feeling in my chest that flares every time I think of his name. I didn't come back for Patrick. I didn't come back here to fix things with him. It's the wrong timeline.

"Are we finally going to talk about it?" Dina's question slices through my spiraling thoughts, pulling me back to the present.

"Talk about what?" I ask, trying to remain calm and composed.

"Come on, June." She shakes her head, her curls bouncing slightly. "I know you're hiding something from me, and I know it has to do with Patrick."

I stare down at my short, round nails, my heart pounding in my chest. "It's your birthday. Can't we just enjoy it without worrying about why I'm here?"

Dina shifts in her chair, her expression a combination of frustration and sympathy. "I don't understand why we can't discuss your feelings for him."

"Because they're irrelevant," I say, lifting my head to meet her gaze. "They don't matter right now. Patrick and I... We don't have any contact in this part of my life."

"You talked to him yesterday," she counters, her tone incredulous. "You asked him to take Kira on a date, and he said yes. I can't even get him to go to the gas station with me. Why would he do that for you, June?"

"You'd have to ask him," I shrug, trying to sound nonchalant. "I really didn't expect him to agree to it."

"But why did he?" she presses, leaning forward, refusing to let this go.

I don't want to tell Dina the truth. Keeping it hidden makes things infinitely easier on me. But deep down, I know I didn't come back here to take the easy way out.

"I think you know why." I utter swallow harshly.

Dina's shoulders slump as she sags back into her chair. "He's in love with you."

The barista calls out our names, breaking the tension. I push back my chair and stand, taking slow, sobering breaths as I grab our coffees from the counter and walk them back to our table.

"So," Dina exhales, wrapping her fingers around her warm coffee cup, "he's in love with you. But you're not in love with him."

"Why does it matter?" I ask, trying to deflect, but knowing deep down it does matter—more than I'm willing to admit.

"Because I know why you came back," Dina declares, a wide smile spreading across her face.

"You do?" I raise my eyebrows in confusion, unsure if I want to hear what she has to say.

"I do." She grins, her eyes lighting up with excitement.

"Why did I come back?" I ask, the sound skeptical.

"You came back to make sure Patrick falls out of love with you," Dina decides, as if she's solved the biggest mystery of all time.

"What?" I tilt my head to the side, genuinely baffled.

"Think about it," she insists, leaning forward. "You came back in time to put an end to whatever happens with Patrick. This way, we're still friends in the future."

My heart tightens in my chest at the gravity of her words. "I don't know if that would change anything."

"Of course, it would," Dina says confidently. "If you make him fall out of love with you, then there's no chance you'll do something to hurt him in the future, right?"

"You think a stop sign whacked me in the head on the eve of the second worst night of my life so I could come back here and break Patrick's heart?" I clarify, the absurdity of it all hitting me.

She nods enthusiastically, her smile unwavering. "You clearly need a friend, Old June."

"I wouldn't have my writing career without Patrick," I tell her, panic flooding my chest. "He's the reason..."

"He's the reason what?" Dina urges, her curiosity piqued.

"He's the reason I found Sissy Barnes," I admit, the truth slipping out before I can stop it.

"Who is Sissy Barnes?"

"My literary agent," I explain, clicking my tongue in frustration at the complexity of it all.

"I'm sure you'll still find another way to publish your stuff," Dina offers, her optimism almost endearing.

My head begins to pound as I take a sip of my coffee. The warm liquid hits my tongue, and I recoil in disgust. "What in the world?"

Dina laughs, the sound light and carefree. "Teenage June's taste buds aren't a fan of your skinny vanilla latte?"

I smack my lips together, trying to rid my mouth of the strange taste. "I guess not."

The conversation stalls after that, and I find myself lost in thought.

Patrick.

Is he really the reason I came back? To break his heart? It just doesn't make sense. When Patrick and I started dating, Dina was weirded out by it, but she never interfered. She never even got mad when I'd have plans with Patrick and couldn't hang out with her. The longer we dated, the more time Patrick and Dina spent together. Eventually, they became close—too close. That's why she ended our friendship when I broke up with him. At some point, Patrick became her best friend, and I faded into the background.

What if Dina's right? What if none of that should have happened? What if my dying writing career was just a fluke? What if I was supposed to do something else with my life? Something more important?

"You look like you're having a stroke," Dina's voice cuts through the noise in my head, pulling me back to the present.

"Just thinking."

"About Patrick?" she asks, her tone gentle.

"About everything," I whisper.

"I've upset you," Dina says, guilt lacing her words.

"No," I wave her off, trying to reassure her. "I... I have a lot of things I need to sort out. I think I might skip school today."

Dina's mouth drops open in shock. "Skip? You'd never skip school. Ever."

"I'm not Teenage June," I remind her. "I'm..." But the words die in my throat, because I don't know what I am anymore.

"I'll skip with you," she insists.

"You have a perfect attendance record," I challenge. "You shouldn't skip."

"I want to, June," she says firmly.

"I, uh, think I need some time alone," I admit, the truth of it settling in.

"But it's my birthday." Dina's lower lip trembles, and I can see the hurt in it. "And you're not supposed to ditch me on my birthday. You're still going to spend the night tonight, right?"

I close my eyes briefly, a sense of dread gnawing at me. "Yeah, I don't know what I was thinking. I can't leave you alone on your birthday."

Dina's face lights up with relief. "Good. Because I have a surprise for you, Old June."

"What is it?" I ask, trying to match her enthusiasm.

"You'll have to wait and see," she sings, her smile wide and mischievous.

I take another sip of coffee, but my stomach twists into tighter knots. I don't know if I came back to end whatever

Patrick and I had before it began, but I know one thing for certain: I can't do it.

Patrick is the most important part of my story. He's the reason I'm a writer. The reason I found something meaningful to do with my life. The reason I found an inkling of self-worth. Enough to believe in myself, anyway.

If I end things before they ever begin, I lose him.

But I don't lose Dina.

When it comes down to it, I'm not sure I'll be able to choose.

CHAPTER NINE
A Scathing Rebuttal

Dina's surprise is not at all what I expected.

"So?" She rocks back and forth on her heels, teeming with excitement. "What do you think?"

I tilt my head to the side, trying to wrap my mind around what I'm seeing. "You didn't."

"I did!" she squeals, practically jumping up and down.

Pinned to the student bulletin board in the library is a scathing letter—an anonymous manifesto of sorts—addressing the recent Book Club President election. The tone is biting, the words sharp, and I can't help but feel a mix of shock and amusement as I read the opening lines.

"You really wrote this?" I ask, unable to hide my disbelief.

Dina glances around the empty library, her voice dropping to a whisper. "It's anonymous, June. Keep it down!"

I clear my throat, suppressing a laugh. "To the esteemed members of the Bloomford High Book Club," I begin, reading the letter aloud in a mock-serious tone.

Dina groans, hiding her face behind her history book as I continue.

"As a concerned member of the student body, I feel compelled to write this anonymous letter to address a grievous error made on behalf of Word Warriors, Story Seekers, and Novel Navigators everywhere. You chose the wrong Book Club President. You chose popularity over character. You chose to follow the crowd instead of stepping out of your comfort zone and choosing the best candidate. Instead, you chose someone who doesn't love books and stories but someone who would rather spend her free time tearing down her fellow classmates. Cheyenne Radcliffe doesn't care about the book club. She cares about adding extracurriculars to her college applications and collecting titles like trophies. You failed lovers of books everywhere, Bloomford High Book Club. You failed Word Warriors, Story Seekers, and Novel Navigators. You should feel ashamed of yourselves. Sincerely, An Anonymous and Disgruntled Member of the Bloomford High Student Body."

I finish with a laugh and watch Dina squirm next to me.

Dina peeks out from behind her book. "Is this good laughter, Old June, or bad laughter?"

"G-good," I manage to say between laughs. "But they're totally going to know it was you."

"How?" Dina's eyes widen in horror.

I grin, leaning in closer. "Word warriors, Story Seekers, and Novel Navigators? That has Dina Noble written all over it."

"It does not!" she huffs, clearly offended.

"I'm not trying to upset you," I say, reaching out to squeeze her arm. "It's just... You're so great, Dina. Seriously, everyone needs a friend like you. Someone who will write a letter like this to defend her best friend. Someone who always has my back. You're so great, Dina. I... You're just so great."

Dina's blue eyes shimmer with unshed tears, and she smiles. "That's the nicest thing you've ever said to me, June. That's the nicest thing anyone's ever said to me."

We hug, and I squeeze her tight, my heart swelling with gratitude. It's been so long since I've had someone in my life who's got my back like this, someone who would go to such lengths just to see me smile.

"We should probably get out of here before someone sees us by the letter," Dina suggests, pulling back from the hug with a mischievous grin.

I nod, wiping a stray tear from my cheek as we slip out of the library. I've missed this. I've missed feeling like I belong, like I'm part of something.

"I know it's my birthday," Dina sighs, "but I wanted to do something special for you."

I give her a soft smile. "That's really sweet of you, Deen, but you didn't have to."

"I know," she replies, her tone light and teasing.

My heart feels heavy, like it's trying to push open a door that's been closed for a long time—too long. It's that same door I've kept shut, not wanting to let in all the things I've tried to keep out. But maybe it's time. Maybe it's time to let in some fresh air.

"Let's get to class," I say, motioning toward the door.

Dina's face brightens. "Sure, but tell me more about New York City."

So, we walk, and I start talking. I tell her about the chaos of the subway system, the best bagels in the city, how the Met is my favorite place to spend an afternoon, and why Central Park is basically my kryptonite—I'm directionally challenged and have gotten lost there more times than I can count. But really, who's keeping track?

"But who do you go to brunch with?" Dina asks, curious. "Who do you hang out with?"

The question catches me off guard, and I falter. "I... don't really hang out with anyone. I spend most of my time in my apartment, writing."

"No one? Like, at all?" Dina's eyebrows shoot up in surprise.

I frown. "No one. I'm pretty much on my own."

Dina stops walking, and I do too. "That sounds so..." she trails off, searching for the right word.

I glance at her, waiting. "So what?"

"Lonely," she muses softly, her eyes filled with concern.

I swallow hard, my throat suddenly tight. "It is lonely," I admit, the words tasting bitter.

Dina looks at me like she's seeing me for the first time. "You've mentioned Sissy, your agent, and Sutton, your ex, but what about your dad? What about Lily? Where are they in all of this?"

I wrap my arms around myself. "My dad... He passed away about a year after I graduated college."

Dina's eyes widen with shock and sadness. "Oh, June, I'm so sorry."

I force a smile, trying to play it off like it doesn't still hurt. "It's okay. Talking about it has never been easy, but I've learned to manage."

"And Lily?" Dina presses gently.

I shrug. "After Dad died, we just... drifted apart. There wasn't any reason to stay in touch."

"So, it's just you and Sissy?" Dina's voice wavers. "I don't get it."

"Don't get what?" I ask, though I think I already know what's coming.

Dina runs a hand through her blonde hair, her brow furrowed. "Why have you isolated yourself so much, June?"

I bite my lip, unsure how to explain the mess I've made of my life. How everything unraveled when I didn't know how to deal with my pain. "It's hard to explain."

Dina looks at me with big, understanding eyes. "I'm your best friend, June. You can try."

I take a deep breath, feeling the weight of the confession I'm about to make. "I'm not proud of who I became after high school. I made a lot of bad decisions."

"You mean with Patrick?" she asks pointedly.

I shake my head. "Not just Patrick. It's the way I handled everything. My mom leaving, Lily's constant criticism. I didn't face any of it until it was too late."

"Why did you wait so long?"

"Because it's easier in high school," I admit, my voice low. "There are distractions. Classes, boys, the drama with Cheyenne Radcliffe. But when you get to college, it's quieter. And the quiet makes everything so much louder. Instead of dealing with my pain, I shoved it down, pretending I was fine. But that only made it worse. I started running from it... and I ran in the wrong direction."

Dina's hand reaches out, warm and comforting on my shoulder. "I didn't realize..."

"Didn't realize what?"

"That I've been a terrible friend," Dina says sadly. "I talk about my stupid dog bite and my nightmares, and you've been carrying all this—real trauma, things that can't be fixed with a few stitches."

I place my hand over my heart, trying to find the right words. "Dina, just because our pain is different doesn't mean yours is any less valid."

"Your mom left," Dina mutters, shaking her head. "And I haven't been there for you the way I should've."

"That's not true," I state firmly. "You've always been there for me. Your friendship is what got me through my mom leaving, and so much more. You've been the best friend anyone could ask for."

Dina's eyes fill with tears, and she pulls me into a hug, holding on like she's afraid to let go. I hug her back just as tightly, knowing that no matter how much I've messed up, I still have this—this unbreakable bond with Dina.

"But... I..." Dina struggles to find the right words, her eyes searching mine for some kind of reassurance, some kind of explanation that would make everything make sense.

"You are 17," I remind her gently. "You don't have the tools or the experience to help me through all the things going on at home."

"But you listen to me ramble on in the middle of the night when I have a nightmare about that ferocious dog," Dina groans, shaking her head. "We should be talking about you. About your nightmares. I'm the worst best friend in the history of the world, June Nelson!"

"Listen to me," I say, placing my hands on her shoulders. "I can't talk to you about it because I don't realize how much it bothers me. And even if you wanted to talk to me about it, Teenage June just isn't ready. Ferocious dogs are the only kinds of nightmares I can handle at this age."

Dina nods slowly, processing my words. "I hear you. I do, but I should be a good enough friend to see where you're struggling. Even if you can't handle it."

"Dina, you are a good friend," I tell her, squeezing her shoulders. "The best friend. But we all have our battles, and sometimes we're just not ready to face them. That's not on you."

Before Dina can respond, a familiar voice interrupts. "June?"

I turn, already knowing who I'll see—Patrick.

"Y-yeah?" I stammer, dropping my hands from Dina's shoulders as if I've been caught doing something wrong.

"Can we talk?" Patrick asks, raising a hopeful eyebrow that makes my heart clench.

"We're kind of in the middle of something here," I reply, but it's no use. Patrick's presence has always had a way of catching me off guard.

"No," Dina interrupts, stepping back and giving me a look that says she knows exactly what she's doing. "You should speak with him. Especially about the thing we talked about."

I blink, trying to find the words to protest, but Dina's already turning on her heel and disappearing down the hall, leaving me alone with Patrick—and a choice I don't think I can make.

"Where's the fire?" Patrick jokes, nodding toward where Dina vanished.

"What's going on?" I try sounding casual, but the edge in my voice betrays me.

"Why are you upset?" Patrick steps closer, concern marring his handsome features.

"Long story." I shake my head and stare down at the concrete walkway, suddenly fascinated by the way the light hits the tiny cracks in the surface.

"Have I done something wrong?" The words spill out of him like a secret he's been holding onto for too long, and it makes my heart throb.

"No," I rush to assure him, lifting my eyes to meet his. "It's not you. It's... me."

Patrick gnaws on his lower lip, the way he always does when he's unsure of something. "I have my date with Kira tonight."

"Oh," I exhale, relief mixing with something that feels suspiciously like disappointment. "That's good."

"We're grabbing pizza and going to see a movie," he continues, but there's a hesitancy, like he's waiting for something.

I nod, trying to keep things light. "Cool."

"You're not even jealous, are you?" Patrick laughs, but there's no humor in it.

"Am I supposed to be?" I frown, genuinely confused by the turn this conversation is taking.

Patrick's teeth sink into his lower lip, his eyes searching mine for something I'm not sure I can give him. "I was kind of hoping you would be."

I tread carefully, knowing that the wrong word could unravel everything. He doesn't know I'm from the future. He doesn't know our entire relationship can be summed up in a single word: tragic.

"I don't have a reason to be jealous," I reply, forcing a smile that I hope hides the turmoil inside me. "I get to sleep under the same roof as you tonight and spend all day with you tomorrow. In the grand scheme of things, what's pizza and a movie compared to that?"

Patrick gives me a boyish smile. "Dina conned you into a sleepover?"

"It's her birthday," I remind him, hoping to steer the conversation away from dangerous territory.

"Did you like her gift from my parents?" Patrick's eyes light up, the way they always do when he talks about his family.

"I loved it," I tell him honestly. "And so did Dina."

"Don't tell her." He leans in close, raising a conspiratorial eyebrow that sends a shiver down my spine. "But I talked them into surprising her with a new car."

I know, Patrick. I know. But instead of saying that, I just smile. "That was very sweet and thoughtful of you."

"She deserved it, you know?" He looks past me, into the distance, his tone softening with emotion. "She spends so much time in therapy and I just wanted her to have something nice."

Despite everything, despite the fact that I'm from the future and Patrick is my first love whose heart I shattered—and that this must break every time-travel rule imaginable—I place a hand on his chest, feeling the steady beat of his heart beneath my palm.

"She's lucky to have you." I look up at him, and the world tilts, just a little. He's so kind, so genuine, that it hurts. It hurts to know what I walked away from. It hurts to know that I let this go.

"She's lucky to have you, too," Patrick whispers, his hand brushing a strand of hair behind my ear, his touch gentle and achingly familiar. "I hear her on the phone with you in the middle of the night. You've helped her through so many panic attacks, June. It's one of the many reasons I—"

"You two look awfully cozy," I hear and it ruins the moment.

I freeze, recognizing who it is before I even turn.

CHAPTER TEN
Bullies and Bloggers

"What is this?" Cheyenne's voice screeches like nails on a chalkboard as she practically shoves a crumpled paper into my face.

I catch it mid-air, my heart sinking as I glance down at the bold words. *To the esteemed members of the Bloomford High Book Club...*

Uh oh. She found Dina's letter.

I force a casual shrug as I hand it back to her. "No idea. What is it?"

Cheyenne's eyes narrow, her glare sharp enough to cut glass. "As if you don't know, June. Typical. You always pretend to be so honest, but your actions? They always miss the mark."

My head tilts in confusion. "What did you just say?"

"I think she called you a two-faced liar," Patrick chimes in with a smirk, clearly enjoying the drama.

"No, not that," I murmur, more to myself. "The thing about missing the mark."

"Your actions, June," Cheyenne huffs, clearly losing her patience. "They miss the mark. Pay attention!"

Her words echo in my mind like a bell ringing in a distant memory. *Miss the mark... Miss the mark...* And then it hits me.

"June Nelson professes to be a romance novelist," I mumble, more to myself than to anyone else, "but her stories always seem to miss the mark, especially when it comes to executing believable love connections."

Cheyenne's face contorts in confusion. "What are you babbling about now?"

My mind races, stitching together the tattered edges of an unfinished blanket. Could it be? Cheyenne Radcliffe... The anonymous book blogger who's been ripping my novels apart in the future?

I shake my head, filing the information away for later. "Nothing. It's nothing."

Cheyenne's still glaring at me, her face red with frustration. "Even if you did know who wrote this letter, you wouldn't tell me, would you? You're such a hypocrite, June. You're always pretending to be better than everyone else, but you're just a bully in disguise."

"I'm not the one bullying people, Cheyenne," I say calmly, locking eyes with her. "You've always been the one throwing around insults and making people feel small. Maybe it's time you get a taste of your own medicine."

Cheyenne's face flushes even deeper, and for a moment, I think she might actually explode. "I'm taking this to Principal Pool," she announces, her voice edged with anger.

"Good luck with that," I smirk, my tone dismissive as I turn my back on her.

Patrick steps closer, a grin tugging at his lips. "Walk you to class?"

"Sure." I nod, but then hesitate. "But we, uh, can't let Dina see us."

Patrick raises an eyebrow. "Why not?"

"She, well, uh..." I fumble for the right words, knowing how much Dina wants me to stay away from Patrick.

"Spit it out, June," Patrick says, clearly amused.

"Dina's made it pretty clear she doesn't want us hanging out," I admit, feeling a little guilty.

Patrick just laughs, shaking his head. "She'll get over it."

As we walk side by side, our shoulders bumping occasionally, I can't help but feel a warmth spread through me. It's a strange combo of nostalgia and something deeper, something I thought I'd long ago buried. *Hope*.

Being with Patrick, it feels like slipping on a favorite old sweater—comfortable, familiar, and safe. But there's a tension too, a reminder that this isn't just any old sweater. This is the boy I once loved, maybe still love in some confusing, complicated way.

"You seem lost in thought," Patrick observes, pulling me back to the present.

"I was just thinking," I reply, my mind swirling with a thousand memories.

"About?" he presses, his tone teasing.

"About you," I say, deciding to be honest for once.

His smirk widens. "What about me?"

I stop at the end of the hallway, turning to face him. "Just... this. Walking with you. It's nice."

He hands me my backpack, and as our fingers brush, a spark of hope, maybe a little regret, flares in my chest.

"I should go," I tell him, though every part of me wants to stay.

"Yeah." Patrick grins. "See you later?"

"Not if I see you first," I reply with a small smile, turning to walk away.

As I head to my first class, I can't resist a glance back. Patrick's still standing there, watching me, a grin playing on his lips. The tightness in my chest refuses to ease as I force myself to keep walking, even as my heart urges me to turn around.

But things aren't that simple. Maybe they never were.

***

"What's your favorite movie in the future?" Dina asks as I unroll my sleeping bag on her bedroom floor.

"Hmmm..." I purse my lips, stalling. "Hard to say."

"Who's the biggest movie star right now?"

My mouth opens, then closes. I can't remember the last time I watched a movie, let alone kept track of Hollywood stars.

"You don't know?" Dina gasps, dramatic as ever.

I shake my head, smiling faintly. "I've kind of been busy writing."

"What do you do for fun?" Dina asks, fluffing her pillow and settling in.

Fun? Fun isn't exactly in June Nelson's vocabulary—at least, not in the future.

"I order takeout, have a glass of wine, and take a bubble bath." I shrug, trying to play it off like it's no big deal.

Dina stares at me, wide-eyed. "That's not fun."

"It is when you're 34 and have no life," I chuckle, but the words sting more than I'd like to admit.

"You should start watching more movies," Dina suggests, ever the problem-solver.

"I should," I agree, though the thought feels more like a chore than a solution.

"And you should make some friends, June," she continues gently. "Or call me. I bet Future Dina misses us."

I click my tongue, deflecting. "I think I'm going to go brush my teeth."

"Good to know you're still avoiding confrontation!" Dina calls after me, laughing. "Even in the future!"

It's not that I'm avoiding confrontation; it's just... Dina and I ended our friendship 13 years ago for a reason. Reaching out now, in the future, would be like opening an old wound. She has her life, I have mine. Would we even have anything in common anymore? She's a teacher with a huge family, and I'm... Well, I'm just me, struggling to keep a few houseplants and a flailing writing career alive. Maybe it wouldn't hurt to send her an email if I ever get back to the future.

Lost in thought, I walk right into someone, nearly bouncing off their solid frame.

"Oof!" comes a soft groan, and then, "June?"

Patrick's voice is warm, and the darkness in the hallway only makes it feel more intimate. His hand finds my arm, steadying me. "You okay?"

"Yeah," I breathe out, smiling even though he can't see it. "How was your date with Kira?"

His hand slips down to mine, fingers tangling together like it's the most natural thing in the world. "Boring. Underwhelming. Nothing to write home about."

I laugh quietly. "Not the answer I was expecting."

"Just being honest." There's a click of his tongue, a sound I've missed more than I realized.

It's so dark I can't make out his expression, but I can feel the honesty of his words.

"Thank you," I whisper. "I know you went on that date for me."

"I'd do anything for you, June."

The silence stretches out, thick with the things we're not saying. No one gets a chance like this—to go back and relive a part of their life, to maybe fix things before they break. Is that why I'm here? To fix my friendships, to mend all the things that will shatter in the years to come?

Right now, standing here with Patrick, I have this one moment. What do I want to say to him, knowing that in a few years, I'll break his heart?

"Patrick," I mutter, the words sticking in my throat.

"Yeah?" His grip tightens on my hand.

"No one's ever been as kind to me as you've been," I confess, the truth pouring out before I can stop it.

"It was just a date, June."

"I know," I say, the truth surprisingly comfortable, "but no one else would have done that for me."

"Dina would have," Patrick points out, ever the protector.

"Yeah, but she wouldn't have agreed to it as quickly as you did," I tease, my heart aching with the bittersweetness of it all.

"You would've been a great Book Club President," he utters, his tone so sure it almost makes me believe it.

My heart sinks a little. "I guess we'll never know."

"Nah, you would've," he insists. "I know it."

"Thank you for saying that."

"You're different, June," Patrick murmurs, his voice tinged with intrigue. It's subtle, but it's there. "You made a deal with Kira for the vote. You took on Cheyenne, you... Never mind."

I swallow the lump in my throat. "I should get back before Dina wonders where I am."

"Can we just..." He trails off, the tension thick in the air.

"Can we what?" I prompt, my heart pounding.

"Just stand here a second?"

"Yeah."

We stay perfectly still there in the dark, holding hands, not saying anything. It's been so long since I've let myself be this vulnerable, since I've let someone get this close.

Since Dad died, I've built walls so high no has been able to climb them. I thought I had to be someone else—someone better, someone different. But with Patrick, I get to be just June. And it feels like coming home.

"Well," I finally say, my voice thick, "I should get back to the room."

"I'll see you tomorrow, June." Patrick sighs softly as he lets my hand slip from his.

"Not if I see you first," I reply, the words lame even as they leave my mouth.

To my surprise, Patrick laughs, a soft, genuine sound that makes my heart twist. "Good night."

"Good night, Patrick."

I slip back into Dina's room, quietly shutting the door behind me, leaning against it for a moment to catch my breath.

"That was fast," Dina remarks, eyeing me suspiciously.

"Someone was in the bathroom," I lie, too easily. "I'll just brush my teeth in the morning."

"Whatever you say, Old June."

I really hate when she calls me that.

CHAPTER ELEVEN
The Place No One Wants to Remember

"Where are we going?" I ask, settling into the passenger seat of Patrick's car.

"It's a surprise," he replies with a smirk.

"I really hate surprises," I groan, crossing my arms over my chest.

"I know, June," Patrick laughs. "Remember your 14th birthday? I think I still have the video somewhere on my camera."

I cringe at the memory. "Please don't remind me."

Lily had thrown me a surprise party, but it was more like the birthday party she would have wanted as a teenager, not what I wanted. Instead of a fun trip to an amusement park with Dina, I was subjected to a flamingo-themed pool party with fruity drinks and blaring 80s music. She even invited the neighborhood kids—who were all at least three years younger than me. It was a disaster.

"Lily had a blast, though," Patrick says, chuckling.

"Ugh." I roll my eyes. "She ruins every good moment."

"I don't know." Patrick shrugs in the driver's seat. "I think her intentions were good."

"Doubtful," I scoff.

"Lily's done some pretty crappy stuff to you, sure," Patrick concedes. "But she's also tried to be there for you in the only way she knows how."

"Are you seriously defending her right now?" I give him a perturbed side-eye.

He shakes his head. "Not defending, just... seeing things from a different perspective."

My first instinct is to snap back, but this is Patrick—the kindest, sweetest guy I've ever known. What if he sees something I don't? If I'm going to do things differently this time, maybe I need to listen to the people who've been around me the longest.

"What's your perspective on the whole Lily situation?" I ask, chewing on the inside of my cheek as he turns onto the interstate.

"You really want to know?" He glances over at me, wary.

"I do," I say, trying to sound more confident than I feel.

"You're different," he notes, almost to himself.

"What do you mean?"

"Well, I expected you to yell something like, 'What perspective, you idiot?' But you didn't. You're... You're different somehow."

I take a moment before responding. "I guess I'm trying this new thing where I don't jump to conclusions."

"Lily tries," Patrick says thoughtfully. "When your mom was around, she never threw you a birthday party, right? She barely acknowledged your birthday. But Lily, she tried to do something for you. I know it wasn't what you wanted, but still... she tried."

I take a deep breath, absorbing his words. "From the outside, it might look like Lily is trying, but she planned that whole party for herself, not for me."

"Okay." Patrick nods, accepting my perspective.

Awkward silence falls between us as we drive down the interstate, long miles between our destination and our hearts.

"I just..." I begin, but trail off. "Finding the right words is hard sometimes."

"You've always struggled with that," Patrick says, almost teasingly.

"Except when they're on paper," I add, staring out the window at the passing landscape.

"Have you ever thought about becoming a writer?" he asks, his tone casual but curious.

I smile to myself. I wish I could tell him that we have this exact conversation three years from now and that he's the reason I wrote my first book. He's one of the reasons I chased the writing dream. I wonder if Future Patrick knows that.

"I've thought about it," I reply.

"I think you'd be amazing at it."

The walls around my heart—the ones I built over the years—tremble. Patrick is making them crumble, brick by brick.

"You say I'd be amazing at everything." I wave him off, trying to play it cool.

Snowflakes begin to splatter against the windshield as Patrick changes lanes.

"Plainer's," he suddenly says.

"What?" I furrow my brow.

"You asked where we're going," he explains.

I glance out the window as tears well up in my eyes. "Plainer's?"

Years ago, Mom used to take me to this little café below a three-story library in the city. But it wasn't just any library—it was full of winding staircases and tiny wooden doors that opened to cozy reading rooms. I can still smell the musty bindings of the old books.

"You alright over there?" Patrick prods gently.

I quickly wipe away a tear. "Sorry, I just haven't been there since…"

"Since she left," Patrick finishes for me. "I know. That's why we're spending the day there."

"I don't think I can go inside," I admit quietly.

"There are places too important to avoid forever, June," he counters. "This place was special to you."

"It was special because it was our place—my mom's and mine."

"Well," Patrick says, taking a deep breath, "we'll go in, look around, and if it's too much, we'll leave."

"I don't know if I can," I whisper, wrapping my arms around myself. "There are too many memories—too much pain."

"You should try," he encourages softly.

"I do miss the smell," I admit, clicking my tongue. "Old musty books."

"And coffee," he supplies. "Don't forget the smell of coffee."

"How do you…" I turn to him, surprised. "You've been there?"

"Where do you think I got you that copy of *Leaves of Grass*?"

I'd almost forgotten. For my 15th birthday, Patrick gave me a worn version of Walt Whitman's classic.

"Do anything," Patrick begins quoting, "but let it produce joy."

"Are you a closet poetry fan?" I tease, though my heart is racing.

He tries—and fails—to hide a smile. "I may have read the book cover to cover before I gave it to you."

My heart swells. "Why didn't you ever tell me?"

"Because we haven't really spent that much time alone together," he volunteers. "Dina's always hovering."

She even hovered this morning after dropping me off at home. I was so nervous Patrick would show up before she left, but they missed each other by a couple minutes.

"No, I meant when we—" Stop talking, June! He doesn't know anything about the future.

"When we what?"

I swallow hard. "I guess you're right. We haven't spent much time together."

"I hope that changes." Patrick sneaks a glance at me, and suddenly Dina's words from the coffee shop echo in my mind, settling like a heavy rock on my chest.

If you make him fall out of love with you, then there's no chance you'll do something to hurt him in the future, right?

I don't know what to do. Dina could be right. Breaking Patrick's heart might ensure I have Dina in the future, but then all the memories I have with Patrick—they'd be gone. The time we get to spend together, it would be over.

"June?" Patrick's voice cuts through the chatter in my head. "You alright?"

"Just thinking."

"About?"

I turn in my seat to face him. "If you knew the future—if you knew everything that was going to happen between now and your mid-30s—would you change anything to avoid heartache?"

Patrick swallows hard. "That's a loaded question."

"I just mean," I pause, choosing my words carefully, "if you had the chance to make everyone's life better, including your own, would you take it?"

"I don't know," he admits. "Do I like my life in the future?"

"Hypothetically?" I raise an eyebrow.

"Hypothetically," he repeats, smiling.

"No," I reply. "You don't like it at all."

Patrick's gaze shifts back to the snowy road. "I don't know if changing the past would make things better, you know?"

"Yeah, I guess," I sigh.

"Part of living is experiencing pain and joy. Isn't that what all the great poets write about? The living parts of life—the parts that make us human."

Sometimes, I forget how much Patrick and I are alike. But while he writes music and sings for the world to hear, I hide behind my words on a computer screen.

"Have you always been this wise?" I ask, half-teasing.

"Of course." He scoffs. "I'm an old soul, June."

"I seem to have forgotten that part."

"The future is far away," Patrick says. "Whatever happens, happens. And if we're lucky, we'll get a few good songs and poems out of it, right?"

I click my tongue. "Yeah, sure."

"We're only young once," he reminds me. "Let's just enjoy the moment. Worrying about the future won't change anything."

If only that were true, Patrick.

"You're right. Let's focus on the here and now."

"Speaking of here and now," Patrick grins, "what did you mean when you said that thing about missing the mark when it comes to love stories to Cheyenne?"

I scratch my nose nervously. "Just something she said to me."

"I didn't know you wrote love stories." I watch out of the corner of my eye as his forehead furrows.

"I, uh, dabble in them," I say, trying to keep it vague.

"Dabble?" Patrick raises an eyebrow, amused.

"What?"

"I'm just not used to you saying that word."

"We don't really talk," I counter. "So how would you know?"

He gazes at me, something a lot like longing in his eyes. "I've listened to you talk for years. I know exactly how you speak."

"I'm not sure what to say to that."

The car comes to a stop, and Patrick puts it in park. "We're here."

I glance out the window, and for the first time in years, I see it—Plainer's. The place that once felt like a sanctuary, the one place Mom actually spent time with me—quality time. The place no one wants to remember.

"We don't have to go inside if you're not ready," Patrick offers, soft and tentative. "But I think this place was really special to you. And I..."

"You what?" I turn to look at him, curious and a little nervous.

He hesitates for a moment, then says, "I hope you give it another chance. Special places can still be special, even if the people we shared them with aren't in our lives anymore. We shouldn't run from the memories just because they hurt. Sometimes, holding onto the good in them can help us heal."

"Who hurt you?" I jest, trying to lighten the mood, but my heart aches a little at how much he seems to understand.

He shrugs, a half-smile playing on his lips. "I've seen you go through some tough times, June. It just kills me that you gave up something you loved because it reminded you of someone who hurt you."

And there it is again—this profound wisdom coming from an 18-year-old. I'm 34, yet Patrick is the one making more sense than anyone I've ever known.

"Are you sure you're still in high school?" I ask, half-joking but genuinely amazed at how insightful he is.

"Not for long." He winks as he opens his car door.

I take a deep breath, unbuckle my seatbelt, and step out of the car. But as my eyes land on Plainer's, something shifts inside me. My vision blurs with unshed tears, and the ground beneath me feels unsteady.

I take a shaky step forward, but I miscalculate. I stumble, and as I start to fall, I squeeze my eyes shut and whisper under my breath, "Please don't send me back yet."

CHAPTER TWELVE
Crossroads

I wave goodbye to Patrick as his car slowly pulls out of the driveway, the winter air nipping at my cheeks. My fingers brush the small bump on my forehead, a reminder of the fall outside Plainer's that briefly knocked me out. For a moment, I feared I might be jolted back to the present, but thankfully, it was just a false alarm.

Snowflakes swirl in the fading light, each one catching the last of the sun's rays before settling onto the ground. It's peaceful, but my mind is anything but.

I know Dina wanted me to end things with Patrick—to put out the small flame between us before it becomes a wildfire that'll leave both of us burned. But how could I when we spent hours at Plainer's, sipping lattes and getting lost in old books? For the first time in what feels like forever, I had fun. Genuine, unfiltered fun.

I almost forgot what that felt like—the flutter in my chest when our hands brushed, the way his laugh made my heart skip a beat, the comfort of being with someone who just gets me. It's that heady rush of first love, the one you read about in books or see in movies, but never think will happen to you. And it did, once. Patrick was mine, and a part of me isn't ready to erase that, even if it means saving my friendship with Dina.

Why does it always come down to this? Friendship or first love? In the end, I know I lose them both anyway.

"June Gloom!" Dad's greeting booms from inside the house as I open the front door, too cheerful to be anything but forced. Uh-oh. That can only mean one thing: Lily's mother is here.

I step inside, the warmth of the house wrapping around me, but it does nothing to melt the icy feeling that creeps up my spine.

As I hang up my coat, Dad's face appears around the corner, his smile as fake as mine. "Dad! So happy to see you!" I say, trying to sound as normal as possible.

He pulls me into a hug, leaning in to whisper, "The witch is in."

Oh, great. Sassafras Dupont, my lovely step-grandmother.

"Is that little Junie I hear?" Sassafras's voice floats in from the living room, dripping with that fake sweetness I've come to dread.

Dad leads the way, and I follow, bracing myself. If Lily's bad, Sassafras is a whole new level of unbearable.

"Come here, Junie," she coos from her throne—I mean, recliner—by the Christmas tree. "Give Grandmama a hug."

Grandmama. I inwardly cringe, but I force myself to step forward and wrap my arms around her, careful to avoid the fluffy collar of her brown faux fur coat that's tickling my chin.

"So, Grandmama," I say as I pull away, already regretting the nickname, "What brings you here?"

"Well, Darling Junie, I was in the neighborhood and thought I'd stop by to check on my daughter. Seems she still hasn't figured out how to dust." Sassafras runs a manicured finger along the lampshade, her disapproval evident. "And while I was in the area, I took a look at the houses in Shampton Estates. Simply gorgeous. I can't quite understand why the three of you are still stuck in this rundown shack."

For the record, our house might be a bit dated, but it's home. Cozy, comfortable, and far from the shack Sassafras likes to paint it as.

"We're just staying here until June finishes school," Lily says, appearing from the kitchen, the lines of her face tight with tension.

"Then file for a transfer." Sassafras yawns, like it's the most obvious solution in the world. "I'm sure the school district would make an exception."

"I'll look into it," Dad replies, his tone too eager to smooth things over. "I was just about to start the grill. How do hamburgers sound for dinner, Sassy?"

Sassafras wrinkles her nose as if he's offered her something truly revolting. "I would rather starve."

Lily jumps in quickly, "We could try that new Indian restaurant on Main Street?"

"Anything but hamburgers or a buffet," Sassafras declares, her voice oozing with disdain.

Dad sighs, muttering under his breath, "Guess I'll get the emergency credit card."

"Pretty sure this is an emergency," I whisper back with a grin.

"Junie," Sassafras snaps, drawing my attention back to her. "Go brush your hair and put on a nice dress. You could be so pretty if you simply tried."

"Mom!" Lily's tone is sharp, but I can see the unease in her eyes.

"You know it's true, dear," Sassafras replies with a dismissive wave of her hand.

"I'm literally standing right here," I say, refusing to be brushed aside. "And I'm not changing. I'm going to dinner in this." I motion to my jeans and bright blue sweater, feeling a rare surge of defiance.

For a moment, Lily looks at me, and I see something I've never noticed before—fear. Fear of her mother's judgment, fear of not measuring up. And I get it. I really do. We either become our mothers or do everything we can to be their opposite.

"I'm only going to say it once more, Junie," Sassafras warns icily.

"It's June," I correct her firmly. "And I'm not changing."

Before Sassafras can respond, Dad steps in. "June's fine as she is. Let's get going."

Sassafras looks like she wants to argue, but Lily claps her hands, forcing a smile. "It's cold tonight, so don't forget your mittens!"

Just like that, the tension shifts, and Lily's mask slips back into place.

The drive to the restaurant is suffocatingly tense. I'm squished in the backseat with Lily, who's talking nonstop in a desperate attempt to keep Sassafras from saying anything too cutting. It's irritating at first, the way Lily just keeps going on, but soon I realize she's doing it on purpose. The more she talks, the less Sassafras can criticize.

By the time we trudge through the snow and slush, Sassafras teetering on her three-inch heels, there's a twenty-minute wait at the restaurant. A couple offers us their spot on one of the benches near the entrance, but Sassafras and her oversized designer purse take up most of the space, leaving Dad and me to stand near the door, huddled together against the cold drafts that sneak in every time someone enters.

My flip phone buzzes in my pocket, and I pull it out, grateful for the distraction. A new message. I flip it open, a small smile tugging at my lips when I see it's from Patrick.

But before I can read it, the hostess calls out, cutting through the chatter around us.

"Draper, party of three!"

Draper? My heart skips a beat as I scan the room. And then I see him—Connor Draper, the buzz-cut football player from my psych class, standing up with his parents. How did I forget his last name?

More importantly, who in the world is C.R. Draper? A book blogger determined to destroy my writing career in the future? Or could it be someone I went to high school with? Someone who's known me for years?

"June Gloom?" Dad says, pulling me back to the present.

I look up at him, trying to calm my racing thoughts. "Yeah?"

"You okay? You look like you've seen a ghost."

I run a hand over my face, trying to push away the wave of panic threatening to overtake me. All this time, I thought C.R. Draper was just some faceless person behind a screen who didn't like my books. But what if it's more personal than that? What if it's Connor Draper—or worse, Cheyenne Radcliffe—who's been trying to take me down? How do I even begin to process that?

"I'm fine," I murmur, more to convince myself than Dad. Sassafras snaps her fingers, motioning for us to join her.

Dad places a hand on my shoulder, giving me a reassuring squeeze. "I appreciate you trying with Sassafras. I know she's a lot to handle, but you always manage it like a pro."

His words feel like a knife twisting in my chest. I didn't ask for any of this. I didn't ask Dad to move on so quickly after Mom left. I didn't ask for Lily to take over our house or for the wedding that felt more like a funeral than a celebration. I certainly didn't ask for Sassafras and her uninvited opinions.

But here I am, playing my part, just like I always do.

I never understood why my relationship with Patrick ended so abruptly, why I walked away from it all without a second thought. But now, it's starting to make sense. My life has always felt like a performance, especially after Lily entered the picture. I kept smiling through the pain, pretending everything was okay when it wasn't. Eventually, that facade crumbled, and I took everything I loved down with me.

And for what? Because I felt out of control and powerless. Because it was easier to destroy everything than to face the truth.

Tears sting my eyes as the realization hits me. I thought I was doing what was best, that I was protecting myself. But all I did was push away the people who mattered most. I was selfish, and I let fear dictate my choices.

But I don't want to be that person anymore. I want to be better. I want to find a way to rise above, not someone who burns it all down.

"You should know," my voice trembes as I look up at Dad, "I don't handle it like a pro. I handle it because you've never given me any other choice."

Dad's face hardens, a flicker of something I can't quite read—regret, maybe?—passing through his eyes. "I'm sorry you feel that way, June Gloom."

"Why?" I whisper, wrapping my arms around myself as if that could somehow protect me from the truth I'm about to say. "Why wasn't I enough for you after Mom left?"

"BUD!" Sassafras's irritating squeal cuts through the tension, sharp and demanding. "Get over here, NOW!"

"We'll talk about this later," Dad dismissively responds before hurrying over to his mother-in-law.

"Nelson, party of four!" the hostess hollers, and I feel the crushing weight crashing down.

I know what I'm supposed to do—smile, push everything deep inside, and get through dinner. But I spent too many years doing that and look where it got me. I've always tried to keep the peace for Dad's sake, but in doing so, I lost myself. I pushed away the one person who truly saw me—Patrick—and chose a path that led to nowhere.

I used to think I needed to be seen and heard by others, but now I realize I needed to see and hear myself first.

I have a chance right now to make things right, to be honest with myself and with the people around me. I have a chance to break this cycle.

"I have to go," I say, barely more than a whisper.

Then, without waiting for a response, I turn and bolt out the door into the cold, frozen night.

CHAPTER THIRTEEN
Only So Many Chances

"What are you doing here, June?" Dina gasps, her eyes widening as I stand shivering on her doorstep, my teeth chattering from the biting cold.

"We need to talk," I say, my breath visible in the frosty air as a sharp breeze whips past us.

"Come in, then." Dina quickly steps aside, holding the door open wider.

I slip out of my jacket and kick off my snow-covered boots in the entryway, the warmth of the house wrapping around me like a cozy blanket. The familiar smell of cinnamon and fresh laundry fills the air, reminding me of all the times I'd rushed through this very door, eager to hang out in Dina's room.

"My parents are having dinner with the neighbors next door, and Patrick's at band practice," Dina explains as she heads for the kitchen. "I'll make us some tea."

"Thanks." I swallow hard, running my fingers through my damp hair as I take in my surroundings.

It's strange how some things never change. The Noble house looks exactly the same, from the rooster-shaped cookie jar on the counter to the fading daisy wallpaper on the kitchen walls. This place was like a second home to Teenage June, a sanctuary when things got too tough at my own house. Ken and Alicia always made me feel welcome, offering me a safe place to land when I needed it most.

"Where's your head at, Old June?" Dina teases lightly, catching me lost in thought.

I shrug, offering a small smile. "Just thinking about all the time I spent here when we were younger."

"We've had a lot of good years in this house," Dina says with a wistful smile.

I nod, feeling a pang of nostalgia. But I didn't come here to reminisce. "We need to talk about the night our friendship imploded," I say, getting straight to the point. "There are some things you should know."

Dina's eyes widen in surprise. "You're finally ready to talk about it?"

I lick my lips nervously. "You wanted me to break Patrick's heart, but I'm not sure I can."

"Why not?" Dina asks, her forehead creasing in confusion.

I take a deep breath, searching for the right words. "Patrick is the only person I've ever been in love with. He's the only person, besides you, who really saw me—saw the real me. And in all the years that followed, I never fell in love again. My life... It's been incredibly lonely, Dina. I don't expect you to understand, but when I lost you and Patrick, I lost my dad, too. And I never really recovered."

Dina shakes her head, clearly struggling to grasp what I'm saying. "I don't get it."

"I know." I sigh as the truth settles over us like an early autumn fog.

"No," Dina insists, frowning. "I don't get why you're alone in the future."

"It's complicated," I try, knowing that's not the answer she wants to hear.

"You keep saying that, but it doesn't make sense," Dina replies, tucking her blond hair behind her ear in a gesture that shows her growing frustration.

"Remember when I got strep throat and was out of school for a week in sixth grade?" I ask, trying to explain it in a way she'll understand.

Dina nods, her expression softening. "Worst week of my life. I had to eat lunch alone, and Connor Draper threw a hot dog at my head."

I manage a small laugh. "It's kind of like that. I didn't want to eat lunch with anyone else—only you. So, I've spent most of my adult years eating alone, getting metaphorical hot dogs thrown at my head."

Dina chuckles despite herself. "June, don't make this funny."

"I'm not trying to," I say softly, my smile fading. "I just know I need to start being honest."

"Then tell me what happened," Dina urges, quiet but firm.

I take a deep breath, bracing myself. "Patrick was looking at rings, and I freaked out."

Dina's face falls. "He was going to propose to you?"

"I'm not proud of myself," I admit, the words breaking as they leave my mouth. "But I wasn't ready to get married. And instead of telling him that, I ran."

Dina's blue eyes fill with unshed tears. "Why did you do that?"

"Relationships are hard." I shake my head, trying to find the right words. "And at 21, I didn't have the tools to communicate what I needed or wanted. I think that's why first love is so tragic. You're madly in love, but you're also dealing with all these conflicting emotions. Instead of following my heart, I listened to my head. I didn't want to end up like my mom. I didn't want to hurt anyone the way she hurt me. So I thought if I stayed—if I married Patrick—I was terrified I'd ruin everything."

"Oh, June," Dina exhales, her ocean blue eyes full of understanding.

"I don't want you to think I'm using my mom as an excuse," I continue, willing away the tears. "Back then, I was. But I'm not anymore."

"So, what does this all mean?" Dina asks, clearly struggling to keep up.

I gnaw on the inside of my cheek, my confession suspended in the air like a guillotine. "It means I made mistakes. Big, life-altering mistakes. And somehow, those mistakes led me back here. I'm not sure I want to change anything."

"Then why did you get blasted into the past?" Dina argues. "If it's not to right a few wrongs, then why?"

"I don't know," I say quietly.

"Then we need to figure it out," she demands, her hands gripping the edge of the counter as if she can somehow force the answers to come.

Dina's never done well with uncertainty. She likes plans, goals, charts, and order. It's why the dog bite traumatized her so much all those years ago—it came out of nowhere and shattered her sense of control.

But life isn't wrapped up neatly with a bow. It's messy and unpredictable, like a worn bungee cord tossed around in the trunk of a car. It stretches and grows, then snaps back into place. It gets tangled and jumbled, but somehow, it survives.

For too long, I've avoided the hard things, the painful things. But what has that gotten me? Nothing. Absolutely nothing.

"I know you're determined to figure out why I'm here but, as you get older, you'll realize you can't control everything that happens to you. Only how you respond to it."

Dina blinks, her expression softening just a bit. "That's the dumbest thing I've ever heard."

"To be 17 again," I mutter, waving her off.

"No, June," Dina protests, her voice firm. "It's dumb to think you have no control over what happens to you. You've made choices, and they led you where you are. Hurting Patrick was one of them."

I sigh, running a hand over my face. "I know that. I lived it, remember?"

"Then just fix it," Dina snaps, throwing her hands up in exasperation.

The thing is, not everything that's broken is meant to be fixed.

"I'll work on it," I promise, pulling out my cell phone as it buzzes again. Nine missed calls from Dad. "But I think I should go home."

"Why?" Dina asks, concerned.

"You're a great friend, Dina, but there are some things I don't think anyone will ever fully understand about me. Not until they've lived my life."

"You're mad at me," Dina guesses, her voice wavering.

I shake my head. "Not at all. I just wish I could wave a wand and make everything better. But that's not how the real world works."

"You don't know that," she insists.

"I do," I say. "I'll call you tomorrow."

"I'm still confused." Dina lets out a broken sigh. "Why are you choosing Patrick over me?"

A sharp pain slashes through my chest, and I do my best to ignore it.

"I'm not choosing anyone," I reply. "That's what I came to tell you. I don't want to try and change things. I want to enjoy whatever time I have with my dad before he's gone. I want to spend as much time as I can with you. I miss having lunch with you every day, Deen. When you grow up, you don't get to eat meals with your best friend every day."

Dina's eyes fill with tears. "What if you don't get to go back to the future?"

I click my tongue and glance out the dark kitchen window. "Then I make the most of it."

"You're not worried?" Dina crosses her arms over her chest, flabbergasted.

"I haven't given it much thought, honestly."

"Stay and have a cup of tea with me?" Dina pleads.

"Okay," I give in. "But I have to call my dad first. He's blowing up my phone. Sassafras is in town."

Dina shudders. "Poor Lily."

"Yeah." I suck in a harsh breath. "I never realized how hard Sassafras was on her until tonight."

"Do you think that's why Lily is..."

"Insecure?"

"Insecure," she repeats, her tone contemplative.

"Yeah, maybe," I say, clearing my throat. "You know, for the longest time, I thought Lily was just out to make my life miserable. But now... I'm starting to realize it's probably not even about me."

"She still says some pretty awful things to you," Dina points out, raising an eyebrow.

"I know," I admit, staring into the distance. "But maybe that's more about what's going on inside her than anything to do with me."

"Lily definitely has that whole 'evil stepmother' vibe down," Dina mutters, shaking her head.

Before I can respond, the teapot lets out a piercing whistle, making both of us jump. Dina scrambles to take it off the stove, and the sudden burst of noise seems to echo my own internal panic.

As she hands me a mug, the warm steam swirling between us, I realize that I might not make it back to the future and it hits me like a tidal wave, leaving me breathless.

***

Dad's standing in the entryway when I walk through the front door, his arms crossed like he's been waiting for me. "You know you've got a curfew, June Gloom. Or have you forgotten?"

The truth is, I had forgotten. It's been 17 years since I've had to worry about a curfew. But I can't exactly say that, can I? Instead, I mumble, "I'm sorry I'm late," as I hang my snowy coat on the rack.

Dad doesn't let it go. "What's been going on with you lately?"

Despite the fact that I'm 34 and haven't had to explain myself to anyone in years, the question tugs at something deep inside me. "What do you mean?"

He gives me a pointed look, one that says he's trying to figure me out. "You've been pretty vocal with Lily, you argued with Sassafras about your outfit, you ran out of the restaurant without a word, and now you're coming home well after midnight. That's not like you."

I can feel the tears prickling behind my eyes, but I refuse to let them fall. "It's just... I've got a lot on my mind."

"Like what?" His voice is soft, inviting.

I shrug. "Just stuff."

I try to move past him, but Dad gently stops me with a hand on my shoulder. "June, you know you can talk to me, right? About anything."

"I know," I reply, the words leaving a bitter taste in my mouth.

"Did Lily do something to upset you?" he asks, his concern clear.

I shake my head. "No, it's not that."

"You know she loves you, right?" Dad tries reassuring me.

"Can I ask you something?" I blurt out before I lose my nerve.

"Of course."

"Why wasn't I enough for you?" The question spills out before I can stop it.

Dad looks like I've just hit him with a wrecking ball. "What are you talking about? Why do you keep asking me that?"

"When Mom left, why did you... You and Lily... It all happened so fast, and I just... Why wasn't I enough?"

He lets out a long, forlorn breath. "June, you've always been enough."

"But I didn't feel that way," I confess, the words coming from the 34-year-old me who's carried this heartbreak around for years.

Dad drops his hand from my shoulder, his expression softening. "I didn't plan on falling in love with Lily. Your mom and I were high school sweethearts. I never imagined we'd get divorced. When she left, it was like my whole world fell apart. And then, by some chance, I met Lily in that grocery store parking lot after she backed into my truck. I didn't expect to feel anything again, let alone love. But it happened. I fell in love again, and I didn't want you to think that just because someone leaves us, we stop loving. We don't. We have to keep going, keep believing in love. We don't shut down just because something didn't work out."

I bite my lip, holding back a flood of emotions. "I guess I just needed more time to grieve the family I lost. It felt like you replaced Mom so quickly."

Dad exhales, rubbing a hand over his face. "I didn't replace her, June. Your mom gave me you, and you are the best thing that's ever happened to me. I could never replace her."

"I just..." I trail off, the words escaping me.

"You've always been enough," he says firmly, his eyes locking onto mine. "And nothing, no relationship I'm in, will ever change that. As you get older, you'll see that life doesn't give us endless chances. If we don't take them when we can, we'll regret it."

Tears finally spill over, blurring my vision. If only he knew how many chances I've already let slip through my fingers.

"I love you, June Gloom," Dad declares, opening his arms. "And nothing could ever replace you. Not now, not ever."

I step into his embrace, wrapping my arms around him as tightly as I can. He smells like the woods, all birch and cedar and oak, and it makes me feel safe.

As tears streak down my cheeks, I hold on to him, vowing not to let any more chances pass me by.

CHAPTER FOURTEEN
A Starry Night

Dina elbows me as we walk past a dark blue poster hanging in the quad. "Look at this," she says with a dramatic sigh, nodding toward the sign that reads: WINTER FORMAL: A STARRY NIGHT.

I let out a breath as I take in the words. I didn't go to Winter Formal junior year, but I remember senior year, when Patrick took me.

"Poor Van Gogh," Dina grumbles. "People still can't get the name of his painting right. It's *The* Starry Night, not *A* Starry Night."

"Maybe the Prom Committee thought *A* Starry Night sounded better," I suggest, trying to suppress a smile.

"What kind of world are we living in when artists can't even be quoted right?" she laments, raising a fist dramatically in the air.

"Oh, Dina." I chuckle and drape an arm over her shoulders, "just wait until you get on social media in the future. It's full of misquoted creative geniuses."

"I can't wait." She rolls her eyes as we round a corner in the hallway.

Straight ahead, I spot Patrick, his guitar slung over his shoulder, and Cheyenne Radcliffe, her finger trailing up his sweatshirt-clad chest. Dina stops dead in her tracks and grabs my arm.

"Ugh, don't look, June, but it's a total puke fest." She pretends to gag, and I can't help but laugh.

"You're something else, Dina Noble."

"How can you watch that?" Dina groans, still pretending to vomit.

"I know he doesn't like her," I say with a shrug.

"You're so confident, Old June," she sighs, smacking her lips together. "I want to be more like you."

"I don't think I'm confident," I reply, my gaze lingering on Patrick as Cheyenne inches closer. He takes a step back and bumps into the wall.

"Why are you always so quick to put yourself down?" Dina presses, tapping her foot impatiently.

I lick my lips nervously as I watch the scene unfold. "So many reasons," I answer cryptically.

"I mean, Patrick is in love with you," Dina somehow manages to say without a trace of envy. "You should feel good about yourself."

"I thought you were against Patrick being in love with me," I challenge, raising an eyebrow.

"I still am." Dina swallows harshly. "But if I had to choose someone for him to love, it'd be you, June. Even if you're going to blast his heart to smithereens."

"For the record," I exhale heavily, "I blasted my own heart to smithereens, too."

"It's crazy to think we were almost sisters," she muses, and the silence that follows hangs between us like the last wisps of summer dandelion fuzz.

"We should get to class," I suggest, breaking the moment.

Dina shakes her head, her face falling. "I'm sorry, June. Knowing what the future holds is a little heartbreaking."

"I know." I nod. "I shouldn't have told you."

"I'm glad you did."

"You are?"

"Even if the future is going to be... disappointing, I think I'd rather know now. That way, I can enjoy every second I get with you."

I place a hand over my heart, hoping Dina can't hear how painfully it's throbbing. "Me too."

"Uh oh," Dina tuts, her voice a low warning. "Looks like Cheyenne's not happy."

I glance over just in time to see Cheyenne storming off, leaving Patrick heading straight for us.

"Should I scatter?" Dina mumbles under her breath.

"No, stay," I say, though I can't help but feel a little guilty.

Patrick gives me a coy smile. "Hey."

"Hi," I reply, trying to keep my cool.

"So," Dina drawls, "what did Cheyenne want? To make out with you?" She doesn't even try to hide her disdain.

Patrick rolls his eyes. "No. She asked me to Winter Formal."

"And?" Dina's eyes narrow in on him, demanding an answer.

"And I have a gig that night," Patrick reveals with a grin.

"You do?" I ask, genuinely surprised.

"I do," he confirms.

"That's amazing," I tell him, feeling a rush of pride. "Where at?"

"Just this little place in the city," he says, downplaying it.

"Be more cryptic," Dina challenges.

"It's not a big deal, Deen. Move on," he chides, but I can tell it means something to him. Playing shows is Patrick's passion. He once told me music was what he was made to do.

All these years later, I'm still figuring out what I'm supposed to be doing.

"You're so dumb," Dina whines, clearly unimpressed.

"Can you, uh," Patrick clears his throat, "leave us alone for a sec?"

Dina's mouth drops open in mock outrage. "You're such a loser."

"No, you are," Patrick retorts.

"Oh my gosh, you two," I lament. "Stop bickering."

"I'll see you in class," Dina says, giving Patrick a playful shove as she passes him.

"She's so immature," Patrick says with a smirk, stepping closer to me.

"Uh…" I glance around, feeling the heat rise in my cheeks.

"Are you embarrassed to be seen with me?" he teases, his voice soft and warm.

"It's just…" I trail off as I catch Cheyenne's eye from down the hall. "People like to talk."

"So?" He steps even closer, his fingers grazing mine.

"What's up?" I ask, trying to sound casual.

Patrick smiles, his eyes locking with mine. "I was going to ask you to Winter Formal, but the guys and I got a gig, and I really can't let them down."

"I'm flattered," I say, returning his smile. "But I understand the band needs you."

"We're playing till midnight, so if you're bored Friday night, you should stop by," he suggests, his grin widening.

"Can I bring Dina?" I ask, already imagining her reaction.

"Yeah, of course." The bell rings just as Patrick's fingers twine with mine. "I'll see you at lunch?"

I shake my head, laughing softly. "We don't eat lunch together."

Patrick moves backward, pulling me with him. "We should really change that, June."

As he slings his arm over my shoulder, Cheyenne's glare burning into us from the shadows ahead, I say, "I doubt Dina would be okay with that."

"She'll get over it," Patrick responds confidently.

I lay my head on his shoulder, letting myself breathe him in as he walks me to class, the flutter in my stomach telling me that, right now, this moment is all that matters.

***

Johnny Williams cuts in front of me in line at the cafeteria, making no effort to hide the gloating on his face. "Whoops, were you in line?" he asks, glancing over his shoulder.

"Yeah, I was," I reply, trying to keep the annoyance out of my voice.

"Sorry," he says with a shrug, though it's clear he isn't sorry at all.

I shift my weight from one foot to the other, trying not to let his immaturity get to me. Then, I remember—Johnny asked me to Homecoming our freshman year, and I turned him down. Maybe he has a right to be a little bitter. But what if I could make it up to him?

Winter Formal is coming up on Friday. What if I asked him to go with me? It might be the perfect way to smooth things over. If he rejects me, we'll be even.

"Johnny?" I say tentatively.

"Yeah?" he replies, his expression guarded.

"I was wondering... Would you want to go to Winter Formal with me?"

His shoulders stiffen, and he turns to face me fully, disbelief written all over his face. "What?"

"Winter Formal," I repeat, trying to play it cool. "Would you like to go with me?"

He just stares at me, like he's trying to figure out if I'm messing with him. "Are you serious, June?"

"Yes, I'm serious."

"You want to go to Winter Formal with me?" The sound a mix of shock and excitement.

"Yes," I say again, feeling a bit flustered by his reaction.

"This Friday?"

"Yes," I confirm, laughing a little now.

"Are you sure?" He's practically vibrating with excitement now.

"Yes, Johnny," I say, smiling despite myself.

"What color should I order your corsage in?" he asks, as if it's the most natural next question.

I blink at him, taken aback. "Is that a yes?"

"Yes!" he squeaks, clearly thrilled. "I've been wanting to take you to a dance since freshman year."

This isn't exactly how I pictured this going.

"Really?" I say, still trying to process his enthusiasm.

"What color is your dress?" He's all business now.

"Honestly," I admit, "I didn't think you'd say yes, so I don't have a dress yet."

"That's fine," Johnny assures me with a dismissive wave. "I'll order white flowers. White goes with everything."

"It does..." I trail off, still reeling from how quickly this conversation has escalated.

"I have so much to do before Friday." He steps out of line, already pulling out his phone. "I have to go tell the guys that June Nelson is my girlfriend!"

"Wait—" I start to say, but he's already running across the quad.

"Why does Johnny Williams need to tell people you're his girlfriend?" Dina asks, appearing beside me with her sandwich in hand.

"I asked him to Winter Formal," I explain, still a bit dazed.

"You did?" she sputters, nearly choking on her sandwich.

"I did."

"And he said yes?"

"I'm just as shocked as you are," I admit.

"But what about the P word?" Dina asks, raising an eyebrow.

"Patrick?" I blink, caught off guard by the question.

"Yeah," she says, looking at me like I've lost my mind.

"Patrick has a gig," I reply, as if that explains everything.

"I can't wait until he hears about this," Dina chuckles, her tone a bit wicked. "He's going to freak."

"I didn't think Johnny would say yes," I whisper, suddenly overwhelmed by the situation. "I figured if I asked him and he rejected me, we'd be even."

"Didn't work out the way you planned then, huh?"

"Nope," I say, grabbing a slice of pizza and a fruit punch. This whole time-travel thing is really throwing me off my game.

"Just think of it this way," Dina says between bites, "now you've fixed one thing while you're here."

"Yeah." I frown, the victory feeling hollow. "One thing off the list."

"Bet you didn't think this would be one of the things Old June was going to have to fix, did you?" she teases.

I let out a sigh. "No, I really didn't."

"Do you think Johnny will make you his #1 friend on MyPlace?" Dina jokes, nudging me with her elbow.

I raise an eyebrow at her. "I can't wait until you discover FriendBook."

"I already have one," she says nonchalantly.

"What?" I whip my head around to look at her.

"Yeah, my cousin Molly sent me a request to join."

"Seriously? And you didn't invite me?"

Dina shoves the rest of her sandwich into her mouth, conveniently avoiding the question.

"You're so on my list," I narrow my eyes at her.

"Or onnn eye ist, ooh," she says with her mouth full.

I roll my eyes, following her to a little green picnic table in the middle of the quad. We sit down, and just as I'm about to take a bite of my pizza, I notice Patrick waving at us from across the way.

"Oh," I say, suddenly nervous. "Patrick wants to eat lunch with us."

Dina's nostrils flare in annoyance. "No."

"Well, uh, he's heading this way," I point out.

"Right now?"

"Right now," I confirm, watching as Patrick approaches.

"Just break his heart," Dina mutters through gritted teeth.

"I might when he finds out who I'm going to Winter Formal with," I mumble in response.

"Hey guys," Patrick greets us, his usual easy smile in place.

"June's going to Winter Formal with Johnny Williams!" Dina blurts out before I can say a word.

My mouth drops open. Seriously, Dina?

"Johnny Williams?" Patrick repeats, his eyes narrowing slightly as he looks at me. "The guy you rejected like, two years ago?"

"How do you remember that?" Dina asks, clearly impressed.

"Yeah." I clear my throat. "I figured if I asked him, he'd reject me, and he could stop hating me. But he said yes and ruined that plan."

"And now he's telling everyone that June is his girlfriend," Dina adds, not-so-helpfully.

I send her a death glare, but she just shrugs.

"That's cute," Patrick says, smirking as he peels an orange.

"That's cute?" Dina scoffs. "That's all you've got?"

Patrick shrugs, popping a slice of orange into his mouth. "I'm playing the long game, Deen. Johnny doesn't even know who he's competing with."

Did Patrick just admit—out loud—that he likes me? My heart does a little flip as I try to process everything that's just happened.

CHAPTER FIFTEEN
The Truth Hurts

I tip my pink piggy bank upside down, letting the coins and crumpled bills tumble onto the bedspread. I sift through the small pile, my hopes sinking with each passing second. 7 quarters, 4 pennies, and 5 measly dollar bills. Seriously? Why did I think there'd be more in here?

I groan, staring at the pitiful pile of change. There's no way this is enough to buy a Winter Formal dress. The thought of having to ask Dad for money makes my stomach churn. I might look 17 on the outside, but 34-year-old June is cringing on the inside. I haven't asked anyone for money since I was 18—since I moved out. Back then, I was desperate to escape Lily's suffocating presence that I didn't realize what I was leaving behind—precious time with Dad that I can never get back.

But that's the thing about life. No one hands you a roadmap to the future. You don't get to see the twists and turns ahead. All you can do is live in the moment, taking it one second, one breath at a time.

"Dad?" I call out hesitantly as I pad down the narrow hallway.

"Yeah, June Gloom?" his reply echoes from the living room.

I find him lounging on the couch, a basketball game flickering on the TV. He's running his fingers through Lily's bleached-blond hair, and I have to resist the urge to roll my eyes.

"I, um, was wondering if I could possibly, maybe, uh—"

"Spit it out, June," he chuckles, his voice gruff but amused.

"I'm going to Winter Formal, and I was wondering if I could have some money to shop for a dress?" The words tumble out in a rush.

Dad sits up a little straighter, a surprised smile tugging at the corners of his mouth. "You're going to Winter Formal? Did Patrick finally ask you?"

I blink, tilting my head. "What do you mean did he finally ask me?"

"He's been in love with you for years," Lily chimes in with a yawn. "Everyone knows it."

Well, 17-year-old me certainly didn't. It would've been nice if someone had clued me in. Then again, maybe things turned out exactly how they were meant to.

"Why don't you and Lily go shopping tomorrow?" Dad suggests, his eyes bright with excitement.

"Oh," I wave my hand dismissively, "I can manage on my own."

"No, I'd love to go with you," Lily offers, her tone surprisingly sincere.

I resist the urge to sigh. "It's really okay. I'll be fine."

"I'm free tomorrow after school," she insists, clasping her hands under her chin like she's practically begging to take me.

"Um... Yeah, I guess we can do that," I relent, trying to muster some enthusiasm.

"I'm so excited!" Lily beams, glancing at Dad, who looks like he's won the lottery.

"I'm going to head to bed," I say, throwing a thumb over my shoulder. "See you guys in the morning."

"Love you, June," Dad calls after me, the sound following me down the hallway.

I pause, closing my eyes for a moment, letting his words wash over me. If I ever make it back to the future, I want to remember this—him telling me he loves me. I want to remember that once upon a time, June Nelson was truly loved.

As I crawl into bed, I plug in my cell phone, just in case Dina needs me in the middle of the night.

Even after all these years, it's the people who were part of my childhood that I miss the most.

***

"What about this one?" Lily asks, holding up a bright pink dress covered in sparkles.

"It's nice," I say, trying to sound enthusiastic. "But it doesn't really scream 'June.'"

Lily's eyes narrow slightly. "Then what does it scream?"

Outlandish? Grotesque? Too much? "Fancy," I finally say, choosing my words carefully.

"It is very fancy," Lily agrees, running her French-manicured nails over the sequins and glitter, her expression softening.

"I'm looking for something more… sophisticated," I explain gently.

Lily frowns, as if the word doesn't quite compute. "Pink is sophisticated."

"Pink is fun," I reiterate, trying to keep the conversation light. "But I'm thinking more like black."

"Black?" Lily repeats, as if the color is a foreign concept.

"Black," I confirm with a nod.

"Okay." Lily nods too, though her enthusiasm has dimmed a little. She returns the dress to the rack. "Black it is."

"What about this one?" I pull out a floor-length black dress. It's simple but elegant, with a touch of old Hollywood charm.

"It's boring, June," Lily whines, her nose scrunching up as she looks at it.

"Well, maybe I'm boring." I let out a nervous laugh, holding the dress close. "But I love it."

"Let's try it on, then." Lily sighs, leading the way to the dressing rooms as I juggle the silky material in my arms.

In the changing room, I take my time slipping into the dress, feeling both anxious and excited. Mirrors and I haven't always been on the best terms, especially in my teenage years. I spent so long avoiding anything that reflected my own image—mirrors, windows, even shiny surfaces. I was always so hard on myself, convinced I never measured up. I let people like Lily and Connor Draper get into my head, and somewhere along the way, I started believing them.

I take a deep breath and turn to face the mirror. My reflection stares back at me, and for a moment, I hardly recognize myself. When I walk into Winter Formal on Friday night, I won't be Plain June anymore. I won't be hiding. I'll be June Nelson, the girl in a pretty black dress.

I step out of the dressing room, ready to show Lily, but the sight that greets me stops me in my tracks. Lily isn't sitting poised on the edge of the pale yellow couch like I expected. She's doubled over, clutching her midsection, her face scrunched in pain.

Panic floods my chest as I rush to her side. "Lily, are you okay?"

"I'm f-fine, June," she stammers, though her paling face tells a different story.

"Lily," I say more firmly, kneeling beside her. "What's hurting?"

She tries to sit up straighter, but the pain seems to grip her tighter, making her wince and close her eyes. "I'm f-fine. Stand up so I can see the whole dress."

But she can't even manage that without crying out in pain, and suddenly, I'm not thinking about the dress anymore. "Can someone call 911?!" I shout, my voice trembling. My purse and phone are back in the dressing room, and I feel helpless.

A woman working at the register raises her hand and quickly picks up the phone.

"I'm—" Lily starts to say, but the pain is too intense, and she lets out a wounded cry that makes my heart ache.

"I'm going to change out of this dress and grab my things," I tell her, hurrying back to the dressing room. My hands shake as I fumble with the zipper, and it feels like an eternity before I'm back at Lily's side.

"The d-dress," she mutters weakly as a few concerned shoppers gather nearby. "Did we like it?"

"I think whatever's happening with you right now is a little more important than the dress," I say, trying to keep calm.

"I'm going to be alright," she insists, giving me a watery smile. "I've been through this before."

Through what before? I sift through every memory I have of Lily, trying to recall a time when she was ever in this much pain, but nothing comes to mind.

"Are you going to tell me what's going on?" I ask softly. "Or am I going to find out from the paramedics when they arrive?"

"They're here!" Someone calls out, and sure enough, two women in navy uniforms arrive with a stretcher.

"This is embarrassing," Lily mumbles, looking mortified as the paramedics check her out. She whispers something to them, her voice cracking as she does.

My heart lurches, but I don't pry. I can see how upset she is, and the last thing I want to do is make her feel worse.

I grab her hand and squeeze it tight. "I'm going to call Dad."

I follow the paramedics through the department store, both mine and Lily's purses slung over my shoulder. I try calling Dad three times, but he doesn't pick up. I send him a flurry of texts, leaving a voicemail that it's an emergency and that we're heading to the hospital.

By the time the paramedics have Lily settled inside the ambulance, a small crowd has formed, and I know Lily's having a silent meltdown. I squeeze her hand again, trying to offer some comfort. "It's okay," I reassure her, even though I have no idea what's happening.

"It's not going to be okay," she tearfully informs me. "But I appreciate you trying to make me feel better."

"What's going on, Lily?" I tread carefully, feeling my own throat tighten with emotion.

"I'm pregnant, June," she whispers. "And I'm pretty sure I'm losing the baby."

My heart sinks as the ambulance starts moving. A paramedic begins checking Lily's stats again, but all I can do is sit there, stunned. "I-I didn't know."

"Of course, you didn't," Lily cries. "This is the third time."

"The third time you've been pregnant?" I falter, barely able to process the words.

She nods, her tears falling faster now.

"I'm so sorry." I'm stunned. "I had no idea. You never said anything. I wish I would have known."

"I didn't want you to feel the heartbreak each time," Lily says with a sad shrug.

"I'm sorry you didn't feel like you could tell me."

"I never felt that way," she admits. "Your dad and I thought it would be best if you didn't know… We didn't want you to feel like you were losing anyone else."

Her words hit me like a surge, and my heart quivers in my chest. "Lily…"

"I know I haven't been easy to live with," she begins, her voice cracking. "I thought my life was going to look different. I thought we'd have another kid or two. But I… My body has a hard time staying pregnant. And your dad, oh Bud, he's going to be so devastated."

"We'll get through this," I promise her, even though I have no idea how.

"And my mom," she adds, letting out a strangled sob. "She expected this one to stick. How am I going to tell her it might not?"

"You know, Lily, you don't have to be perfect for your mom. You don't have to make her happy. That's not your job."

"She just doesn't understand me." Lily shakes her head. "I'm not like her."

"Living a life most people don't understand," I say as the tears drip down my cheeks, "is one of the hardest, most honest things anyone can do."

Lily reaches out, running her fingers through my hair, the first motherly affection she's ever shown me. "When did you get so wise, June?"

Since life threw me a curveball and sent me back here, I think to myself. But instead, I say, "I just hope you never feel like you can't be who you are, Lily. You deserve to be unapologetically you."

"I'm working on it." She gives me a small smile. "We can't all be as brave as you are."

"I'm not brave," I mutter, shaking my head.

"I beg to differ," Lily argues, wiping a tear off my face. "You're the bravest person I know, June Nelson."

After that, we don't say anything more. I just sit quietly beside Lily, holding her hand tight as we ride to the hospital. When we finally arrive, Dad is waiting for us, his face drained with worry.

I watch as he rushes to Lily's side, leaning over the stretcher to kiss her forehead. Slowly, I make my way to the waiting area in a daze.

I never knew. They never told me. I could have had siblings. I could have... More pieces of Dad could have existed in this world.

My throat clogs as more tears slip down my cheeks. I always thought Lily was selfish and distant. I had no idea she was carrying so much pain.

...we didn't want you to feel like you were losing anyone else.

I don't even know what to think. Dad and Lily thought they were protecting me from more pain by not telling me. That's both the sweetest and stupidest thing they could have done.

Maybe at 17, I was too fragile—too broken—to handle this. But at 34? I just want to hug Dad and Lily tight, to tell them that I'm here, that I understand now. Lily lost just as much as I did when Dad died. She lost her family. She lost the love of her life. She lost me.

I sink into one of the hard plastic chairs in the waiting room, the fear and regret and guilt pressing down on all sides. I never saw Lily as someone who could be hurting, too—someone who needed love and understanding just as much as I did. Maybe I was too caught up in my own pain to see it.

But now, sitting here with all this knowledge, I feel something shift inside me. It's not just about me anymore. It's about us—about the family we could still be if I let go of the past and start being a part of the present.

Oh, June Nelson, what do we do now?

I wipe away the last of my tears and take a deep breath. The answer is simple, really. I stand, resolve settling in my bones.

We heal.

CHAPTER SIXTEEN
Everything

My eyelids keep drifting shut as I struggle to focus on the endless drone of Mr. Garcia's history lesson. We got home late from the hospital last night, and sleep was impossible after everything that happened. There's just too much to untangle, too much that doesn't make sense. The lines between what's happening now and what I remember from before are starting to blur.

Lily miscarried for the third time. She lost another baby, and I never even noticed what she was going through. How could I have missed something so big?

Because, June, you were 17. Give yourself a break.

Lily has always been the person I resented the most, the one who made me feel small and inadequate. She's the woman I've had to grudgingly share Dad with, the person who seemed to thrive on making me doubt myself. But now, I see her differently. All that time I spent rebelling against her, she was silently carrying her own agony and heartbreak.

I used to think I was so perceptive, that I could see people's pain as clearly as the blue sky. But now, I'm starting to wonder how many others have been suffering while I was too wrapped up in my own hurt to notice.

"Pssst!" Dina whispers from beside me, jolting me out of my thoughts.

I glance over at her, my world a bleary gray. "What?"

"Johnny keeps staring at you," she says, her voice laced with curiosity.

I lick my lips, trying to muster up some interest. "Okay."

Honestly, Johnny is the last thing on my mind right now.

"That's all you're going to say?" Dina presses, clearly expecting more from me.

I shrug, feeling too drained to care. "I'm kind of dealing with some personal stuff."

"What personal stuff?" Dina's eyebrows knit together in concern.

"Shhh!" someone hisses from across the room, cutting our conversation short.

"Fine," Dina whispers back, pouting a little. "We'll talk later."

"Can't wait," I mumble, more to myself than to her.

The rest of the class drags on painfully slow. Johnny keeps flashing smiles my way, Dina's huffs of frustration are impossible to ignore, and Mr. Garcia's monotonous lecture feels like nails on a chalkboard. No wonder history was always my least favorite subject.

"June?" Mr. Garcia cuts through the haze. "Can you tell me what year the Declaration of Independence was signed?"

"1776," I answer automatically, stifling a yawn.

"Correct year, but which month?"

I give a half-hearted shrug. "I don't know."

"It's on the test Friday," he reminds me, his tone a bit sharper.

The class lets out a collective groan, and someone whines, "But Winter Formal is on Friday."

"Dances do not dictate test schedules in this class," Mr. Garcia retorts, clearly unimpressed. He turns back to me, his gaze expectant. "So, Miss Nelson, what month was it signed?"

"August," Johnny calls out, and I can't help but notice the slight hint of pride in his tone.

"I thought it was July 4th," Dina pipes up, looking confused.

"That's when Congress adopted it," Johnny explains. "It was actually signed on August 2nd."

"Well, that's confusing," Dina grunts, frowning.

"History is full of confusing details," Mr. Garcia says with a yawn, already moving on to another topic.

But I've stopped listening. How am I supposed to sit here, 17 years in the past, and pretend everything is normal when my whole world feels like it's falling apart?

"Are you sure you're okay?" Dina's quiet question pulls me back to the present.

"Actually..." I start, raising my hand before I can talk myself out of it.

"June?" Mr. Garcia looks at me, his expression a mix of concern and impatience.

"I'm not feeling well. Can I go see the nurse?" I ask, hoping I sound convincing.

"What's wrong, my love?" Johnny blurts out from across the room, concerned. A wave of oohs and laughter ripples through the class, but I barely notice.

"Uh," I blink, trying to focus, "stomachache."

"Go ahead." Mr. Garcia waves me off, clearly not wanting to deal with any more interruptions. "Just don't get sick on the carpet."

I quickly stand and head for the door, ignoring the murmurs and jokes behind me. For once, I don't care what anyone thinks. I just need to get out of here, to clear my head and figure out how to deal with everything that's spinning out of control.

My feet wander aimlessly until I find myself standing in the quad near the culinary building, where the only boy who's ever really loved me is sitting on a bench, looking lost in thought. As if sensing my presence, his eyes flick up, and for a moment, it feels like the entire world narrows down to just us.

"Hey," I say softly, stopping in front of him.

"Aren't you supposed to be in class?" he teases, a smile tugging at his lips.

I laugh, the sound a little lighter than I feel. "Aren't you?"

"Finished my test early, so I snuck out," he explains with a shrug. "What about you?"

"I lied and said I was sick," I confess, sinking onto the bench beside him.

Patrick's expression turns serious. "What's wrong, June?"

I shake my head, the exhaustion winning out. "Have you ever found out something that completely changed the way you see everything?"

He chuckles. "Can't say I have."

Of course not. He's only 18. He hasn't lived long enough to have his world turned upside down as many times as I have over the past 34 years. But here I am, trying to navigate this strange in-between where everything feels both familiar and foreign.

"It's just... so much," I try to explain, but the words stick in my throat. "I don't even know where to start."

"Take your time," Patrick coaches gently. "You don't have to figure it all out right now."

A small part of the tension in my chest eases. With Patrick, I don't have to have all the answers. I don't have to be perfect or put together. I can just be me, messy thoughts and all.

"Something happened with Lily," I say after a long pause. "And it's making me see her differently."

"Good different or bad different?"

"I'm not sure yet," I admit, the confusion still swirling inside me.

Patrick hesitates, then asks, "Can I ask you something about your mom?"

"Sure."

"Do you miss her?"

The question hangs in the air between us, heavy and difficult. I meet his gaze, those navy eyes that have always been so kind to me. "I'm not sure."

"Do you think about her?"

"I call her sometimes," I confide, the confession slipping out before I can stop it. "She never answers, but I leave her messages. Just in case she wants to know what's going on with me."

"She never calls back?" His voice is tender, filled with an understanding that makes my heart ache.

I shake my head. "Never."

"What would you do if she did?"

The question hits me harder than I expected. "I probably wouldn't answer. I'd be too shocked to know what to say."

"But would it change anything?"

I think about it for a moment, really think about it. What would it mean if she finally picked up the phone? "I think I'd feel less lonely."

Patrick nods slowly, absorbing my words. "You're lonely."

It's not a question. It's a certainty I've been carrying for so long that I almost forgot what it feels like to admit it out loud.

"Yeah." There's a brief pause as I let the truth wash over me. "It's complicated," I add, feeling the need to justify it somehow.

"I know you didn't ask for advice," Patrick says, his thumb gently brushing over the back of my hand, "but I think you need to hear this. Your mom calling you back wouldn't fix anything. The person who hurt you... They can't make it right. Only you can."

There's so much truth in his words that my heart sloshes around in my chest. "I'm supposed to fix myself."

"No." Patrick's grip tightens, pulling me closer. "That's not what I mean. You need to be around people who love you, people who would never leave you."

But I left. I left him, just like my mom left me. And maybe that's what scares me the most—that I'm more like her than I want to admit.

"I guess you're right," I sigh.

"Do you want to talk about Lily?" he asks.

"Not yet. I'm still trying to wrap my head around it."

"Do you want to just sit here? We don't have to say anything."

I squeeze his hand, grateful for the offer. "I'd like that."

So, we sit in silence, the cold breeze occasionally ruffling our hair, but it doesn't matter. For a few moments, everything feels simple. Easy. Just two people who care about each other, finding comfort in each other's presence.

"This is nice," I observe, breaking the quiet.

"Yeah," Patrick agrees with a grin. "I should write a song about it."

"You can call it 'Sitting Silently Beside June,'" I joke, earning a laugh from him.

"I think I'd just call it 'June.'"

I look over at him, a flood of memories filling my head. Memories of the life we had together, the love we shared, the way I hurt him. And in that moment, I realize just how much he still means to me.

"What about you?" Patrick nudges me playfully. "What are you going to name after me?"

Everything, I want to say. Every word I've ever written, every character I've ever created—they all have a piece of him in them.

"I'm sure I'll think of something," I reply, a sad smile tugging at my lips.

The bell rings, pulling us back to reality. I wish we could stay here forever, just the two of us, where nothing else matters. But life keeps moving, whether we're ready for it or not.

"I should get to class," I say reluctantly, standing up.

"Are you coming to the show Friday night?" he asks as we both rise.

"I wouldn't miss it," I promise, letting go of his hand and start heading toward the gym.

"June!" he calls after me, making me stop in my tracks.

I turn back, and the look on his face makes my heart skip a beat. "You look beautiful today."

A blush rises to my cheeks. "Thank you, Patrick."

He gives me that goofy grin I've always loved, and I wave awkwardly, wondering how he still manages to make me feel things no one else ever has.

"Don't forget to save the last dance for me," he adds with a wink.

"Always," I reply, my heart feeling a little lighter as I walk away.

There's still so much to figure out, so much to process. But sitting with Patrick, feeling his warmth, makes everything just a little bit better.

CHAPTER SEVENTEEN
June or August

Snowflakes collect on my bedroom window as I grab my coat from the bed and catch a glimpse of myself in the mirror. It's funny how time changes things. 17 years ago, I couldn't stand looking at myself. All I saw were my flaws—freckles I wished away, chubby cheeks I pinched, and that left eyebrow that never seemed to grow right, no matter how much I tried to tame it.

But now, I see something different. I see a girl who's been through so much, a girl who's stronger than she ever knew. A girl who's been loved deeply, even when she couldn't see it.

A soft knock at the door pulls me from my thoughts.

"Yeah?" I call out.

The door creaks open, and Dad slips inside, his presence filling the room with warmth. "Lily's resting, so I thought I'd check on you. But it looks like you've got everything under control."

I smooth down my curled hair, feeling a small smile tug at my lips. I've gotten much better with a curling iron and makeup since the last time I was 17. I'm even wearing my red, sparkly Christmas dress from last year. The one I used to hate because Lily and I had matching ones. I spent most of that Christmas hiding the shimmer under a sweatshirt, embarrassed by the attention it drew.

But now, I'm starting to wonder if Lily saw something in me that I never did—never could. Something that sparkled just as much as that dress.

"I figured it out," I say with a smile.

Dad shoves his hands into the pockets of his jeans, his expression softening as he looks at me. "You look beautiful, June."

"Thanks, Dad."

There's something in his eyes, a sadness that clings to him like a heavy coat. It's in the way his shoulders slump, in the way he forces a smile that doesn't quite reach his eyes.

"Are you okay?" I ask softly.

He tries to brush it off with a shrug. "As long as you're healthy and happy, I'm always fine."

I used to think that was true. I used to believe that as long as I was okay, Dad was okay. But now I see it—the grief lines etched into his face, the way his eyes have lost some of their sparkle over the years. I was so wrapped up in my own pain that I never saw his.

"I'm sorry." The words come out in a rush. "I'm sorry that life has been full of so much disappointment for you and Lily."

He waves off my apology, but I can see the cracks in his composure. "We'll be just fine."

"You're allowed to be sad, Dad," I tell him, squeezing his hand. "You don't always have to be strong for us. It's okay to have weak moments."

For a split second, his tough exterior slips, and I see the man who's been holding everything together for so long. "I didn't want you to find out like this, June. I wanted to protect you."

My heart tightens in my chest. "Can I tell you something?"

He nods, his salt-and-pepper hair catching the light.

"All this time, I thought Lily was unhappy because of me. I thought I was the reason for all the tension in the house. I didn't realize what was really going on, and it made me feel so alone, like I didn't belong."

Dad's expression crumples, and he shakes his head. "I didn't want you to be sad like we were—like we are. I thought if I could keep you from that, everything would be okay."

I take his rough, work-worn hand in mine. "I know you were trying to protect me, but grief isn't something you can protect someone from. It's something we have to go through together."

"I didn't realize," he murmurs, his voice thick with emotion. "I didn't know how much you needed to know."

As I see the tears welling in his eyes, my heart breaks a little more. Coming back here wasn't just about rediscovering myself—it was about making peace with my father, too.

"When Mom left, it was horrible," I begin, a little shaky. "We were both devastated, but we got through it. You and me, Dad—we made it through."

"Did we?" he asks, a sad smile tugging at his lips.

"You found love again," I remind him. "And I've got so many people who love me. Mom leaving was hard, but it brought new people into our lives. We made it, Dad. And even if things are hard and sad and scary right now, we'll get through this, too. Because we're Nelsons, and Nelsons don't give up."

"You're not my little girl anymore, are you? You're growing up into someone I'm so proud of."

Hearing him say that, knowing that he's proud of me—it means everything. It makes all the hard times worth it.

"I love you, Dad," I say, my heart in my throat. "You're the best dad anyone could ever ask for."

He opens his arms, and I step into them, hugging him tight. It feels like a weight has lifted off my chest, a weight I've carried for so long. A weight that feels an awful lot like forgiveness.

The doorbell rings, interrupting our moment.

"Sounds like someone's here to pick you up," Dad says with a soft smile.

"Yeah," I reply. "My date."

"You sure you're okay?" he asks, his concern evident.

I nod, giving him a reassuring smile. "I'm okay, Dad."

My feet carry me down the hall to the front door, each step feeling heavier than the last. I'm just going through the motions at this point, trying to get through the dance so I can watch Patrick's show. It's been so long since I've seen him perform. I didn't realize how much I missed it, how much I missed him.

When I open the door, my breath catches in my throat as his familiar navy eyes meet mine.

"Patrick?" I gasp, shocked to see him standing there.

He gives me a lopsided grin. "I'm heading to my gig, but I wanted to stop by and see you first."

I step aside, waving him in. "Come on in."

But Patrick shakes his head, still smiling. "Actually, would you mind coming out here?"

I laugh softly, stepping out into the chilly night. The cold bites at my skin, making me shiver instantly. Without a word, Patrick slips off his coat and drapes it over my shoulders. The warmth and scent of him wrap around me, filling me with a sense of comfort I didn't realize I needed.

"I have something to show you," he says.

"Okay," I reply, curious.

He takes my hand, his touch balmy against the cold as he leads me down the snowy driveway to his car. When he opens the passenger door for me, his fingers linger on mine for just a moment before he lets go. I slide inside, wrapping his jacket tighter around me, and sink into the cozy passenger seat as he joins me in the driver's seat.

"I wrote something for you," Patrick reveals.

"For me?" I ask, surprised and touched.

He nods, a bit of nervousness creeping into his usual confidence. "I wrote a song. The one we talked about—the June song."

My heart skips a beat. "You did?"

"It's just the first verse and chorus," he says, almost shyly.

"Play it," I urge with a smile, feeling my excitement build.

He hesitates for just a second before turning on the car stereo. A soft melody fills the car, and then his voice—familiar, and full of emotion—begins to sing.

"Walking down the sandy shore,
Hand tucked in mine, I've always wanted more,
The summer breeze, well, it whispers low,
Uttering secrets only we know
June, you light up my gray sky
With your gentle eyes and your sweet summer high
June, under the sun's warmest rays,
Every second with you feels like a holiday."

My breath catches in my throat. I know this song. I know it because I've heard it a thousand times before. But in the future, it's called "August," not "June." I never realized... I never knew...

"What do you think?" Patrick asks, his tone tinged with nervous anticipation.

"It's wonderful," I manage to say, my throat tight with emotion. "It's really wonderful, Patrick."

"Yeah?" He smiles, relief washing over his face.

I nod, my heart pounding in my chest. After we broke up, I used to check his MyPlace page, just to see what he was up to. His band released "August," not long after I ended things, and it became their biggest hit. I never knew it was about me. I never realized how much I was still a part of him, even after all this time.

"I can't wait until you finish it," I say, giving him a watery smile. The song that once brought me so much pain now feels like a gift, a piece of him that's always been mine.

"Shouldn't be too hard," he says with a grin.

"This is really special," I tell him. "Thank you for sharing it with me."

Patrick looks down, uncharacteristically shy. "I was worried you might not like it."

"Patrick." I reach over to touch his hand, "I love everything you write. Always have."

The dashboard light casts a soft glow over his face, highlighting the tender lines and curves that I know so well.

"I should be the one taking you to Winter Formal tonight," he says softly, his smile filled with regret.

I shrug, trying to play it off. "I owe Johnny."

Patrick chuckles, shaking his head. "When are you going to tell him you're not his girlfriend?"

I smile, teasing him. "Are you jealous?"

"No," he responds a little too quickly. "I just know how Johnny is."

"Relentless?" I laugh.

"That's one word for it," Patrick replies with a grin.

Just then, a pair of headlights pulls into the driveway beside us, and I let out a sigh. If this were a fairy tale,

Patrick would be my Prince Charming, and Johnny... Well, Johnny would be the clock striking midnight.

"Duty calls." I sigh, reaching for the door handle.

But before I can open it, Patrick grabs my hand, bringing it to his lips. He kisses my knuckles softly, his touch lingering for just a moment longer than necessary before letting me go.

I slip out of his jacket and walk around to his side of the car. As I hand his coat back to him through the open window, our eyes meet, and I see a lifetime of missed opportunities reflected in his gaze.

"I'll see you after," I promise. "Break a leg tonight."

He stares up at me and his longing expression makes my heart ache. I missed out on so much because I ran. I missed out on everything I ever wanted because I was too scared to stay.

Tears sting my eyes, and I blink them back, wishing I didn't have anywhere else to be.

"Are you okay?" Patrick asks, concern lacing his voice.

"I'm fine," I reply, though the truth is far more complicated. "You're going to kill it tonight, Patrick. I just know it."

I turn away from him, heading toward Johnny's parked car. Johnny quickly gets out, adjusting his tuxedo as he rushes over to meet me.

"Why were you in someone else's car?" Johnny asks, his tone drenched with insecurity.

"It's just Patrick." I trying to brush it off.

"Are you two-timing me, June?"

I sigh, already feeling the dread of the night ahead. "No, Johnny."

He presses a hand to his chest, clearly panicked. "Is there something you're not telling me?"

"Let's just go to the dance and have a good time," I suggest, trying to keep things light.

"Why does it feel like you're breaking up with me, June?"

I let out a frustrated breath. This is going to be a long night.

CHAPTER EIGHTEEN
You Don't Deserve to Be Johnny Williams' Girlfriend

I don't remember much about high school except the teasing and the feeling of being invisible. But walking into Winter Formal in my sparkly red dress, something feels different. Maybe it's the dress, maybe it's me, or maybe it's the fact that I'm no longer Plain June. For the first time, I feel like I'm standing tall, like I belong here, like I'm part of something bigger.

"Would you like some punch, my fair maiden?" Johnny asks beside me, pulling me back into the moment. For a second, I forgot he was even there.

"I would love some punch," I reply, flashing him a smile.

He grins and tugs me across the dance floor as the R&B beats pulse through the gym. Everything is white and bright, the lights reflecting off the decorations, casting a glow over the room. This is my last high school dance. Technically, I had my last dance with Patrick 16 years ago, but for 34-year-old June, this feels like a second chance. A chance to soak in the memories, to remind myself that life inside these gym walls wasn't as bad as I once thought. In fact, it wasn't bad at all.

As we weave through the crowd, I search for Dina. She texted me earlier saying she found a last-minute date, which is surprising because I didn't even think she talked to boys. I'm curious to see who her mystery date is.

"For you," Johnny says, handing me a cup of punch. "They've got water too, if you'd rather have that."

"I"m good with this for now," I insist, taking a sip of the punch as a new song starts playing. A smile tugs at my lips as memories rush back with the familiar tune. "Did you know that the music we listen to as teens actually sticks with us in a special way? Researchers call it neural nostalgia."

Johnny blinks, clearly not following. "No, I didn't know that."

"Yeah," I say, nodding as I let the music wash over me. "It's why these songs feel different, more... meaningful."

"But you're still in your teen years," Johnny points out, confused.

"Right," I quickly correct myself. "I just meant that compared to when I was younger, this music really resonates."

Johnny frowns, not quite getting it. "So, uh, you wanna dance?"

"I'm still working on my punch," I remind him, holding up my cup as an excuse.

"Then let's sit," he suggests, gesturing to the bleachers.

"Yeah, sure," I agree, following him as we climb up a few steps and find a spot in the middle. Johnny sits so close that his warmth radiates off him, making me feel slightly uncomfortable. But I don't say anything. I'm not ready to break the news to him that I'm not interested in being his girlfriend. Maybe after the dance. I hate hurting people, and the thought of making someone feel less than or undeserving just because we're not right for each other... It's awful.

"Wow," Johnny guffaws, breaking my train of thought. "Since when are Connor Draper and Cheyenne Radcliffe a thing?"

My heart skips a beat. "W-where are they?"

Johnny points to the center of the dance floor, and sure enough, there they are, moving together in perfect sync, dressed in matching black outfits.

"I thought Cheyenne was with Jose Martinez," Johnny says, sounding genuinely surprised.

"How did you know that?" I ask, trying to keep my voice steady.

"Jose and I are in drama class together," Johnny explains with a shrug. "They sneak into the storage room during rehearsals."

"Interesting," I mutter, my mind racing.

"You ready to dance yet?" Johnny inquires, clearly eager.

Before I can answer, I spot something that makes my stomach drop. "Uh oh," I groan. "You'll never guess who Jose showed up with."

Johnny follows my gaze and sucks in a breath. "Dina?"

I can't believe what I'm seeing. Dina, my best friend, just walked in with Jose Martinez, Cheyenne's secret boyfriend. What on earth is she thinking?

"Give me a minute," I tell Johnny as I stand.

"Then we can dance?" he asks, hopeful.

"Yes, we'll dance," I promise, making my way down the bleachers as quickly as my heels allow. I dodge a few people, my eyes locked on Dina and Jose as they head toward the photo booth.

"Deen!" I call out, catching up to them.

Dina turns, flashing me a bright smile. "Hey, June!"

I pull her into a tight hug and whisper, "We need to talk."

"After pictures," she replies through gritted teeth.

I can't believe she's doing this. She knows about Cheyenne and Jose. Why would she go to the dance with him?

"You ready?" Jose asks Dina, barely acknowledging me.

"Yep," Dina says, taking his hand with a grin.

I have no idea what's going on, but this can't end well for anyone involved.

"You ready to boogie?" Johnny's sudden appearance startles me.

"Yeah," I reply, still confused by what's happening.

Johnny tugs me onto the dance floor and twirls me around, catching me off guard. "Didn't know you had moves, Williams," I tease.

He shrugs, grinning. "I'm full of surprises, June."

We dance for a while, Johnny showing off his surprisingly good moves. But eventually, I'm out of breath, and sweat is dripping down Johnny's face.

"To refreshments!" he announces, leading me back to the punch table.

I grab a blue snowflake-shaped cookie, taking a bite as Johnny suddenly whispers, "Ooh, drama at three o'clock."

I glance over, and my heart sinks. Cheyenne has cornered Dina and Jose outside the bathroom. Nope, this isn't going to end well.

"Should we... intervene?" Johnny asks, looking concerned.

"I don't think so," I respond, watching the scene unfold as I take another bite of my cookie.

"Dina's your best friend," Johnny says, sounding determined. "If things get messy, I'll step in. I'll protect her just like I'd protect you."

"That's sweet of you," I say, appreciating the sentiment.

It's now or never, June. Just tell him the truth.

"Listen, Johnny," I start, clearing my throat and tossing my half-eaten cookie into the trash. "There's something I need to tell you."

"Oh no," Johnny gasps, his attention back on the unfolding drama. "Cheyenne just shoved Jose."

"Can you focus on me for a second?" I implore, trying to keep him from getting distracted.

"What's going on, June?" he asks, turning to face me.

I take a deep breath. "I don't want to be your girlfriend."

Johnny's eyes widen in surprise. "What?"

"I asked you to the dance to make up for hurting your feelings freshman year," I explain. "Not because I want to be your girlfriend. You're great, Johnny, but we're just incompatible."

"You've got to be kidding me," Johnny says, his mouth dropping open. "You begged me to come with you, and now you're dumping me?"

"I didn't beg," I protest. "I asked. There's a difference."

"You threw yourself at me, June." Johnny shakes his head, clearly upset. "And now you're dumping me?"

"To be fair," I say, trying to be gentle, "we were never really together. This was just a date to a school dance."

Johnny raises his hands in frustration. "You know what? You don't get to dump me because I'm dumping you. We're over, June. You don't deserve to be Johnny Williams' girlfriend."

"You're right," I concede, nodding. "I don't deserve to be your girlfriend."

"Just do me a favor, okay?" Johnny says quietly. "Don't ever talk to me again."

"I can do that, Johnny," I reply, feeling a pang of guilt.

"Peace out," he says, flashing two peace signs before turning and moonwalking through the crowd.

"Ciao," I say awkwardly. Ciao? That's the best I could come up with?

As I watch Johnny disappear onto the dance floor, I can't help but feel relieved. Breaking up with Johnny was by far the easiest breakup I've ever had. I expected more drama, maybe some tears, but it was surprisingly... simple.

"So," Dina exhales, laying her head on my shoulder. "Johnny dumped you, huh?"

"Is he already telling everyone?" I laugh, a little incredulous.

"He is." Dina chuckles, lifting her head to meet my eyes. "And by the way, Cheyenne and Jose are making out in the girls' bathroom."

I twist to face her, my eyebrows shooting up. "Wait, you came with Jose?"

She shrugs casually. "I might have messaged him."

"You IM'd him?" I smack my forehead in disbelief.

"You told me he was going to be famous, June," she defends herself with a grin. "I needed just one picture with him so that when someone does a 'Where Are They Now?' special, I'll be the girl he almost dated in high school."

"Pretty sure no one does those anymore," I tell her, shaking my head.

"He needed a last-minute date," Dina reveals with a smirk. "I offered, and I have zero regrets. Even if my date is currently making out with the head cheerleader."

"You are... something else," I say, unable to hold back my laughter, just as a slow song starts playing from the speakers.

"June?" Dina tilts her head to the side, offering her hand with a mischievous glint in her eyes. "Would you like to dance with me?"

"There's literally no one else I'd rather dance with."

Since I'm taller, I wrap my arms around her waist while she loops hers around my neck. We sway back and forth, laughing as we move to the slow rhythm.

In a surprise twist, fake snow begins to fall from the ceiling, and we both ooh and ahh, taking turns twirling each other as the gym transforms into a winter wonderland.

"You're pretty cool, Old June," Dina finally says, her voice soft and sincere.

"Yeah?" I lift an eyebrow, smiling down at her. "You think so?"

"What am I supposed to do when Teenage June comes back?" she asks, a hint of worry creeping into her tone.

I chew on the inside of my cheek, thinking it over. "Don't tell her I was here."

Dina exhales heavily, her brow furrowing. "That's a big secret to keep from my best friend. Especially if I'm supposed to find a way to keep our friendship from falling apart."

I've been thinking about that a lot—about what might have happened if we'd stayed friends, if I'd found a way to keep in touch after everything with Patrick fell apart. But the truth is, if I hadn't lost Dina, I might never have made the mistakes that eventually brought me back here. And without those mistakes, I wouldn't have had this second chance to tell Dad I love him, to see Lily in a new light, to realize that Patrick was always the one for me, even if he has a life without me now.

"I know it's a big ask, Deen," I sigh, "but Teenage June needs to go through everything she does so that I can come back here. I needed this more than I can ever explain."

Dina lets out a frustrated breath, her expression torn. "I don't know, June. I don't know if I can keep it."

We continue swaying to the music, the fake snow falling softly on Dina's blonde hair like a delicate crown.

"I've been trying to figure out why I came back," I admit. "I thought it was to fix things, but now I see that I didn't come back to change anything. I came back to fix my focus. I have so many regrets, but they led me right here, dancing with my best friend in the whole world at a high school dance in 2007. And honestly, there's nowhere else I'd rather be."

Dina's eyes well up with tears, and she nods slowly. "I'll keep your secret, but on one condition."

"Anything," I say, gripping her hand a little tighter.

"When you get back to the future, you have to come see me, June," she insists, her tone serious.

I stop swaying, caught off guard by her request. "I-I don't know, Deen…"

"Come on," she pleads, giving me a determined look. "You're asking me to give up our friendship in some way. You owe me this. You owe me big time."

"What if you close the door in my face?" I ask, a note of fear creeping into my voice.

She shrugs, but her eyes are firm. "You're asking me to trust you. I'm just asking for the same in return."

"You're right," I concede with a sigh. "I promise, if you keep my secret, I'll find you as soon as I get back to the future."

Dina pulls me into a tight hug. "I'm sorry you've had to go through so much without me."

Even though she's still so young and has no idea of the terrible things I'll do in the years to come, her words hit me deep. I needed to hear them.

It's been hard without Dina. But maybe this is the first step toward making things better—toward finally letting go of the guilt and pain I've carried for far too long.

CHAPTER NINETEEN
Secrets

I should have brought a change of clothes. Then again, showing up to Patrick's first gig in a red sparkly dress might have made 17-year-old June feel awkward. But 34-year-old June? I think it's perfect. This is a celebration, after all.

"I feel too young to be in this place," Dina whispers nervously, clutching my arm like a lifeline.

Everyone around us has red wristbands, marking them as over 21 and eligible to buy drinks at the bar. Honestly, I wouldn't mind a glass of merlot right now.

I guide us through the muggy crowd toward the front of the room. Patrick's band is in the middle of their set, and everyone is swaying to a slow, alt-rock song they wrote a few years ago. I sing along as Patrick spots us and winks. My knees go a little weak, but I shake off the feeling and smile back at him.

Crowing at Midnight plays a few more songs as Dina and I move to the music. It's been so long since I last saw Patrick perform on stage. I forgot how good he is, and it stings a little knowing he gave all of this up. I can't believe his band didn't become famous.

"Why are you frowning, Old June?" Dina asks pointedly, her eyes narrowing at me.

I exhale, glancing over at her. "Just thinking."

"About?" She leans closer, her curiosity piqued. "What's on your mind, Old Lady?"

"First," I roll my eyes, "stop calling me old. It hurts my feelings."

Dina throws her blonde head back and laughs. "No, it doesn't."

Well, maybe it does a little. But compared to 17-year-old Dina, I feel like I've lived a hundred lifetimes—and I guess, technically, I have.

"And secondly," I continue, "I was thinking about all the things Patrick gives up, you know?"

Dina's gaze shifts to Patrick. "You mean his band?"

"I mean... All of it." Me. The band. His dreams.

"I'm sorry I call you old," Dina says, her tone softening. "But it's how I differentiate between Teenage June and Future June. It's still confusing to me."

"I know," I say, understanding.

"You said Patrick's band didn't make it," Dina notes as the band transitions into their next song. "But what if it was never supposed to be big?"

"What do you mean?" I raise an eyebrow, curious.

"Maybe it wasn't meant to be a huge success," Dina suggests. "Maybe it was just supposed to be a really important part of his life. A lesson."

I smile at my best friend. "Who are you, Dina Noble?"

She shrugs, a small smile playing on her lips. "I'm trying to see things from all perspectives these days."

"In the future," I say quietly, "we call that character growth."

"I'm pretty sure that's what we call it here in the past, too."

She loops her arm through mine, and we both look up at Patrick. His dark, sweaty hair is plastered to his forehead, but he's grinning ear-to-ear.

"I have to pee!" Dina suddenly yells, loud enough for the entire room to hear.

Patrick smirks as his fingers dance over the guitar strings. He totally heard her.

And because we're best friends, I know that when Dina has to pee, I also have to pee.

By the time we reach the bathroom at the back of the crowded venue, Dina is sweating bullets.

"Are you okay?" I ask, concerned.

She exhales heavily. "I don't think I like crowds. Too loud. Too much chaos. Just... Too much."

"Says the woman who will one day be an elementary school teacher with a minivan full of kids," I tease.

"How do you know I'll have a minivan?"

"What?" I tilt my head, trying to process what's going through her head right now.

"You just said I have a minivan full of kids," she presses, her grip on my arm tightening. "Are you telling me you've seen me in the future?"

I sigh, knowing I can't dodge this one. "I might have FriendBook-stalked you, okay?"

"I don't even know what that means," Dina mutters, moving forward in the line, her expression unreadable.

"It means I looked you up online, found your account, and, well, I saw some pictures. Including one with you and your kids standing in front of a minivan. That's how I know you're married."

"Oh my gosh!" She stomps her foot in frustration. "You did it again, June!"

"Did what?" I throw up my hands in confusion. "What did I do?"

"You don't tell me the whole truth," she accuses in a harsh whisper.

"I haven't lied," I promise. "I've told you the truth this whole time. Even when it was hard."

"But you could have told me you've seen my kids!" she says, clearly upset. "I feel like you're hiding things from me."

"I told you that you had kids," I remind her gently. "I even told you how many."

Dina runs a hand through her hair, clearly overwhelmed. I realize then that it's not just about me seeing her future. She's angry about something much deeper.

"You're mad," I state. "And I'm sorry if I wasn't completely forthcoming. I've... I've had a lot on my mind."

"I have, too," she admits. "This is a lot for me, June. I've been doing better since the Dog Bite Fiasco, but... It's a lot."

"You're only 17," I say, reaching out and squeezing her arm. "It's a lot to take on. I know that. I know everything I've shared with you comes with a price."

"Do you remember when we had that history quiz the first day of sophomore year?" she asks suddenly.

I nod, not sure where she's going with this. "Yeah, I remember."

"You did the assigned reading over the summer and aced the quiz," she continues. "And I didn't read and failed."

"Yeah," I say slowly.

"It kind of feels like that right now."

"If keeping my secret is too much for you," I begin carefully, "then you don't have to. If it's going to cause you this much stress, then forget I asked, okay?"

"I want to keep it, though," she argues, her agitation evident.

"But it's not worth upsetting you, Deen."

"I'm angry with you," Dina finally says. "We were supposed to do everything together. We were supposed to go to college, get jobs together, get married, have kids, and they were going to be best friends like us. You showed up and ruined that dream, Old June. And it makes me so angry."

"I never should have told you I was from the future," I sigh, realizing the burden I've placed on her.

The line moves again, and Dina shakes her head. "I would have figured it out. You couldn't hide this from me. I would have known you were different."

"I'm sorry," I offer, knowing it's not enough.

"I just…" She wipes a tear from her cheek. "I feel like I'm losing you, and it's terrifying."

"What can I do to make this easier on you? Do you want to punch me in the face?" I suggest, half-joking.

Despite her glum mood, Dina laughs. "No, I don't want to punch you."

"Anything," I tell her sincerely. "I'll do anything you need me to."

Dina licks her lips nervously. "There is one more thing you could do."

"Name it."

"Can you and Patrick wait to date until the summer?"

I smile. "That's when we start dating, so you don't have to worry about that."

"No, I need you to tell him, June."

"To wait?"

"Yes," she confirms, her eyes pleading. "I know this sounds selfish, but I want six more months with my best friend before I have to share her with Patrick. Before she eventually breaks his heart and ruins our friendship."

"I will talk to him," I promise.

"I'm happy it's you for him," she says. "But I'm sad for me."

"Wherever you go," I say, my voice thick with emotion, "and whatever you do, I will always be your best friend."

"Even when I don't want to be yours?" she asks, the words heavy between us.

"Especially when you don't want to be mine." I offer her a smile even though the tears are blurring my vision.

"Thank you," she whispers.

"For what?" I ask, curious.

"For being a good friend to me."

"I haven't always been a good one," I acknowledge, "but I'm working on it."

A stall opens up, and Dina disappears inside. I stand there in line, feeling a heaviness settle in my chest. I'm not ready to leave yet, but I think it might be soon.

There's still so much to say, so much to fix. And I'm running out of time.

I need to talk to Patrick. I have to figure out if Connor or Cheyenne is the book blogger who's been single-handedly trying to destroy my writing career in the future. I need to make sure Lily and Dad are alright. And Johnny—what about Johnny? Should I even bother apologizing for the abrupt breakup? Can it even be called that?

I'm running out of time.

My heart starts racing, and my palms turn clammy. The walls of the bathroom feel like they're closing in, too hot, too suffocating. I need air. I need space.

I leave Dina behind, my footsteps quickening as I push through the bathroom door and head back into the main area of the venue. The cooler air hits me, but it does little to ease the frantic beating of my heart.

The crowd roars with excitement, and I glance up at the stage. *Crowing at Midnight* is playing their final song of the night, and it's one of my favorites—*Helene*. Patrick co-wrote it with Bodhi last year. He once called it an ode to first love.

As the familiar melody washes over me, I feel my heartbeat start to steady. Patrick's voice, so full of emotion, wraps around me like a comforting blanket, and for a moment, everything else fades away. The anxiety, the confusion, the fear of running out of time—it all quiets down, replaced by the soothing sound of his voice.

I wrap my arms around myself, letting the music anchor me. This song has always felt special, like it was written just for us.

I think back to our breakup. To that night at the bar. I was so lost and he was so... perfect. I can't believe I ended things. I can't believe I didn't realize what I had until it was too late. Until I set it all aflame.

Then again, maybe everything works out the way it's supposed to. Maybe I was always meant to come back here. To figure things out when I was mature enough—when I was ready.

But just as I'm starting to feel some semblance of calm, something sharp and sudden disrupts the moment. A dark object flies out of nowhere, striking me squarely in the head.

Pain explodes in my skull, and the world around me tilts. The last thing I see is the blurry image of Patrick on stage, his face twisted in concern, before everything fades to black.

Complete darkness.

CHAPTER TWENTY
The Breakup

I'm dreaming. I know I am because I'm standing outside the college dorms I used to share with Dina, but everything feels... off, like watching a movie you've seen a thousand times before.

I see 21-year-old me getting into the driver's seat of my old car, the one with the broken radio that only played static stations. This can't be real. It's like I'm watching my life on a screen, a story that I know all too well.

And just like that, the scene changes. Suddenly, I'm outside The Cobalt Room, the dimly lit bar where everything fell apart. My heart starts pounding as I look around, realizing this is the night I ended things with Patrick. The memory is so vivid it's suffocating. I don't want to be here—I can't relive this. But the universe, or my subconscious, has other plans.

I blink, and I'm standing by the stage. 21-year-old Patrick is there, singing into the microphone, his voice full of that raw emotion that has always made my knees weak. The pain hits me like a wave, harsh and relentless, and my ears start ringing. This is the worst night of my life. Why am I dreaming about the worst night of my life?

In the crowd, I spot 21-year-old June and Dina slipping into a table at the back. I watch myself from afar, a ghost in my own past, trying to get closer but feeling a million miles away.

"Are you sure you're feeling alright?" Dina asks, concerned. "You seem off tonight."

21-year-old June shakes her head, dismissing Dina's worry. "I'm fine, Deen," she says before downing a glass of wine like it's water. But I can see it—she's not fine. I wasn't fine. I knew I was going to break up with Patrick that night, but I didn't expect it to hurt this much, even now.

"You don't seem fine, June," Dina presses, her eyes searching for something, anything, to help.

"Nothing's wrong," 21-year-old June snaps, the lie rolling off her tongue so easily it's painful to hear.

I wince as I watch this unfold. Dina was trying to help, trying to break through the walls I was building around myself, but I wasn't ready to let anyone in. Not even her.

"I want to help if I can," Dina says softly, her voice a lifeline I ignored.

"There's nothing going on," 21-year-old June insists, the concrete walls rising higher.

Dina glances up at the stage, where Patrick is pouring his heart into the music. I wonder if she sensed what was coming, if she knew that our lives were about to change forever.

"I need a refill," 21-year-old June says, slipping out of her chair and heading for the bar.

I should follow her, but I can't. I stay with Dina, watching as she fidgets with her phone, probably trying to distract herself from the sinking feeling in her stomach. Then, the band announces their final song—*Helene*, dedicated to Patrick's longtime love, June.

My breath catches as Patrick scans the crowd, searching for me—21-year-old me. His face lights up with that familiar lopsided grin that always makes my heart skip a beat.

The song begins, and all I feel is dread. I know what's coming. I know how this ends, and it's tearing me apart as I watch it unfold again.

"You're dreaming, June. Just wake up!" I yell at myself, desperate to escape this nightmare.

But I don't wake up. I'm trapped, forced to relive the moment I shattered Patrick's heart.

I continue to watch as 21-year-old June drinks another glass of wine, avoiding the stage, avoiding him. The weight of all my insecurities and fears is so heavy, I can almost feel it drowning me again.

Patrick finishes the song and jumps off the stage, making a beeline for 21-year-old June. He's still riding the high of performing, his smile so wide, so full of love. He has no idea what's about to happen, no idea that everything is about to fall apart.

I want to look away, but I can't.

Patrick wraps his arms around 21-year-old June, but she stiffens in his embrace, turning her face away when he leans in for a kiss. He kisses her cheek instead, his smile faltering.

He still doesn't get it. He doesn't see what's coming. He's too caught up in the moment, too in love to notice that she's about to break his heart.

"You look amazing," he says, his voice soft and full of adoration.

But she's already pulling away. "I need another drink," 21-year-old June says, the words cold and distant.

Patrick's face falls, the hurt already starting to creep in. "How was the interview today?" he asks, trying to keep the conversation going, trying to keep her from slipping away.

"I bombed it," 21-year-old June replies, not even bothering to look at him.

Come on, you idiot. Can't you see how much he loves you? I wish I could reach through time and shake some sense into myself.

"I found you an agent," Patrick reveals with a big smile. He slips something out of his pocket and hands it over. It's a piece of paper. "S. Barnes. She's an up and comer in New York City. She said she's interested in your writing."

21-year-old June takes the paper from him and shoves it into her pocket without saying a word.

Patrick reaches for her again, but she ducks out of the way. "I'm not in the mood, Patrick," she says, the sound charged and dismissive.

He takes a step back, wounded. "In the mood for what?"

"For you," she snaps, the words like daggers.

"What's going on with you lately?" Patrick asks, the words tinged with desperation.

"I'm fine," 21-year-old June lies so easily it's sickening.

"You're not," Patrick insists, his eyes searching hers for the girl he fell in love with. "You're not the June Nelson I fell in love with."

And there it is. The truth I'd been trying to avoid, the truth I wasn't ready to face back then. But instead of admitting it, instead of letting him in, I pushed him away.

"Then maybe we shouldn't do this anymore," 21-year-old June coldy proposes.

"Do what?" Patrick challenges.

"Us," she says, motioning between them. "It's too hard, Patrick. You expect so much out of me, and I can't... I'm drowning."

Tears well up in my eyes as I watch this unfold, as I watch myself destroy the one good thing I had. I needed help, I needed support, but instead of reaching out, I pushed everyone away.

"Are you saying that I'm suffocating you?" Patrick asks, panic etched in the corners of his face.

"Maybe," she replies, my heart breaking with every word.

"Say it then," Patrick tells her. "I know you've wanted to say it for months. Say it, June. Out loud this time."

"We're over, Patrick," 21-year-old June says, the final nail in the coffin.

He takes a step closer, pressing his lips to her forehead. "I'll give you space, June. But if this is really what you want, you need to think long and hard about it."

"It's what I want," she says, flat, emotionless. "I don't want to be with you anymore."

"You're not you right now," Patrick argues softly, defeat and resignation evident in his tone. "Let's talk about this in the morning."

"I'm not going to change my mind," she says. "I've felt this way for a while."

Patrick nods slowly, his heart breaking right in front of me. "I love you, June. I'll always love you. But it's been pretty obvious for a while that I don't make you happy." There's a long pause, almost as if he's waiting for 21-year-old June to argue. When she doesn't, he says, "I hope you find whatever it is you're looking for."

And with that, it's over. The love we shared, the dreams we had, all shattered in a moment of weakness and fear.

I watch myself down another glass of wine, trying to numb the pain, trying to forget the damage I've done. But I can't forget. I can't undo what's been done.

There are so many things I wish I could tell her, tell my younger self. You'll never find anyone like Patrick. You'll never have another friend like Dina. Stop punishing yourself because Mom didn't choose you. Love yourself enough to fight for the people who love you. Don't give up, June. Don't ever give up.

But I can't change the past. All I can do is watch it play out, again and again, like a nightmare that never ends.

A blur of blond, curly hair races past me as I wipe the tears from my cheeks. Dina, with that determined look I know too well, grabs 21-year-old June's arm and yells, "What are you doing?"

21-year-old June shrugs, her tone laced with a cold detachment. "What does it look like I'm doing? I'm drinking, Deen."

"Patrick said you just broke up with him," Dina shouts, the words cracking with disbelief.

"And?" 21-year-old June hitches a shoulder, the indifference in her tone like a slap to the face.

"You're joking, right?" Dina guffaws, searching her face for any sign of a cruel prank.

"No," 21-year-old June scoffs, her words sharp and biting. "I've outgrown Patrick. I don't want to string him along anymore. Honestly, I should have broken up with him a year ago."

Dina stomps her foot, anger radiating off her in waves. "I don't ever want to see you again, June Nelson! How could you? How could you do that to him? How could you break his heart so carelessly? He... He's loved you for years. He loved you when no one else knew you existed. He loved you when you didn't even like yourself. No one, I mean no one, is ever going to love you the way he did. I can't believe you're being so selfish. Go back there and fix this. I don't even know you anymore. I don't think I can be friends with someone like you. Someone who chooses substance over heart. You always said you'd never turn into Lily, but you have. You have, June."

21-year-old June's face remains stoic, but I can see the cracks forming. "What does it matter anymore?"

Dina's lower lip trembles as she whispers, "This is it, isn't it?"

"I don't know," 21-year-old me replies.

"Give me your keys," Dina demands, leaving no room for argument.

"Why?"

"Give me the stupid keys, June!" Dina hollers.

21-year-old June pulls them out of her denim jacket pocket and hands them over, her movements mechanical, devoid of emotion.

"You're drunk," Dina says, her voice softening as she pockets the keys. "Call a cab when you're ready to go. I'll drive your car back to the dorms. After tomorrow, we're done. Forever."

Dina brushes past me, her face red and her eyes brimming with tears. I can feel the finality in her words, the pain of a friendship crumbling before my eyes.

"Can I get another one?" 21-year-old June slurs from the bar.

"How about a cab instead?" the barkeeper suggests as if he's seen this all too many times.

"But I was just getting started," she mumbles, stumbling through the crowd until she reaches the door.

21-year-old June pauses for a moment, staring at the stage where Patrick was just performing, realizing what she's lost. But then, as if resigning herself to the destruction she's caused, she shoves the door open and steps outside into the cold night.

I follow, my heart hammering in my chest, feeling the heaviness of the choices I made all those years ago.

21-year-old June sits on the curb, her head dropping into her hands. Her shoulders shake, and I know she's sobbing, the weight of everything finally crashing down on her.

I sit beside her, even though I know she can't see me. I want to reach out, to comfort her, to tell her that it's not too late, that she doesn't have to keep making the same mistakes.

Eventually, after the tears run dry, 21-year-old June stands and fishes her cell phone out of her pocket. She dials a number, and when someone answers, she says, "Dad?" small and broken into the phone

As the dream fades, I wake up with a dull ache in my chest, the reminder of my past cold as stone. It's a warning, I think. A reminder that the choices I make now could shape the rest of my life.

"She's alive!" 17-year-old Dina shouts, relieved, as she hugs me tight on the sticky floor.

I'm still stuck in the past.

For now.

CHAPTER TWENTY-ONE
Making Plans

Waking up to the concerned faces of Dina and Patrick is a jarring contrast to the emotional nightmare I just relived. It takes a moment for reality to settle in, but when it does, I'm grateful to be back—back to a time when I still have a chance to make things right.

Dina helps me sit up as Patrick hands me a glass of water. I rub my forehead before taking a tentative sip, feeling the bump forming—a reminder that tomorrow morning is going to be rough.

"You blacked out, June," Dina whispers. "You scared us half to death."

It takes me a minute to gain my bearings, to talk. "I'm fine," I say finally, trying to wave her off as I attempt to stand. But the moment I do, my head spins, and I quickly sit back down on the sticky floor.

"Drink," Patrick urges, gently pushing the glass closer to me. Part of me wishes I could just stay here, in this moment, where everything feels right. But I know better than to think time will stand still for me.

I take another sip, trying to steady myself, but my mind is swirling just as much as my vision. I want to warn Dina—and Patrick—about what's coming, about how things are going to fall apart for all of us. But... Is that really why I'm here? Or is there something else I'm supposed to understand, something I need to see clearly for the first time?

Every time I've tried to change something—whether it was running for class president or making things right with Johnny or my relationship with Patrick—things have stubbornly remained on their original course. It's like the universe is reminding me that I didn't come back to rewrite history or prevent heartbreak. I came back to understand it, to let go, to learn.

A small crowd has gathered around us, their hushed whispers and curious looks adding to the surreal feeling of the moment.

"I'm okay," I force out before finishing the last of the water and handing the glass back to Patrick. "But I need to get up."

Dina hooks her arms under my shoulders and helps me to my feet, and Patrick's laughter fills the space between us as I wobble on unsteady legs.

"When did you get so strong, Deen?" Patrick teases his sister.

"Since always," Dina retorts, still holding onto me as if I might topple over at any second. "I think it's the adrenaline."

I manage a smile as Dina guides me to an empty table. Patrick, with a sheepish grin, admits, "I jumped off the stage. You really scared us, June."

I swallow hard, trying to recall what happened before everything went black. "What hit me?"

Dina chuckles softly. "A shoe."

"A shoe?" I repeat, incredulous. "Someone threw a shoe? Why?"

"We don't know why. Are you sure you're okay?" Patrick asks, his eyes not leaving my face.

I nod. "I'm fine. Really."

"I have to help the band pack up," Patrick says, throwing his thumb over his shoulder. "But I'll drive you both home afterward."

"I can call Mom to pick us up," Dina offers.

"No," Patrick quickly counters. "She dropped you off. Don't make her drive all the way back when I'm already heading that way."

His dark hair falls into his eyes as he glances at me one last time, as if to make sure I'm really okay.

"I'm fine," I reassure him again. "I'll be right here until you're done."

Satisfied, he heads back to the stage.

Dina frowns as she looks at me. "You sure you're okay? You're as white as a ghost."

"I'm fine," I repeat, though my voice is quieter this time. "Just had a scary nightmare while I was out."

Unlike Patrick, Dina doesn't just take my words at face value. "Then why don't I believe you, Old June?"

"I'm telling the truth," I say, trying to convince both her and myself. "I did have a nightmare."

"Do you want to talk about it?" Dina asks, her concern evident.

I hesitate, unsure if I want to share the details of reliving the most painful moments of my past—the breakups, the mistakes, the regrets. "I'd rather focus on something else," I say honestly.

Dina picks up on the change of topic immediately. "What rumors do you think will be swirling around school on Monday after Johnny tells everyone about your Winter Formal breakup?"

I let out a small laugh, grateful for the distraction. "Knowing Johnny, it'll be both creative and exaggerated."

Dina smiles, but it quickly fades as she says, "I'm sorry we got into that fight in the bathroom. When you were out cold, I was terrified that 17-year-old June was going to reappear, and I wouldn't get to tell Old June how much I love her."

I smile back, warmth flooding my chest. "Old June loves you, too."

Dina leans in and hugs me tightly. I reach up to squeeze her wrist on my shoulder. I know I shouldn't be here—I should be in the present, moving forward with my life. But right now, sitting here with Dina, it feels like maybe this is exactly where I'm meant to be.

"You two ready to go?" Patrick's voice breaks through my thoughts.

Dina and I pull apart, both of us nodding.

"Yep," I say, my knees still a little shaky.

The car ride home is quiet, with Dina playing with the radio while Patrick steals glances at me in the rearview mirror. I try to smile back at him, but my mind is elsewhere, lost in thoughts of what's to come.

Tomorrow, it's supposed to snow. The sky tonight is so clear, so peaceful, like it knows everything will change soon. I wish I could be that calm before the storm.

"Why don't you drop me off first," Dina suggests from the front seat, pulling me out of my reverie.

Patrick nods and turns down their street.

When we pull up to the curb, Dina opens the door and reaches for mine. "Front seat, June," she says, her tone leaving no room for argument.

I chuckle and unbuckle my seatbelt, stepping out into the cold night air.

Dina pulls me into a tight hug, whispering, "I love you, Old June. You'll remember that when you get to the future, right?"

I nod against her blond hair. "And you know I'm always going to love you, too, Deen. Right?"

Dina releases me, a small smile playing on her lips. "I think you're going to go back to the present soon."

"Maybe," I say, though I'm not entirely sure anymore.

"Remember your promise to me," she pleads.

"I haven't always been great at keeping my promises," I admit, "but I will keep this one. No matter what."

The moon casts a soft glow over Dina as she smiles, her eyes bright. "Then I'll keep mine, too."

As I watch her walk toward the house that's been my refuge, my safe place, I realize it wasn't really the house that made me feel safe—it was the people inside it.

And that's what I'll carry with me, no matter where I end up.

"You're awfully quiet tonight," Patrick notices, breaking the silence as he drives me home.

I let out a tired breath. "My head is still hurting."

"You got hit pretty hard," he replies, concern lacing every word.

I shake my head, the absurdity of it all hitting me. First, the stop sign, then I tripped and fell outside Plainer's. Now, a shoe? It feels like the universe is trying to tell me something—though I'm not quite sure what.

"I like your dress," Patrick mumbles, his awkwardness almost endearing.

"Thank you," I say.

"What did you think of the show?" he asks. "What little you saw of it, anyway."

"It was amazing, Patrick. You guys," I pause, searching for the right words, "you really have something special."

"Do you think you might want to come to our next show?" He glances at me, anticipation in his eyes.

I turn slightly in my seat to face him. "Did you book a second show already?"

He shrugs modestly. "We find out tomorrow."

"I'm not even surprised," I say, my heart picking up speed in my chest. "People really connect with your music."

"Do they?" Patrick scratches the back of his neck, a rare moment of self-doubt.

"They will," I rephrase, leaning back and resting my head against the headrest. "They definitely will."

"I, uh..." He stumbles over his words, something unspoken hanging in the air between us. "I'm glad you came tonight."

"I wouldn't miss it for the world," I say sincerely.

Silence settles over us, but it's not uncomfortable. It's a silence filled with possibilities, with everything that could be. After a while, Patrick clears his throat and reaches for my hand. "June, I—"

"Before you say anything," I interrupt gently, "can I go first?"

"Yeah, of course," he agrees, his grip on my hand tightening just a bit.

I take a deep breath, steadying myself. "You're the most honest, kind-hearted person I've ever met, Patrick."

The glow of the streetlights plays across his face, highlighting the softness in his expression. "I feel the same about you."

"I'm glad to hear that," I mutter, my voice barely above a whisper.

Patrick's fingers curl around mine, warm and safe. "I've always liked you, but I didn't want to make things weird with Dina."

I nod, understanding the delicate balance he's trying to maintain. "I get it."

The car fills with a quiet tension, the kind that makes my heart race and my thoughts scatter. Even after all these years, Patrick is still the only person who can make me feel like this—nervous, excited, completely out of my depth.

"Would you want to," he hesitates, taking a deep breath, "go on a date with me?"

I smile, feeling the glow of the moment. "I'd love that, but I think we need to ease Dina into the idea of us going out."

"Good point." He laughs nervously, the sound a little shaky.

I'm not sure how to tell Patrick that we need to wait six months before that date can happen. It seems impossible to explain without sounding completely insane.

"Do you have a timeline in mind?" he asks, his tone hopeful.

"Well," I clear my throat, grateful that he's leading the conversation, so I don't have to, "there's a lot going on between now and summer."

"Summer?" Patrick chuckles in disbelief.

I exhale, trying to make it sound less ridiculous. "I just think things will be easier once you've graduated. That way, Dina doesn't have to share me at school, you know?"

Patrick grips the steering wheel, thinking it over. "That actually makes sense. Dina can't get too mad when we hang out outside of school if she gets every minute with you inside of it."

"And you'll be starting college," I add, hoping it sounds like a natural progression.

He shrugs. "It's only a twenty-minute drive."

"Are you going to stay in the dorms?" I ask, curious about his plans.

Patrick laughs, shaking his head. "No, I don't think so. I have band practice every day and I can't see roommates being cool with that. My parents offered to let us use the garage since Bodhi's moving and his will soon be out of commission."

"You're lucky to have the parents you do," I say, a bit of envy slipping into my voice.

"I am," he agrees.

I squeeze his hand, feeling emotions I can't quite put into words. "After graduation, you'll ask me on that date, right?"

"I'm already counting down the days, June," he says, warm and sincere.

My heart flutters in my chest. "You're really willing to wait that long?"

Patrick shrugs again, but there's a tenderness in his eyes that makes my breath catch. "What's six more months when you get to take your dream girl on a date?"

I blush, a smile spreading across my face. "Dream girl, huh?"

"Smart, creative, and kind," he lists, like it's the most obvious thing in the world.

"I'm glad you see me that way," I whisper, feeling something shift inside me.

"How else would anyone see you, June Nelson?" he asks, his tone genuinely puzzled.

I give him a small smile, touched by his words. "I think we all see what we're looking for, Patrick."

"Then maybe you should start looking for the good," he suggests gently. "Especially in yourself."

"I should," I affirm, feeling a weight lift off my shoulders. "I really should."

"I should let you go so you can get some sleep," Patrick says, though there's a tinge of disappointment wrapped in every word.

"Yeah," I say, reluctant to let go of his hand.

I slip out of the car, feeling a dull ache in my chest as I walk away from him. There's this nagging sensation, like I'm supposed to look back, just once.

So, I do.

I pause in the middle of the driveway, letting the moment wash over me. There are times in life when you just know something is important and you'll carry it with you forever. This feels like one of those moments, and I want to remember it—the simplicity, the ease, the feeling of being right where I'm supposed to be.

The weight in my chest lifts, and I head inside, grateful for at least one more night under the same roof with Dad and Lily.

CHAPTER TWENTY-TWO
A Box of Dreams

Dad is passed out on the couch when I hang my coat up on the entryway rack. I walk over and gently drape a fuzzy blanket over him, watching as he stirs slightly, his soft snores filling the room like the ticking of a clock. It's a sound I've always associated with comfort, but tonight, it feels more like a reminder—time slipping away, moments that I've taken for granted.

I stand there for a brief second, taking in the sight of him. The laugh lines and grief lines that map his face, the tenderness etched around his closed eyes, the way his left eyebrow hairs refuse to be tamed, just like mine. I didn't realize how much I'd miss this—how much I'd miss him—until now.

Down the narrow hall, a light spills out from under the door of Dad and Lily's bedroom. I hesitate, unsure if I should check in on her, but then I remember that life is short and sometimes you need to reach out, even when you're not sure what to say.

I knock softly, not wanting to startle her. Lily glances over her shoulder and offers me a wistful smile. "Hey, June."

"Can I come in?" I ask.

"Of course," Lily says as she closes the lid on a shoebox resting in her lap. "How was the dance?"

"Good," I answer, taking a seat beside her on the bed. "I had a lot of fun."

I notice the tear tracks on her cheeks, the way she tries to discreetly wipe them away. But I see it—her sadness, her quiet pain.

"What's in the shoebox?"

Lily shrugs, her fingers tracing the edges of the box. "It's just a silly box of dreams."

"Silly?" I laugh softly, though it comes out more nervous than I intended. "Why would it be silly?"

She hands me the box, her gaze distant. "Take a look inside."

I swallow hard and lift the lid, my heart splintering as I see what's inside. A pale yellow bib, a pair of tiny knitted baby blue socks, a delicate pink bonnet. There's a Baby's First Christmas ornament and a little onesie covered in tiny ducks. And beneath it all, nestled at the bottom, three positive pregnancy tests.

My chest tightens. "This isn't silly."

"It is," Lily says, her voice breaking as a sob escapes her. "It is, June."

I set the box down gently between us, trying to steady my breath. "It's not silly. It's a beautiful box full of beautiful things. And it's not silly to honor what you've lost."

Lily sighs, the sadness in her eyes deepening. "It feels that way sometimes."

Silence falls over us, the kind that feels heavy with things left unsaid. It's strange, sitting here with Lily, sharing this moment of loss. It makes me realize that, in a way, loss has been the thread weaving through my life. Losing things, losing people—it all comes down to that, doesn't it? Nothing lasts forever.

"I'm sorry you found out about all of this the way you did," Lily says softly, regret marring her face.

I reach out and take her hand, giving it a light squeeze. "I'm sorry you felt like you had to hide this to protect my feelings."

Tears well up in Lily's eyes, and she blinks them away. "We've been through a lot together, June, but... We didn't really go through any of it together, did we?"

I nod, feeling the truth of her words settle deep in my chest. "Yeah, I know what you mean."

We've lived under the same roof, called the same man family, shared more hard times than good ones, but it always felt like there was a door between us. We were separated by our own misunderstandings and the walls we built to protect ourselves.

"Can I ask you something?"

"Of course," Lily replies, her gaze steady on mine.

I chew on my lower lip, trying to find the right words. "Have I... Am I not... Why do you have a problem with the way I look?"

Lily lets out a long sigh, as if she's been carrying this question herself for years. "I guess we all inevitably become our mothers, don't we?"

I clear my throat, shaking my head slightly. "I hope not."

Lily's eyes grow impossibly large. "My mom drilled it into me for so long that the only way anyone would like me was if I was pretty or well-dressed. I've known for a long time that's not true, but... I don't know why I tried to do the same to you, June. I'm really sorry, and I promise you—I'll do better."

"I appreciate that, Lily." I place a hand over my heart, feeling the words slosh around in there. "More than you know."

Lily shifts, her expression softening. "You look lovely in that dress," she says, her tone carrying a hint of pride.

I swallow, feeling a small lump form in my throat. "You think so?"

"I know so, June," Lily replies, firm and sincere.

Something inside me—something I didn't even realize was still broken—starts to mend as she smiles at me through her own pain. It's like a piece of my teenage heart that had been missing all these years has finally found its way back.

34-year-old me understands that one conversation can't undo years of hurt, but it can start to soften the edges. It can open a door to healing that I wasn't sure even existed before now.

"I'm sorry we didn't get you the black dress you wanted," Lily says, wiping a tear from her cheek.

I glance down at the sparkly red fabric, running my fingers over it as I consider her words. "I think this dress," I pause, letting the tenderness of the moment wash over me, "suits me better."

Lily chuckles softly, a sound that feels almost foreign in this room filled with so much unspoken sorrow. "Yeah?"

I nod, a small smile tugging at the corners of my lips. "Yeah."

For so long, I've believed that Lily owed me an apology for the way she treated me. And maybe she does—did. This conversation might be the closest thing I'll ever have to closure. And maybe that's enough.

I want to hold onto this moment, to prolong it just a little longer, because I, too, have a box of dreams. But unlike Lily's, mine isn't filled with baby items. My box of dreams is full of intangible things—Dad being alive, my family whole, a sense of belonging that's been missing for so long, the friendships I've lost.

I miss the life I had before I messed it all up. I miss the person I was before the pain I couldn't—or wouldn't—face took over. I miss the simplicity, the feeling of being part of something that mattered.

"I hope to one day give you a sibling," Lily whispers, her voice so delicate that I almost miss it. "I want that for you, and I want it for your dad and me."

My heart aches. As far as I know, Lily never has children of her own. After Dad died, she didn't even remarry.

Sitting here with her, watching hope flicker and fade, I wish I knew the right words to say. I wish I could make things easier for her, for all of us. But maybe that's not the point of all this. Maybe I'm not here to change anything but to understand. I don't know why that stop sign hit me in the head, but I do know I've seen myself and the people I love more clearly than ever before. I've found pieces of myself I didn't know were missing—pieces that fit perfectly into the puzzle of who I am.

I don't know how much time I have left here, but I know this: I'm going to love everyone the way I should have, with all my heart, while they're still a part of my life. Life is too lonely without family, too empty without friends. It's unbearable when you run from the person staring back at you in the mirror.

I don't want to live a lonely life anymore.

I want it to be full and honest and messy and beautiful. Living any other way is just a waste of time. And now, finally, I understand that.

"I should head to bed," I say.

"I'm glad you had fun tonight." Lily smiles at me, a warmth in her eyes that I didn't expect. "I love you, June."

Tears well up, threatening to spill over. "I love you too, Lily."

We hug, and as I quietly slip out of the room, I catch one last glimpse of Lily holding her box of dreams close to her chest. Empathy wasn't something I ever thought I'd feel for her, but now I'm grateful for it. I'm grateful that I can finally see things clearly.

I change into my pajamas, plug in my pink flip phone, and sink into the sheets. Just as I'm about to drift off, my phone rings.

Dina.

I quickly pick it up, a pang of worry hitting me. "Hey, everything okay?"

"Just calling to make sure you're still... you."

I laugh softly. "Still Old June here."

She sighs in relief. "I want to ask you one more thing about the future."

"Sure," I respond, closing my eyes.

"Am I happy in it?" Dina asks, the words small and uncertain.

I clear my throat. "You look happy in pictures."

"But pictures lie, Old June. You know they do. On the outside, everything looks different. What matters is how things feel on the inside."

"When I make it back to the future—if I make it back," I clarify, "I'll make sure you're happy, okay?"

It's a promise I'm not entirely sure I can keep, but 17-year-old Dina needs to hear it.

"Phew," she lets out a long sigh. "My biggest fear is that when I'm old, I won't be happy."

I exhale slowly. "I believe that you'll be happy, Dina Noble, no matter what your life looks like on the outside."

"I hope so," she whispers. "Well, I'll let you get some sleep, Old June."

"Goodnight, Deen," I say.

"Night."

My eyes grow heavy as I close the flip phone and lay it beside me on my pillow. I start drifting between sleep and wakefulness until I hear something beeping steadily in the background.

Confused, I force myself awake.

My heart drops when I look around and realize I'm lying in a hospital room. In the future.

"June?" a familiar voice calls out from my right.

I turn, and there she is—Lily, sitting beside my bed, her face etched with relief.

CHAPTER TWENTY-THREE
Mirrored Lives

I blink slowly, my heart racing. The last time I saw Lily in the present was at Dad's funeral, over 11 years ago. And now... Now she's here?

"I'm still your emergency contact," she explains, as if she can read the confusion on my face.

I inhale sharply, trying to steady my breath, trying to make sense of how I went from the past to this moment in the present, Lily sitting beside me.

"I was so worried about you," Lily rushes to get out as she tucks a strand of bleached-blonde hair behind her ear. She looks almost the same, just a little older, with a few more lines around her eyes. "I drove through the night to be here. When they called, I..." Her voice catches, and her eyes glisten with unshed tears. "I'm so glad you're awake."

I'm still trying to process it all. One minute, I was in the past drifting off to sleep after talking to Dina, and now I'm here, and Lily—of all people—is sitting by my side. It's like my mind can't catch up with what's happening.

"I, uh," I clear my throat, trying to find my bearings. "What happened?"

She inhales sharply. "You took a pretty hard hit to the head."

I reach up and touch my forehead, feeling the tender bump there. "I got hit by a stop sign, right?"

Lily chuckles, as if she can barely believe it herself. "A traffic vehicle was setting out stop signs for the snowstorm, just in case the power went out and the traffic lights stopped working. One fell off the back of the truck and hit you. It was a freak accident, and everyone said it's a miracle you weren't killed."

"A m-miracle," I echo, the sound shaky. "Yeah."

"I can get the doctor if you need—"

"No," I interrupt her. "I'm fine hearing it from you."

She smiles, but there's a sadness behind it. "I should have called you before now. I can't believe I let so much time go by without reaching out. The truth is, I meant to, but the more time that passed, the harder it got. I never stopped thinking about you, though. I even have a storage unit full of boxes for you. It's mostly your things from the house, but there are some of Bud's things in there, too."

"You... You saved the stuff from the house?" I ask, genuinely surprised.

Lily shrugs, looking a little embarrassed. "I couldn't afford to keep the house. After your dad died, I... I didn't do well. Just getting through each day felt impossible. I almost lost the house, but I worked out a deal with the bank to sell it. I tried to tell you. I wanted to, but I was so ashamed of the mess I was in that I couldn't bring myself to reach out."

I try to sit up, but the room spins, and I quickly lay my head back down.

"Are you okay?" Lily stands, concern etched on her face. "Can I help prop you up?"

I nod, still trying to process everything she's saying. There's so much information, and I'm not sure if I can hold on to all of it.

Lily gently helps me up, then pulls her chair closer to my bedside, grabbing my hand. "I was terrified that I'd lost you too," she admits as she gnaws on the inside of her cheek. An old, familiar habit. "I was scared that I'd never get the chance to tell you how sorry I am for not being there for you. I should have tried harder, June. I should have done better."

Before I can respond, a nurse in blue scrubs enters the room, a warm smile on her face. "Good, you're awake," she says, grabbing the clipboard off the wall and giving it a quick glance. "You gave us all quite a scare, Ms. Nelson. That bump on your forehead is looking a little better."

Ms. Nelson? Ugh. The title makes me feel old—maybe Dina was right.

"How long was I out?" I ask, surprised at how steady the words sound despite the unease swirling in my stomach.

"About twelve hours," the nurse replies, placing the clipboard back in its holder. "Let's check your vitals."

As she speaks, the blood pressure cuff on my left arm starts to inflate, and I glance down at the IV in my right forearm, the reality of the situation settling in.

"Twelve hours?" I shake my head slightly, my forehead still tender from the bump. "It felt so much... longer."

The nurse nods as she listens to me, her expression calm. "You also hit the back of your head when you fell, Ms. Nelson. You've suffered a concussion, so we'll need to keep you here for a little while to monitor you."

"Okay," I respond quieter now, resigned to the situation.

"If you have any questions, just hit the call button on the bed."

When the nurse leaves, Lily takes a deep breath, concern still laced into every line of her face. "Is there anything you need?"

My chest tightens with the weight of everything I wish I could ask for—all the people who aren't here anymore. But Lily *is* here. She's still here.

"Thank you for coming," I tell her. "It means more than you know that you'd drop everything after all this time and be here for me."

Lily's eyes glisten with unshed tears. "Anytime, June. I'll always be here for you."

I wish I had known that years ago. I wish she would have told me sooner. But after my trip back to the past, I know things happen the way they're supposed to, in their own time.

"Tell me about your life, Lily," I say, settling into the bed, the hum of the machines a steady background noise.

She shrugs. "I live in a one-bedroom apartment with my cat. My mom passed away a few years ago. She left behind a mountain of debt, and it was... hard."

Hard. That's a struggle we've both faced since Dad died.

"My life has been hard too," I confess, the words coming out heavier than I expected. "Very hard."

Lily frowns, her eyes searching mine. "But June, you're an author. You did it. I have every book you've written, and I've got a scrapbook filled with every article I could find about you and your writing."

"W-what?" I stammer, the lump in my throat making it hard to speak.

Lily bites her lower lip, regret and something like hope mingling in her expression. "I hope that doesn't sound like I'm stalking you or anything."

"No," I quickly interject. "Not at all."

All these years, I've been calling the wrong person. I've been leaving messages on Mom's answering machine when I could have been reaching out to Lily and hearing a real voice on the other end.

"Why has it been hard for you?" Lily asks, pulling me back from my thoughts.

I shake my head, trying to hold in the flood of emotions. "I've made a lot of mistakes. I have no friends. And I lost the one parent who loved me—who stayed."

"Life doesn't always make sense, June," Lily says, her voice full of understanding.

I reach for her hand, the connection feeling like a lifeline. "You would have been a wonderful mother. It's not fair that my mom had a child and abandoned her when you didn't get the chance to have children at all."

Lily smiles, but it's tinged with sadness. "I've made peace with life being unfair. It's in the unfairness that we discover who we really are and what we're built for."

There's something deeply heartbreaking about how our lives have mirrored each other's struggles.

"We've wasted so much time," I mutter regretfully.

Lily's tears spill over, streaming down her cheeks. "We have, haven't we?"

For years, I've held onto so much anger—anger over things I deemed unfair, over things I had no control over. And what did it get me? I alienated myself, clinging to that anger like a bottle of poison. One sip at a time, it's slowly been killing me.

"I'm sorry if I made things harder for you," I apologize for whatever part I played in her suffering. "I'm so sorry that I... That I was so selfish. It's not an excuse, but I was drowning in pain, and I... I blamed you for most of it."

"Oh, June," Lily says, waving her hand dismissively, "you don't owe me an apology. You were young, and you needed me to be the adult in our relationship. I failed you in that.

I... It's not an excuse," she repeats my words with a sad smile, "but I didn't love myself. And it wasn't until Bud died and I started going to therapy that I figured out how to."

"I should probably go to therapy," I joke, trying to lighten the mood.

"Your books," Lily beams with pride, "they're so beautiful. Your words... They've been a great comfort to me for the past few years."

I'm not sure what to think or even how to feel. Lily is literally the last person I ever expected to show up for me.

"Can we start over?" I suggest, my heart hopeful.

Lily nods. "I would love that." She wipes the tears from her cheeks before reaching into her purse and pulling out a book. I instantly recognize the cover—an hourglass on the front.

"You're reading *Retrospective*?"

"It's beautiful." She smiles, eyes shining with joy. "I think it's your best work yet."

"You don't think it's..." I hesitate, "lacking substance?"

"I think it's honest and real," she sighs before her joyful expression falls flat. "I think that vile Draper Diaries blogger got it all wrong."

Draper Diaries blogger? I'd completely forgotten about the damaging article. I need to figure out who the person is behind the screen—I have a sneaking suspicion it's someone from my past.

"My publisher is probably going to drop me," I explain to Lily, grateful to get it off my chest. "And so will my agent, if she hasn't already."

Oh! The launch party. I never showed up. Sissy Barnes is going to be livid.

"Your agent was here," Lily divulges. "She was really worried about you. She told me to tell you to call her when you're ready."

"I don't know what to do," I admit, feeling the heaviness of everything.

"About what?" Lily asks, her tone kind.

"My life," I laugh, though it barely masks the sadness. For some reason, Patrick flashes through my mind, and my heart aches. "I've messed it up."

Lily shakes her head, a determined look in her eyes. "We'll just have to clean it up then."

"We?" I ask, raising an eyebrow.

"That is, if you'll let me help."

I take a deep, calming breath. "There's a lot to do."

Lily shrugs, smiling. "Then rest up, and we'll get started once you're better."

My chest feels lighter as I close my eyes and drift into a peaceful sleep.

CHAPTER TWENTY-FOUR
Waiting Forever for You

I slide the key into the lock and push the door open, glancing over my shoulder at Lily. She gives me an encouraging nod, but I still feel a twist of nerves as the door creaks on its hinges. As soon as we step inside, my eyes dart to the stack of past-due bills scattered across the counter. I try to casually nudge them aside, but Lily's gaze lands on them instantly.

She raises her eyebrows but shrugs. "I'm not judging you, June. I've been there. I get it."

"Sorry," I mumble, clearing my throat. Hiding the messy parts of my life feels like second nature now, something I don't even think twice about.

Lily shakes her head gently. "You've got to stop apologizing for everything."

If only it were that simple.

"Tea?" I offer as I hobble into the kitchen, my head still pounding from the fall.

"Why don't you sit down?" Lily suggests, slipping off her coat and scanning the cluttered table for a spot to place it. She ends up folding it over a chair, then adds, "I'll handle the tea."

I nod, surprisingly not in the mood to argue, and shuffle over to the couch. As I sink into the cushions, my gaze lands on a bright red notebook sitting haphazardly beneath the TV remote on the coffee table. I grab it and stare down at it. Scrawled across the cover in bold letters is, "Sutton's Diary."

Curiosity gets the better of me. I flip it open to the first page, which my former boyfriend dated a week ago. The words seem to blur for a second before coming into focus:

Sutton's Life Goals

#1: Meet the love of my life.

I roll my eyes. Is he serious?

#2: Become a rock star.

Sure, Sutton. You can carry a tune, but not without a little help from autotune.

#3: Get washboard abs.

Of course. How Sutton of him.

But then, I hit the next line and my breath catches:

#4: Tell June the truth about her writing. It sucks.

The truth?

"Where do you keep the tea bags, June?" Lily's question cuts through my spiraling thoughts, pulling my attention away from the last item on Sutton's Life Goals list.

"Cabinet above the microwave," I reply on autopilot as my mind stays glued to Sutton's bizarre little notebook.

I can't believe I let him live with me. Rent-free, no less! Was he busy searching for the love of his life the entire time? What was I to him—just a distraction? A free place to crash?

My chest tightens, not with sadness over our breakup, but with frustration. How could I let someone trample all over me like that?

I think of Patrick—he would never have done this to me. Regret lodges itself deep inside me, heavy and suffocating. I had something real and good, and I threw it away because I thought I could find something better. But this? This is undeniably worse.

"What's wrong?" Lily asks, handing me a mug, steam coiling from its surface.

I hold up the notebook, still in shock. "My ex-boyfriend apparently didn't like me very much."

Lily takes it from me, skims a few lines, then walks to the trash can and tosses it in without a second thought. "There. One mess cleaned up."

Despite the sinking feeling in my chest, I can't help but laugh. "But he said my writing sucks."

"So?" Lily shrugs as she sinks onto the couch beside me. She still smells like roses, and the familiar scent makes me feel strangely nostalgic, longing for a time I know I can't return to.

"Between Sutton and that Draper Diaries blogger, I'm starting to think I really do suck."

Lily scoffs, shaking her head. "Not everyone is going to like you, June. And that's okay. Life isn't about being liked by every single person you meet. That's never going to happen. It's about growing, dreaming, building something that matters."

I glance over at her, my heart heavy. "But in my line of work, being well-liked kind of matters."

Lily chuckles softly. "After reading Sutton's Life Goals, it's pretty clear that people who don't like you are the ones who can't get their own lives together."

"Sutton's a model and an aspiring musician," I remind her. "He's got it together better than I do."

Lily raises an eyebrow. "Hardly." She gestures toward the trash can. "These people who tear you down are the ones sitting on a couch, scribbling their bitterness into a notebook, or hiding behind a computer screen. They're more focused on dragging you down for chasing your dreams than figuring out their own. Don't listen to that noise, June. Keep moving forward. Keep creating. Keep dreaming."

A wave of relief washes over me. "You're right," I admit, feeling a bit lighter, the weight of Sutton's judgment finally starting to lift.

"Of course, I am." Lily's smile is wide, warm.

I take a slow, sobering sip of my tea, the chamomile working its calming magic. Sitting here beside my stepmom, I can't help but marvel at how much she's changed since Dad died. She's softer now, more grounded. She's nothing like she used to be. Then again, neither am I. Grief changes us. For some, like Lily, it seems to have made them stronger, more resilient. But for people like me? We end up lost, wandering in the echoes of our old lives.

Lily breaks the silence with a question that surprises me. "Why do you write?"

I shift slightly, careful not to spill my tea. "For a lot of reasons," I say, but I know that's not the answer she's looking for.

"But what's the main reason?" she curiously presses.

I pause, really thinking about it. Why do I write? I write because I have so much to say but never feel like I can say it out loud. I write because it's my way of being heard when the world feels too noisy for my voice. I write because there are stories inside me that need to come out.

"I guess... I write because it's how I communicate with the world," I finally confess.

Lily shakes her head, a knowing smile tugging at her lips. "No, June. You write because you feel everything so deeply, and so do other people. You write because some of us need an escape from our hard lives, and you offer that. You write because you see the world not just as it is, but as it could be."

Her words hit me hard, breaking something open inside me. I let out a shaky exhale, a half-sob caught in my throat. All this time, I thought I was writing into the void. But Lily—Lily saw me. She saw me in that sparkly red dress all those years ago, and she sees me now, in every word I've put out into the world.

"You're right," I agree, my voice thick with emotion. I try to hold back another sob, but it escapes anyway.

Lily just shrugs, the crinkles in the corner of her eyes softening. "I may not have said it enough before, but I'm proud of you, June. Always have been."

"I'm tired," I say, giving in to the weight of everything I've been fighting for so long.

"I know you are," Lily replies. She reaches for the remote on the coffee table, her movements gentle, reassuring. "Let's watch a movie. Something light, okay?"

I nod, too drained to protest, as I lay my head on her shoulder. The warmth of her closeness is comforting, and for the first time in a long time, I feel safe.

She flips through the latest releases, her finger pausing on a rom com with bright colors and big smiles. It's the kind of movie I would have rolled my eyes at a few months ago, but tonight, it feels like exactly what I need.

As the opening credits roll, I let out a slow breath and close my eyes for just a second, letting myself be here in this moment. Just Lily and me, watching a movie like everything is normal, like everything is okay—even if only for tonight.

***

The cool December breeze wraps itself around me as I stand on the snowy sidewalk outside Dina Noble-Peterman's house in the suburbs. Her lawn is sprinkled with Christmas decorations—twinkling lights strung across the roof in alternating red and green, and inflatable snowmen scattered across the yard. Abandoned bikes and scooters, with helmets carelessly tossed beside them, litter the driveway. A large wooden sign sits next to the door with a cheerful greeting: "Welcome."

Welcome. It's the last thing I feel right now. But I made a promise to 17-year-old Dina, and I keep my promises, no matter how hard they are to face. So, here I am, standing like a fool in front of my former best friend's house, shivering not just from the cold but from the fear gripping my insides.

I know I should walk up to the porch and knock, but I can't bring myself to move. What if she slams the door in my face? I've made so many mistakes—too many to count—and I've been working on fixing them, but this one... This one feels heavier than the rest. The kind of mistake that could shatter what little hope I have left.

"Hey, lady!" a tiny voice snaps me out of my thoughts. I look up to see a blond-haired boy standing in the doorway, dressed head to toe in a bear costume. "Whatcha doin'?"

I force a smile and start walking up the path. "I'm June," I say steadier than I feel when I reach the bottom step of the porch.

"June?" he repeats my name, rolling it around his tongue like he's tasting it. "Like the month?"

A laugh escapes me—something light, something grateful for this moment of ease. "Yeah, like the month."

"What do you want, June?" He crosses his furry arms over his chest, his eyes narrowing in curiosity.

What do I want? If only it were that simple.

"Is your mom home?" I ask, feeling my nerves creep back in.

"Yes," he says matter-of-factly, then abruptly slams the door shut.

Well, I guess that door slamming in my face wasn't so scary.

My heart pounds in my chest as I stand there, trying to pull myself together. The boy's quick dismissal wasn't what I expected, but somehow it still made my palms sweat, and I can feel my pulse racing in my neck.

Other than a few FriendBook photos of her family, and an InkedIn profile telling me that Dina's now a teacher, I have no idea what her life looks like. That unfamiliarity stings more than I care to admit. She was my best friend, and yet now, we're strangers.

The door swings open again, this time revealing Dina's familiar curly blond hair. She's calling over her shoulder to her kids, "Stop running through the house!" When she turns back to me, her expression freezes as her eyes widen slightly as they lock onto mine. In the fading light, the necklace I got her for her 17th birthday—a gold narcissus pendant she never took off—glows like a lighthouse in a stormy sea.

My heart clenches as I take in the sight of her—older, but still Dina. "Hi," I manage to say, my voice breaking.

Dina swallows hard, her hand gripping the doorframe so tight her knuckles whiten. I wait, every second feeling like an eternity, praying she'll say something. Anything.

Then, slowly, the corner of her mouth lifts into a smile. "It's about time, Old June," she says warmly despite the tears welling up in her eyes. "I've been waiting literally forever for you."

CHAPTER TWENTY-FIVE
Hank the Tank

Dina's house feels like stepping into another world—a world full of warmth, color, and noise. The cream walls are dotted with sticky fingerprints, the forest green curtains billow gently by the windows as heat cranks out of the vents, and the unmistakable scent of home hangs in the air. It's chaotic in the best way—cracker crumbs on the couch, vibrant construction paper covered in crayon scribbles covering the coffee table. There's life everywhere. So much life. And I can't shake the feeling that I missed out on all of it.

"I can't make you a skinny vanilla latte," Dina says with a teasing grin, "but I can offer you a strong French roast with a dash of heavy cream."

I laugh softly. "I'll take it."

Suddenly, a deep, booming bark echoes through the house, startling me so much I nearly jump out of my skin.

"That's just Hank the Tank." Dina waves off casually. "He's upstairs playing with the kids."

"You have a dog?" I gasp in disbelief.

Dina chuckles, shaking her head. "June, I don't just have any dog. I have a Great Dane who stands taller than me on his hind legs."

I blink, processing her words, then feel warmth spread through my chest as I smile. "You... have a dog."

She grins back at me, her eyes twinkling. "I have a dog."

We both laugh, and I can't help but marvel at the change. The girl who was once terrified of dogs now has one as part of her family. It's something I never would've expected, and yet, here she is. It's beautiful—everything I didn't know I needed to see.

The sound of a baby fussing crackles through the baby monitor. Dina laughs softly. "Hang on, I've got to get the baby."

I nod, left alone in the kitchen, the distant giggles and shrieks of her kids playing in the background. I take a slow, deep breath, trying to ground myself in the reality of this moment. I'm really here, standing in Dina's kitchen after all these years. And she didn't slam the door in my face. Part of me expected her to—maybe even deserved it. What I don't deserve is her kindness.

"This is Bob Junior," Dina announces, reappearing with a tiny bundle of baby tucked securely in her arms. "My fifth and definitely last." She grins, her eyes sparkling as she motions for me to take him.

I've never held a baby before, so I awkwardly reach out, cradling him like he's made of fragile porcelain. Dina chuckles. "He's not made of glass, you know." But I can't help feeling like he is. We're all fragile, in a way—delicate, breakable, but somehow still able to withstand the heat of life's fire.

"I just..." I trail off, staring down at Bob Junior, his little button nose and chubby cheeks melting my heart on the spot. "I want to start by saying..." I glance up at Dina, summoning the courage I didn't think I had. "I'm sorry. For everything. For all the ways I hurt you and your family."

Dina rests her elbows on the counter across from me and smiles, the kind of smile that's been earned through years of both joy and pain. "Thank you for saying that, June."

"I made so many mistakes," I continue, feeling the weight of my words settle in the room. Bob Junior babbles softly, his tiny hand brushing my cheek, and I nearly crumble. "I never meant to hurt you, but I know that I did. And I am so, so sorry."

Dina sighs, her expression softening as she looks at me. "You're forgiven, June."

My breath hitches in my throat. "I am?"

She nods. "I forgave you a long time ago. The truth is, it's not really me who needs your apology."

I feel my heart skip a beat. "You mean Patrick?"

Her smile turns sad, but there's a glimmer of understanding in her eyes. "Yeah."

I bite my lip, trying to keep the nerves at bay. "I don't know if I'm brave enough to face him."

Dina's grin widens. "You're the bravest person I know, June Nelson."

I roll my eyes, but it's more out of disbelief than disagreement. "Hardly."

"You showed up here, didn't you?" Dina raises an eyebrow in challenge.

"I guess I did." I exhale, the tension in my shoulders loosening ever so slightly.

Dina leans back, crossing her arms. "I was angry for a long time, you know. But then Beau Blaze asked me to marry him." She laughs at my expression. "I would've said yes, but you once told me I didn't end up marrying him. So, I turned him down. Three months later, I met Bob on a train to New York, and, well, we've been inseparable ever since."

I blink, processing what she just said. "So... I really did go back in time?"

Dina's smile widens. "Yeah, you did."

"And you never told anyone?"

She shakes her head with a soft chuckle. "I wanted to tell Bob, but I made a promise to you. And, well, I've kept it."

I can't help but laugh as a tear slips down my cheek. "Tell me about Bob."

"Where do I even begin?" Dina sighs dreamily, a look of pure contentment on her face. "He's amazing. Looks just like a lumberjack—tall, strong, with a scruffy beard and an endless supply of flannel. But more than that, he's kind. Gentle. He's... everything I've ever dreamed of and more."

"You're happy," I say, feeling an unexpected sense of peace settle over me.

"No," she corrects with a knowing smile. "I'm more than happy. I'm content. I love my life, I love my family, and June," her voice softens, "I love you, too."

A lump forms in my throat. "You do?"

She nods, her eyes filling with fondness. "I do. I've always loved you. I've been waiting for you, because I knew you had to do what you needed to do. You had to find your way. But I never doubted that one day, you'd come back."

I swallow hard, her words settling deep in my chest. "I wouldn't say I've found my way just yet. But I'm trying."

Dina reaches across the counter and squeezes my hand. "That's all that matters. I'm sorry I didn't call you after your dad passed," she adds quietly. "I wanted to, but I didn't know if you'd want to hear from me. I didn't want to derail whatever progress you were making. But I am sorry, June. I know how much you miss him. He was one of the best."

My chest tightens, the familiar ache returning. "I do miss him. Every single day."

"I know," Dina whispers. "I miss him, too."

I'm on the verge of breaking down, so I change the subject. "You're a teacher."

"I was," Dina corrects, giving me a warm smile. "And I loved it. But after Bob Junior made his grand entrance, I decided to take a few years off to be at home with the kids. I want to soak up these moments while they're little. When Bob Junior starts kindergarten, I'll go back."

"That sounds like a good plan," I reply.

"We're avoiding the elephant in the room," Dina says suddenly, cutting straight to the point. "My brother."

I lick my lips, feeling my heart pick up pace. "I wasn't purposely avoiding the topic. I came here to see you—not him."

Dina raises an eyebrow. "Don't you want to know what he went through after you left?"

The question lands hard, and I feel the heaviness of it on my shoulders. Do I want to know? Yes. But am I ready to hear it? I'm not so sure.

"I don't know," I admit, feeling like a coward for dodging the truth.

"I need you to know," Dina insists. "I need to get it off my chest."

I brace myself for whatever is coming. "Okay," I say quietly. "Tell me. What did he go through after I left?"

Dina takes a deep breath, closing her eyes for a moment as if she's gathering her thoughts. "He waited for you, June. He thought you just needed time to figure things out. He was convinced that you'd come back when you were ready. But as the years went by, and you didn't, he kept waiting. It was frustrating. I tried to talk to him, to get him to see that maybe you weren't coming back. But he always said I didn't know you like he did. And the thing is... I did know you. But he wouldn't hear it."

I stare at her, my heart thudding painfully in my chest.

"The band did well for a while," Dina continues. "But eventually, Patrick and some of the guys got tired of the grind. They decided to take a break, and that's when Patrick went back to school for architecture. He fell in love with restoring old buildings. You should see his work, June. It's... It's incredible. While working on this old, abandoned schoolhouse, he met someone. Georgina. She was the interior designer on the project. They hit it off, obviously. They got married nine months after meeting, and then my niece, Stella, was born. Two years later, Rory came along."

I let out a breath I didn't even realize I was holding. As much as I'm happy for him, it feels like someone's twisting a knife in my chest.

"I... I'm glad he found someone," spills out, though I'm not sure I really believe the words I'm saying.

Dina gives a sad chuckle. "The marriage didn't work out."

My eyes snap back to hers. "Oh."

"Do you want to know why?" she asks, her gaze sharp.

I shrug, unsure. "I don't know, Deen."

"You."

"Me?" The word barely escapes my lips.

"Every time you released a book, he bought it. He read everything you wrote. Georgina could never quite shake the feeling that he was holding onto you, even after all these years. They tried counseling, but in the end... Patrick never really let go of you. And I don't think he ever will."

I place a hand over my chest, guilt and regret swirling together. "I never wanted to break up his marriage, Dina. I didn't mean for any of this to happen."

Dina reaches over and gently squeezes my forearm. "It's not your fault, June. You didn't come back for him. You didn't reach out or try to interfere. Patrick just... He couldn't let go. He was banging on a door you'd already closed."

I'm about to respond when the front door creaks open, and I hear the sound of small footsteps thundering down the stairs.

"Bob's home," Dina says, her eyes lighting up.

I instinctively stand up. "I should get going."

"Absolutely not," Dina insists, scooping Bob Junior into her arms as she turns to me with a grin. "You're staying for dinner and dessert. And maybe the night? We can have a sleepover, just like old times. Watch some of our favorite movies?"

I hesitate, racking my brain for a reason not to stay. But I don't have one. I don't have a job waiting for me in the morning. No one's expecting me back home. Lily went back to check on her cat, and there's nothing really pulling me away from this moment.

"Yeah," I finally agree, my voice soft. "I'd like that."

Dina squeals with excitement just as a dark-haired, flannel-wearing man walks into the kitchen.

"Bob," she beams, "this is June. My best friend, June."

I extend my hand awkwardly, but Bob surprises me by pulling me into a bear hug instead.

And for the first time in a long time, I feel like I can breathe without it hurting.

CHAPTER TWENTY-SIX
The Most Unexpected Place

I swipe on a final layer of lipstick, flick off the bathroom light, and grab my purse. Tonight's the night I'm meeting Dina and Bob for cocktails—just the three of us. It's their 11-year wedding anniversary, and they've managed to sneak away from the chaos of kids for a night in the city. Why they'd want to spend that time with me is anyone's guess, but I'm not about to pass up an evening with Dina.

There's a knock at the door, and I check the time. 8:08. Dina doesn't even know where I live, so it can't be her. Who could it be this late?

I swing the door open, and there she is—Sissy Barnes, my agent, standing in the hallway with her arms crossed and a look that could stop traffic.

"Do you not own a phone, June Nelson?" she snaps, pushing past me into the apartment without waiting for an invitation. "I've been calling you for days!"

Sissy takes a quick glance around the place, her expression softening just slightly. "Did you hire a cleaning service?"

"Uh," I fumble, tucking a loose curl behind my ear. "My stepmom, actually. She kind of organized for me."

Sissy barely registers the response as she waves it off, her eyes sparkling with something I can't quite place. "Not important. June," she says seriously, grabbing both my shoulders, "you made the list."

I blink, trying to process her words. "The list?"

"The list," she repeats, her face glowing with pride.

My heart skips a beat. "Wait—are you talking about *the* list? As in, the New York Times Bestseller list?"

Sissy's grin grows wider, and there are tears shimmering in her eyes. "Yes, June. *That* list."

I stagger back a little, gripping the door frame for balance. "*Retrospective*?" I manage to squeak out.

"I told you, June." She pulls me into a tight hug. "I told you it was a romance for the ages."

I'm speechless. "But... What about the Draper Diaries review? I thought that was going to sink me."

Sissy waves her hand dismissively. "I found a blogger bigger than Draper who adored your book. She posted a video, it went viral, and now... Now, you're officially a bestselling author, June Nelson."

I stumble back, catching the arm of the couch just before my legs give out. My mind spins, thoughts swirling together in a tangled mess.

"You're in shock," Sissy notices with a hearty laugh, shaking her head like this was the reaction she'd been expecting. "I never thought I'd see the day."

"That one of my books would become a bestseller?"

She smirks, her eyes gleaming with pride. "No, that you'd finally realize you're an amazing writer."

I swallow, still trying to wrap my head around it all. "Are you absolutely sure? This isn't some joke or cruel prank, right?"

Sissy rolls her eyes dramatically, as if the very idea is absurd. "June, you were just a kid when I found you. You had so much to say, and I could see the fire in your words even then. But success? That takes time, persistence, and hard work. And you've poured everything into this. You've earned it."

My heart pounds as I stare up at her, hardly believing her words. "The publisher isn't dropping me?"

"Quite the opposite." She grins, wide and full of excitement. "They're eager to see what your next book will be."

I press a hand against my chest, feeling the frantic rhythm of my heart. "I... I don't even know what to say."

Sissy nods knowingly. "You're going on a book tour. No dates confirmed yet, but it's happening."

My ears start ringing as I try to process everything she's saying. This has to be a dream. It doesn't feel real. There's just no way that I could've written something that people love enough to buy in droves. But the words echo in my head like a loudspeaker. *You're Enough, June Nelson. You've always been enough.*

"Have a great weekend," Sissy says, her laughter trailing behind her as she heads for the door. "We'll iron out the details for your press tour on Monday."

"Book *and* press tour?" I repeat, the words feeling foreign on my tongue.

Sissy chuckles over her shoulder. "Oh yeah. People are lining up to interview you."

I watch her walk out, the soft click of the door closing behind her leaving me alone with the quiet hum of my thoughts. For so long, I thought it was over. I'd made peace with the idea that maybe writing wasn't my future, that I'd have to find another path.

And yet, here I am. My bottom lip trembles as the realization crashes over me like a downpour of rain.

This is real. This is really happening.

I check the time on my phone and gasp. I'm supposed to meet Dina in ten minutes. My legs feel surprisingly steady as I grab my purse and head toward the door, pausing for a second to glance back at my apartment. Clean, organized, no longer the chaotic mess it once was. Funny how life has a way of falling into place when you least expect it.

I manage to hail a cab in record time and settle into the backseat, scrolling through my contacts. The one person I most want to share this news with flickers through my mind. My thumb hovers over "Mom," and I hesitate, my chest tightening. But instead of pressing the call button, I scroll back up and click on Lily's name.

The phone barely rings once before she answers, breathless with concern. "June! Is everything okay?"

I take a deep breath, feeling the words bubble up from somewhere deep inside me. "Lily," I exhale, "I made the bestseller list!"

Her reaction is instantaneous—screaming and laughing bursting through the speaker and filling the cab with her joy.

"I'm meeting Dina for drinks," I say, grinning from ear to ear. "But I'll call you tomorrow."

"Congratulations, June!" she shrieks. "We have to celebrate! I'm so proud of you!"

Warmth floods my chest, and I smile wider. "Can't wait."

I hang up just as the cab pulls up to a cozy lounge on the Upper East Side. After paying the driver, I step out into the crisp night air, the chill wrapping itself around me like an old friend. I tilt my head back, gazing up at the sky. A handful of stars sparkle overhead, defying the bright city lights that try to drown them out.

Not too long ago, I stood on the sidewalk asking the universe for a sign, desperate for something—anything—to show me the way. But now? Now, I don't feel like I need one anymore.

Everything is finally starting to fall into place.

The lounge is dimly lit, with soft candlelight flickering on every surface, casting a warm glow over the intimate space. Small tables are scattered throughout, and a stage at the back holds the promise of music. The atmosphere is homey, almost magical.

"June!" Dina calls out, the sound cutting through the low hum of conversation. I hurry over to where she and Bob are sitting, both of them looking their best. Dina's wearing a sapphire blouse that shimmers in the light, and Bob, as always, is in his finest flannel, a soft smile on his face.

As soon as I reach them, I blurt out, "I made the bestseller list!"

Dina hugs me tightly, her voice a whisper only I can hear, "You did it, Old June." Her words tug at something deep inside me, something that's been buried for a long time.

"*We* did it," I murmur, my heart swelling with a mix of relief and nostalgia.

She waves me off with a playful smile, and Bob, ever the gentleman, asks what I'd like to drink. "Something tropical," I say, and he nods, heading over to the bar in the corner.

"Retrospective?" Dina asks, her eyes gleaming with pride for me.

I nod, unable to hide my smile. "Yeah."

"I really loved *Midnight Crown*," she confesses, her tone softening. "It's my favorite."

I chuckle, a little embarrassed. "Even though it sounds an awful lot like *Crowing at Midnight*?"

She laughs, a sound that's both warm and bittersweet. "It's the story the two of you should have had."

Her words hit me like a punch to the gut, and I swallow down the sudden lump in my throat. "Sometimes, stories are just meant for books, Deen. Not the real world."

She raises an eyebrow, clearly disagreeing. "I beg to differ."

Before I can respond, Bob returns with an orange drink topped with a little umbrella. "Something tropical," he says as he sets it down in front of me, then settles into a chair that seems way too small for his broad frame.

I take a sip of the sweet, tangy drink, grateful for the distraction. "Tell me something, Bob," I say, trying to steer the conversation away from the ache in my chest. "What was it about Dina that made you sit down next to her on that train?"

Bob smiles, the kind of smile that reaches his eyes and makes them sparkle. He drapes his arm over the back of Dina's chair. "She looked a little sad," he admits. "I thought I'd take a chance and try to make her laugh."

Dina rolls her eyes playfully. "I was going through a breakup, Bob. I was allowed to be sad."

Bob chuckles softly, his gaze full of adoration. "I thank my lucky stars every day that you didn't marry Beau Blaze."

I swallow hard, my throat tight with emotion as Dina replies, "And I thank mine that I got on that train."

Bob's eyes twinkle with mischief. "She was heading to find a friend. Some girl who broke Patrick's heart. But she never ended up finding her," he says with a grin. "We had dinner, then we stumbled upon this little gem of a bar, and the rest, as they say, is history."

My heart drops, realization washing over me. Dina got on that train to find me and instead, she found her future with Bob.

I raise my glass, forcing a smile. "To train rides."

Bob raises his glass in return, his grin wide. "To finding the love of your life in the most unexpected place."

We clink our glasses, the sound light and cheerful, but there's a heaviness in the air. Dina gives me a small smile, her eyes filled with things we've both left unsaid.

Just as I take a sip of my drink, a soft strumming of a guitar fills the room. I start to say something, but then I freeze. The melody is familiar, achingly so. And then I hear the words.

"Walking down the sandy shore, hand tucked in me, I've always wanted more..."

My heart stops, and my mouth drops open. Slowly, I turn to face the stage, and there he is—Patrick. His eyes are closed as he sings, his fingers moving effortlessly over the strings of his guitar. It's the song he wrote for me all those years ago. The song that never left my heart.

Time stands still as I watch him, every note, every word pulling me back to a moment I thought was lost forever.

CHAPTER TWENTY-SEVEN
Thirteen Years

I blink slowly, my heart suspended in a state of disbelief. It's as though time has rewound, but everything feels distant, unreal. Tears brim in my eyes as I stare at Patrick—my first love—for the first time in nearly 13 years. *13 years*. It seems impossible that so much time has passed.

The song plays on, his voice weaving through the notes, but it's like I've gone deaf. The words slip past me, the melody a blur, drowned out by the whirlwind of emotions crashing inside me.

I never let myself imagine this moment. Running into Patrick again was too painful a thought to entertain, too bittersweet. What if we spent our whole lives apart, our paths never crossing again? Worse, what if they did, and he looked right through me? What if he didn't care at all?

The song drifts to a close, and I feel like I'm holding my breath. Patrick opens his eyes, scanning the room, unaware that the entire world hinges on the moment he sees me.

At first, he doesn't notice, and I almost let out a breath of relief. But then, his gaze sweeps over me, and everything stops. His eyes widen, just a fraction, but enough to tell me he's just as caught off guard as I am. He falters for a second, the slightest hitch in his posture, before he recovers, clearing his throat as he introduces himself and the band.

But his words are lost on me. My heart pounds in my ears, so loud it drowns out everything else. All I can do is watch him, standing there, as if the past isn't suddenly rushing back between us, as if the weight of everything we were and could have been isn't crashing down.

Even though I know I should, I can't tear my eyes away from Patrick. He's older now, more mature, with his dark hair cropped short, but those eyes... They're the same deep navy that used to unravel me with just a glance. Soulful. Steady. They hold a thousand memories I've tried to forget but never seem to.

Tears blur my vision as Patrick begins singing one of *Crowing at Midnight's* songs. I blink them away, trying to keep it together, but the melody hits too close to home, stirring up all the feelings I've kept buried for so long.

I tear my gaze away from him and glance over at Dina. She gives me a small, apologetic shrug, and I know, without a doubt, she planned this. She's always been good at pulling the impossible off, but I don't think even Patrick or I expected our reunion to happen like this.

I wipe a stray tear from my cheek as Dina and I exchange a look. She mouths, "I'm sorry," but I shake my head softly, reassuring her. Yes, I feel blindsided, caught in the whirlwind of old emotions, but the truth is, I wouldn't want to be anywhere else right now.

Turning back toward the stage, my heart hammers in my chest. I don't know how long I sit there, watching Patrick and the band play, but with every passing minute, regret rises to the surface, tightening its grip around my heart. I should have fixed things with him. I should have fought harder, proved to him that I loved him, that he was enough. That he was everything.

So many words left unsaid, so many feelings I kept hidden, all charging back now. Maybe if I'd said them back then, we wouldn't be here, on opposite sides of the room, strangers with too much history between us.

When the set ends and the intimate crowd begins to clap, I take a deep, steadying breath. Watching Patrick from across the room had been safe, manageable even. But the idea of actually talking to him? I have no idea where to start.

I'm sorry. I messed up. I've missed you.

"You're not mad?" Dina whisper-yells from across the table as I quickly down the rest of my cocktail, the tropical sweetness doing little to calm my nerves.

I shake my head slowly. "You planned this?"

She scratches the side of her face, clearly caught. "I did."

"Wait," Bob interrupts, his eyes darting between us. "What am I missing?"

Dina and I share a laugh. "June's the friend who broke Patrick's heart," she explains, nonchalantly, as though it's ancient history and not the most significant relationship collapse of our lives.

Bob's head whips back in disbelief. "You hid this from me for... 11 years?"

Dina hitches her shoulder in an unapologetic shrug. "It was so long ago, Bob."

"We have a deal." Bob raises his eyebrows, feigning sternness.

"Yeah, yeah." Dina brushes him off, but her eyes sparkle with amusement as she looks up at him. "I'm supposed to tell you all the relationship drama, but this was before we got together. And besides, it was... complicated."

"It was a hard breakup," I say, jumping in to defend her. "For all of us. Talking about it... Well, I'm sure it wasn't easy for her."

Dina gives me a grateful smile, and in that moment, it's clear that even after all this time, no one knows her better than I do.

"You can tell me the whole story on the train ride home tomorrow," Bob says to her gently as he tucks a blond curl behind her ear, his voice tender.

Dina starts to respond, but before she can, a tall, dark figure approaches our table. *Patrick*. My heart skips, and for a second, I swear it's trying to leap out of my chest to get to him.

"Hi," I blurt out, and immediately regret it. *Hi?* That's the best I could come up with after 13 years?

"Hi, June," Patrick says, and the sound of his voice wraps around me like a familiar embrace.

"It's been so long," I breathe out, watching as he grabs a chair from a neighboring table.

Bob's eyes widen in surprise, glancing between Patrick and me, and for some reason, I get the distinct impression that he's silently shipping us.

Patrick places the chair beside mine, closer than I expect. His scent is different now—earthier, richer, like bergamot and a hint of leather. It catches me off guard, but I almost like it better than the one I used to cling to in a crowd, hoping for a glimpse of him.

"So, you and June patched things up?" Patrick asks, directing the question at Dina.

Bob watches the exchange with a hint of amusement, his eyes flicking between Dina and Patrick like he's trying to catch up on some inside joke he missed.

Dina huffs dramatically. "We've always been friends, Patrick."

Patrick lets out a low, raspy chuckle, and the sound sends a jolt through me, my heart flipping at the familiar cadence. "Like you were friends with Linc Hunt?"

Dina throws her head back with an exaggerated groan. "Are you seriously still holding on to the fact that I had a crush on Jed?"

"Yep." Patrick smirks, leaning back in his chair, arms crossed casually over his chest. As he does, his elbow brushes against mine, and I suddenly forget how to breathe.

"Grow up," Dina says with an exaggerated eye roll.

"You grow up," Patrick shoots back, grinning.

"You first," she retorts with a smirk.

"No, you first," he counters, and their sibling banter feels like slipping back in time.

"Alright, that's enough," Bob interjects with a long yawn, stretching his arms over his head.

"You tired?" Dina asks, glancing up at him.

"No," Bob protests, only to yawn again immediately after.

Dina laughs softly, her hand brushing against Bob's. "We should probably head back to the hotel."

I hold my breath as Patrick flicks his eyes over to me for just a second before turning back to his sister.

"You set all this up, didn't you?" he asks, one eyebrow raised.

Dina stands and grabs her purse from the back of her chair. "Who me? I'd never. Pure coincidence," she says, feigning innocence.

Patrick shakes his head, laughing. "You're the worst liar."

Bob nods, grinning. "She really is."

I rise to my feet as Dina walks over to me. She wraps me up in a tight hug, her curls brushing my cheek as she whispers into my ear, "Talk to him."

My heart beats erratically as Bob steps in next, giving me a brief side hug. "Good seeing you, June," he says warmly.

"Goodnight," I murmur, my pulse racing as I turn back toward the table, and the man I never thought I'd see again is finally standing in front of me after all this time.

Patrick tries—and fails miserably—to hide a smile. "So," he begins softly, almost hesitant.

"So," I echo, swallowing hard. My nerves feel like they're about to get the best of me.

"How do you feel about a cup of coffee?" he asks, his tone shy but hopeful.

I nod quickly, trying to mask the relief and excitement coursing through me. "I'd love one."

Patrick nods too, his lips curving into a small smile. "Let me grab my guitar."

The chill of the New York City night wraps around us as we step out onto the sidewalk. The air is brisk, filled with the faint scent of roasted chestnuts from a nearby cart. Even though Christmas is just a few weeks away, the city is as alive as ever—bustling, loud, and always in motion. Even at this hour.

"I'm glad the band is still together," I say, trying to ease into conversation as we walk side by side.

Patrick adjusts the guitar strap slung across his chest, his profile catching the soft glow of the streetlights. He looks like a dream, if I'm being honest. I sneak another glance, taking in the strong lines of his jaw, the warmth of his gaze.

"We broke up for a while," he admits. "But we found our way back to each other. Eventually."

My heart tightens in my chest. I can't tell if he's just talking about the band or if he's hinting about us.

"I heard you became an architect," I say, shifting the conversation.

Patrick moves closer as a rowdy group brushes past us, their laughter filling the crowded sidewalk.

"I did," he confirms with a nod. "When did you and Dina reconnect?"

"About a week ago," I answer truthfully.

Patrick chuckles, his lips quivering into a smirk. "Didn't take her long to push us together, did it?"

I frown slightly, not wanting him to think I orchestrated this. "I didn't know I was going to see you tonight. I didn't ask Dina to set this up."

Patrick's expression softens. "I know," he reassures me. "I know my sister. She means well."

The honking of cabs and the steady hum of the city's nightlife fills the air as we walk. There's a charged silence, thick with all the years between us.

Finally, we reach a small café nestled on the corner. Patrick holds the door open for me, and I step inside, instantly grateful for the warmth that wraps around me.

We order our drinks and find a table tucked away in the back of the café. Patrick props his guitar up against the wall while I slip off my scarf and jacket, surprised by how easy it feels to be sitting here with him after so many years.

"I saw you made the bestseller list," Patrick says, his smile widening. "Congratulations."

"Thank you." I return his smile, the words simple, but the thought behind them makes me feel lighter.

"I knew you'd do it, June," he continues, pride in every word.

"You did," I reply, our gazes meeting across the table. There's something familiar about this moment. "Tell me about your daughters."

Patrick's face lights up as he launches into stories about Stella and Rory. Stella's the athletic one, balancing ballet and soccer, while Rory's more the creative type—painting and drawing. His eyes glow as he talks, his love for them evident in every word, and I find myself captivated by the way he speaks about the little girls who clearly mean the world to him.

"They sound amazing," I tell him when he finishes.

"They are," he responds with a proud smile.

"You're a good dad," I say, my own heart swelling just hearing how much he loves them.

He shrugs modestly. "I have my days."

"They're lucky to have you."

Patrick leans back in his chair. "I'm the lucky one."

There's a lull in the conversation, but it doesn't feel awkward. Even after 13 years apart, there's still a sense of ease between us. It's like no time has passed at all—just the same quiet, steady comfort that's always been there.

"I..." I begin, but then hesitate, unsure if I should say what's on my mind.

"What is it, June?" Patrick leans forward, curiosity sparking in his eyes.

"You always dreamt about the band making it big," I say, quieter now. "That was your dream."

Patrick licks his lips, considering my words for a moment. "Dreams change," he says with a gentle smile. "And besides, we're allowed more than one dream. I still love music, but architecture... it gives me something different. I get the best of both worlds, and I wouldn't trade that for anything."

I take a sip of my coffee, letting heat settle deep into my chest. But the truth is, sitting across from Patrick in this tiny café, surrounded by the hum of city life outside, this is the warmest I've felt in 13 years.

And maybe that's a dream I didn't even know I still had.

CHAPTER TWENTY-EIGHT
They're All Here for Me?

"The line wraps around the corner of the building!" Lily announces gleefully as she peers out of the green room window. I try to steady my hand as I dab on some lipstick, my nerves threatening to get the best of me.

"How many other authors did you say were participating in this event again?" I ask Sissy, who's fully absorbed in her phone, barely listening.

"Hmm?" Sissy hums, her thumb pausing mid-swipe. "Oh, just you."

"What?" I gasp, the lipstick nearly slipping from my hand.

Sissy finally looks up, giving me a sheepish grin. "I lied, June. Just a tiny, harmless lie."

My stomach drops like a rock. "W-what do you mean you lied?"

She shrugs, looking more amused than anything. "I knew you'd freak out if you found out all these people were coming just for you. So, I told a little white lie to keep you calm."

"I'm going to throw up," I squeak, my heart hammering wildly in my chest.

For some reason, I instantly reach for my phone and start scrolling through my contacts. It's like muscle memory, a reflex I can't quite shake, even after everything.

My finger lands on Mom's name just as Lily places a gentle hand on my shoulder.

I freeze for a second, then quickly power off my phone and set it aside, feeling like I got caught doing something wrong.

"Everything alright?" Lily asks, her voice soft, but filled with concern.

I nod, trying to shake it off. "Yeah."

She doesn't buy it. Lily takes a seat beside me, letting out a long, understanding sigh. "Look, I know you don't need—or maybe don't even want—my advice," she starts, her tone careful, "but I think it needs to be said, June. You're not responsible for fixing things with your mom. You're not responsible for keeping communication open just in case she changes her mind."

"I wasn't going to call her," I say quickly, even though reaching for my phone was more instinct than anything else. "It's just... a habit."

"I know," she sympathizes. "But sometimes, it helps to hear it out loud."

I let out a breath I didn't realize I was holding. "Honestly, I don't even know if I want to fix it," I confess with a shrug, though the truth stings a little.

Lily gives a slow, understanding nod. "I've spent years trying to make peace with a difficult parent," she confesses quietly. "It's... hard."

"It is hard," I agree, my heart twisting.

"It's not fair," Lily continues. "But you don't have to let it define you."

"I just wish I knew why," I say. "Why she always chooses herself over... me."

Lily exhales, her expression both sad and wise. "Most of the choices selfish people make have everything to do with them and nothing to do with you."

I give a small, half-hearted smile. "If only I could get my heart to understand that. My head gets it, but my heart... That's another story."

"Sometimes," Lily says, squeezing my hand, "it just takes the heart a little longer to catch up."

"Yeah," I murmur, the word barely making it past my lips.

"It's time!" Sissy exclaims, her excitement bubbling over as she clasps her hands under her chin.

My stomach flips as I stand, Lily still at my side. I've done book signings before, but none of them ever felt like this. Those were smaller, joint events where most people came for the bigger name authors. A handful of people would show up to buy a book from me, but most would breeze right past, their attention elsewhere.

Now, my legs feel like jelly as I follow Sissy. My heart is pounding in my ears, my head spinning. Is this real?

Horace and Morgan on Lexington is packed wall-to-wall with hundreds of people. All I can do is stare in disbelief.

"They're all here for me?" I manage to get out despite the nausea rolling in my stomach.

Lily gives my hand a reassuring squeeze. "You deserve this," she says softly, her eyes shining with pride.

I try to swallow, but my mouth feels like sandpaper. Just then, someone announces my name, and the room erupts in cheers. Cheers? For me?

Sissy turns to me with a beaming smile, motioning toward a chair in front of a beautiful table set up with all of my books—*Retrospective*, *Midnight Crown*, everything. I take a tentative step forward, but the heel of my shoe catches on a wire pulled taut along the floor. I stumble, and for a terrifying second, it feels like I'm going to crash straight into a towering bookshelf.

But then, just as quickly, Lily is there. She grabs my arm, steadying me before I completely lose my balance. "Take a breath, June," she whispers softly in my ear. "Smile, and just breathe."

I shoot her a grateful look, standing up straighter as I smooth down my blouse. With a nervous smile, I wave to the crowd, then slowly settle into the chair behind the table.

This is real. This is happening.

The line begins to move, and soon a woman is teetering back and forth with excitement, practically shoving her book onto the table. "I loved this book *so* much! Harrison and Giselle's love story was incredible. My favorite part was when she found that letter from him, and after reading his words, she just fell to the floor. It was, like, tragic and epic at the same time!"

Her enthusiasm makes me smile as I sign her copy and hand it back. "I'm so glad you connected with it."

"Thank you for writing it!" she says earnestly.

My heart swells as I respond, "Thank you for reading it and giving it a chance."

The line moves at a steady pace. Reader after reader shares their favorite scenes, moments that resonated with them, and I'm overwhelmed with gratitude. A few even tell me they've been following me since my very first novel. It's surreal. Everything blurs together in a whirlwind of compliments, handshakes, and signatures.

As the hours slip by, the line keeps moving. My hand cramps from signing so many books, each signature becoming sloppier than the last. Just when I think I'm nearing the end, a woman steps forward with a wide grin. "June freaking Nelson!"

I blink slowly. "Uh, yeah, that's me."

Her expression shifts into mock offense. "You don't remember me?"

I stare at her, trying to place the face. "Um... No?"

She throws her arms up dramatically. "Kira! Kira Campbell!"

Oh. My. Gosh. "Kira!" I laugh, flabbergasted. "It's been so long."

Kira grins as she slides her book across the table. "I always knew you'd make it. And, for the record, I still think you would've made a great book club president. You've proven your love for books. All Cheyenne does these days is tear people apart online. Once a bully, always a bully."

Her words catch me off guard. My breath hitches. "She tears people apart online?"

Kira rolls her eyes. "She's a book blogger now—can you believe that? Married Connor Draper and everything. Apparently, she spends her days tearing down people like you who've actually done something meaningful with their lives."

I swallow hard. "She wouldn't happen to be the Draper Diaries blogger, would she?"

Kira nods, looking almost too pleased. "That's her! You've read her blog?"

I let out a long breath. "Not... intentionally."

Kira leans in conspiratorially. "I heard she gave you a bad review, and her readers turned against her. Authenticity, June. People crave it. They see right through the fake stuff."

I scratch the side of my face, trying to absorb it all. Cheyenne Radcliffe. It was Cheyenne Radcliffe all along. Of course. Somewhere deep down, I must have known. But hearing it confirmed now is just the icing on the cake.

Kira gives me a knowing look. "Don't pay attention to her. You keep doing what you're doing, June. Your writing? It's brilliant."

I try shaking off the lingering shock. "Thanks, Kira."

She winks before turning away. "See you at the next signing!"

As Kira disappears into the crowd, I can't help but feel frustrated. All this time, Cheyenne Radcliffe has been lurking in the background, trying to tear me down. But Kira's right. Authenticity wins in the end. And I'm not about to let an old bully define my future.

I sign the last few books, the irritation swirling in my chest. But I refuse to let Cheyenne Radcliffe ruin this moment for me—just like she tried to ruin everything else I've done. I finish up the signing, then Sissy whisks me away to a cozy reception area for coffee and pastries. I chat with some of the staff from Horace and Morgan, leaving behind a box of signed copies for them.

Lily links her arm through mine as we step outside. "Pizza?"

I raise an eyebrow. "You eat pizza?"

She laughs. "I do these days."

"I'm shocked."

"I've changed." She shrugs.

"I can see that," I say with a smile.

We order slices from a little pizza joint down the street and sit by the window, watching the city buzz around us. We make small talk, but I can tell Lily's holding something back. Then she grins—almost too widely—and asks, "So, tell me about coffee with Patrick."

A blush creeps up my cheeks. "We just talked."

"And?" Her eyes sparkle with curiosity.

I exhale, trying to play it cool. "Then he left in a cab, and I walked home."

Lily's expression falls. "That's it?"

"That's it." I press my lips together. "Just two old friends catching up over coffee and going their separate ways."

"But why was it so... anticlimactic?" Lily looks genuinely confused.

"Because," I say with a shrug, "sometimes it takes the heart a little longer to catch up to what the mind already knows."

Lily narrows her eyes, clearly connecting my words to what she'd said earlier. "So, are you saying there was no spark?"

"I never said that," I counter quickly. "But Patrick's moved on with his life. He's got two daughters and a career he loves. We're different people now." I pause, remembering what he'd said about the band. "Dreams change."

Lily sits back in her chair, her brow furrowing. "I just thought—" She hesitates, then sighs. "Never mind."

"No, what?" I tilt my head, intrigued. "What did you think?"

She looks down at her pizza before glancing back up at me. "I thought you two were always good together."

I smile softly. "We were. Until we weren't."

"What happened?"

I watch a young couple stroll by, their arms wrapped around each other, lost in a world of their own. "What always happens with first love."

"And that is?" Lily presses.

"I was immature and selfish," I admit, turning back to her. "I thought I needed more."

She shakes her head. "I don't believe it."

I shrug as I finish my pizza. "Patrick was the best thing that ever happened to me, and I threw it away because I thought there was something better out there."

Lily leans forward, her eyes serious. "Maybe now's the time to revisit that."

I shake my head, feeling that familiar pang in my chest. "He didn't seem... interested."

Lily sighs heavily. "He could have been reeling from the shock of seeing you again."

"Maybe," I murmur, biting the inside of my cheek. It's true, seeing him again stirred up feelings I thought I'd buried long ago. Every time his eyes met mine, it was like fireworks going off in my chest. But still... "He didn't even ask for my number."

"Did you exchange anything? Emails?" Lily's voice grows more hopeful.

I shake my head again. "Nothing."

Lily's face softens, her smile tinged with sadness. "Maybe it's not over yet."

I smile weakly in return, but deep down, I wonder if it's really that simple. Patrick's hug before he left was brief, and as much as I wish it meant something more, it felt like goodbye.

CHAPTER TWENTY-NINE
The Story You Write for Yourself

I tug at the red sweater I'm wearing, feeling uncomfortably warm as I help Dina set up for her annual Christmas party. My nerves are getting the best of me, and it's not just the heat. At some point, Patrick will arrive with his daughters, and the thought makes my heart pound, and my palms sweat.

"Stop fidgeting," Dina teases, giving me a playful wink.

"I'm trying not to," I reply, fiddling with the hem of my sweater. "But..."

But Patrick isn't interested in me. I'm about to meet his daughters, and I'll be stuck here in the suburbs for the night with no means of escape if things get awkward. What if he doesn't want me here? Sure, he was civil, nice, and sweet when we met up, but that's just who he is. He should hate me. Sometimes, I used to hate myself for what I did to him. I wouldn't blame him if he felt the same way.

Dina exhales heavily, placing a hand on her hip. "Spill. What's going on?"

"Nothing." I wave her off. It's bad enough Dina had to share me with Patrick in the past. I don't want her to be caught in the middle of our relationship—or lack thereof—here in the present, too. "Just nervous about seeing your parents."

Dina scoffs. "Sure, June. That's who you're nervous to see."

"I *am* nervous to see them." It's true, and the words feel heavy as I say them. "They were like parents to me growing up, and when I fell off the face of the earth..." I pause, my voice trailing off. "I hurt their kids. I know they must harbor some resentment towards me."

Dina smiles, shaking her head. "You overthink everything. My parents could never hate you. They understand that life is messy and people are complicated."

"I guess," I sigh, though the doubt still lingers.

"Junie!" little Clara yells as she slides into the dining room in her socks, her black velvet dress with white lace and red bows fluttering as she runs. "You're here!"

Her tiny arms wrap around my legs, and Dina shoots me a pointed look.

"We're family, Old June. Always have been, always will be. Even if we're apart for 13 years, we're still family."

My chest tightens at the thought, the weight of the past easing up just a little. I still can't fully believe that Dina's not angry.

"You're sure you aren't harboring any resentment?" I ask, needing to hear it again.

Dina throws her head back and laughs. "I had a few years to prepare for your impending departure and 13 years to forgive you for it." She hitches her shoulder as she finishes setting the elaborate table. "I've made peace with everything. I think it's time you do, too."

I blow out a tired breath. "I'm trying."

"Deen!" Bob's voice booms from the living room. "The boys knocked the tree over again!"

Dina rolls her eyes, a hint of exasperation in her smile. "One day. We can't have just one day without the world falling apart."

I help Bob pick up the tree and hastily rehang the ornaments just before the first guests start arriving. I smile and greet them, but it's all mechanical, like I'm just going through the motions. The truth is, I don't know anyone at this party. In the past 13 years, I've accumulated exactly one friend: Sissy Barnes. Meanwhile, Dina's life is brimming with friends, laughter, and connections that make this house feel so full.

Dina introduces me as her "childhood bestie" every time someone walks through the door, and I try to smile, but the title feels heavy, undeserved. Each time she says it, a dull ache pulses in my chest, a reminder of all the years I let slip away.

The doorbell rings again, for what feels like the millionth time. "June, can you get that?" Dina calls out, light and carefree. I swallow hard and head to the door, bracing myself for another unfamiliar face.

But when I open it, I'm met with a familiar pair of blue eyes.

"June," Patrick says, surprised. "I... hh... didn't know you'd be here."

"I'm sorry," I blurt out, though I'm not sure what I'm apologizing for.

"It's okay," he replies, shaking his head, clearly frustrated by something. His gaze drops to the two girls standing in front of him, their dark hair and navy eyes a mirror image of their father's.

"Hi," I say softly, stepping aside to let them in. "I'm June."

The smaller of the two girls looks up at me, her expression curious. "Who are you?"

"She's a friend of Aunt Dina's," Patrick answers quickly, ushering the girls inside. His tone is polite, but there's a coolness that wasn't there before. And for some reason, the way he says it—just a friend—makes my heart ache a little more.

I linger in the corner as the party buzzes on around me. The laughter and chatter are distant, like they belong to another world, one I'm not really a part of. Bob eventually notices my quiet retreat and hands me a drink. I don't ask what it is; I just down it quickly, letting the warm liquid thaw the chill that's settled deep inside me. Despite the drink, I can't shake the feeling that I'm out of place here, that I don't belong.

Dina, on the other hand, glides effortlessly from room to room, talking to everyone, her laughter lighting up the space. She's always been like this—magnetic and lovely.

"You doing okay?" Dina asks when she breezes by me.

"Great," I lie, forcing a wide smile as I hold up my now-empty glass.

She gives me a knowing look, one that sees right through my facade. "Go talk to him, June."

"Who?" I pretend not to understand, but I know exactly who she means.

"My brother," she says with an exaggerated eye roll.

"I think I'll stay here where it's nice and quiet," I mutter under my breath, trying to avoid the inevitable.

"I heard that!" Dina calls over her shoulder as she disappears into the crowd, a gaggle of kids trailing behind her, all excited for the upcoming Christmas scavenger hunt.

I don't know if it's the drink, Dina's not-so-subtle encouragement, or a mix of both, but something propels me off the wall and into the dining room where Patrick is busy clearing plates from the table.

Our hands reach for the same plate at the same time, and when our fingers touch, it's like sparks fly. But instead of holding my gaze, Patrick quickly looks away, his expression guarded.

"Sorry," he mumbles.

"I, uh," I start, fumbling for words. "Are you okay?"

Patrick's shoulders sag, a long sigh escaping his lips. "No, not really."

"Do you want to talk about it?" I offer, hopeful.

"With you?" Patrick asks, one eyebrow quirking up in surprise.

I shrug, trying to play it cool. "Yeah, with me."

He glances around the room, noting that the girls are happily engaged with Dina and the other kids. After a moment, he nods. "Yeah."

I swallow hard, caught off guard by his agreement. "Outside?"

Patrick smiles, and my heart skips a beat. He's so effortlessly handsome, it's almost unfair. "Yeah," he says again, and this time, there's a hint of something warm in his voice.

I slide open the glass door, leading us out into the crisp night air. Bob's been thoughtful enough to set up outdoor heaters, making the patio a warm, inviting space despite the chill. Under the soft glow of twinkling lights strung overhead, Patrick and I find seats across from each other, the distance between us feeling both too far and just right.

"So, what's going on?" I ask, trying to steady my racing heartbeat. On the inside, I'm still reeling from the fact that we're here, together, talking like this.

Patrick sighs, running a hand through his hair, a gesture that seems to carry the weight of the world. "Georgina, my ex, just told me she's taking the girls out of the country for Christmas and New Year's."

I lean back in my chair, feeling a surge of frustration on his behalf. "I'm really sorry, Patrick."

He shakes his head, a resigned smile on his lips. "It's okay. I didn't fight it. I wanted to, but it would only make things harder for the girls. I don't want them to get caught in the middle because Georgina and I can't figure things out."

"That's really wise of you," I say, meaning it. It's not easy to take the high road, especially when it comes to something as important as your kids.

He lets out a short laugh, though there's no humor in it. "Wise, or just a pushover. She knows I'll give in because I don't want to hurt our girls."

I lean forward slightly, drawn to him by a force I can't quite explain. "From what I've seen, kids usually figure out who's making the sacrifices for them. They know who's really in their corner."

Patrick nods slowly, the tension in his shoulders easing just a bit. "Yeah."

I offer a small smile, hoping it conveys the comfort I'm trying to give. "And Christmas doesn't have to be on the 25th. It can be whatever day you get to spend with the girls. The date doesn't matter as much as the time you share."

He looks at me with a hint of surprise, as if the thought hadn't occurred to him. "You're right, June. Thanks." My heart skips a beat every time he says my name.

"Anytime," I reply, feeling a warmth spread through me that has nothing to do with the heaters.

We fall into a brief silence, the kind that feels oddly comforting rather than awkward. But I know there's more I need to say, something that's been weighing on me for years. I lick my lips, gathering the courage to speak. "Listen, Patrick, I want to apologize—"

He raises a hand, stopping me. "No, you don't need to."

"But I do," I insist. "I'm really sorry for the way things ended between us. I didn't handle it well, and I've carried that regret with me ever since. I was young and I made mistakes, but that doesn't excuse how I hurt you. I... I know I was a terrible person and I'm just so sorry."

Patrick tilts his head slightly, his expression softening. "You weren't a terrible person, June. You were just figuring things out like everyone does. If we all got it right the first time, we'd never learn anything."

His words hit me harder than I expected, and I blink back the tears that well up in my eyes. Even after all this time, he's still as kind and understanding as he ever was. "I guess you're right."

He smiles, that same easy, comforting smile I remember so well. "I know I'm right."

I laugh, a genuine sound that feels like it's been bottled up inside me for too long. The weight on my chest lifts, replaced by a lightness I haven't felt in years.

For so long, I've been telling myself this story—one where Patrick hates me, where every bad thing in my life is just karma coming back to bite me for the choices I made all those years ago. But sitting here with him now, I realize something important: we're not bound by the stories we've told ourselves. We have the power to rewrite them, to give them a different ending.

A rush of boldness sweeps through me. "So," I start, my voice steady but my heart racing, "since you're free on December 25th, would you like to spend it with me? We could go ice skating at Rockefeller Center."

Patrick's eyes lock onto mine, and for a moment, it feels like the world has stopped turning. I can see the thoughts flickering across his face, the memories, the what-ifs, the possibilities of what could be. Then, just when I start to doubt myself, he breaks into a wide, genuine smile—the kind that reaches his eyes and makes my heart skip a beat.

"It's a date," he says softly, the words carrying a promise, a second chance at everything we lost.

And in that moment, I know—we're not just rewriting our story. We're starting a brand new one.

CHAPTER THIRTY
The Deal

"Are you absolutely sure she's going to be here?" I whisper to Dina, huddled beside her in the back of a tiny bookstore on Broadway.

Dina pulls her bucket hat lower, trying to blend in with the crowd. "Positive. I triple-checked her event schedule. She's supposed to be speaking at this book club in," she glances at her watch, "about five minutes."

I peek through my oversized, blacked-out sunglasses, eyeing the small crowd gathering around the coffee station, casually chatting and completely unaware of our intentions.

"You look like a celebrity trying not to get recognized." Dina smirks, adjusting her hat further down.

My heart thumps in my chest, nerves tingling as I scan the room, half-expecting to see her walk through the door any second now. We're here for answers—or maybe just closure—but either way, facing her is going to take everything I've got.

"You're nervous, aren't you?" Dina asks, her voice low as she catches sight of my leg jiggling uncontrollably under the table.

I let out a shaky breath. "Maybe a little."

"You've never liked confrontation," she says, nudging me gently. "But this is your chance, June. She's been sabotaging you for as long as I can remember."

I fidget with the edge of my coat. "What if this just makes things worse? What if she retaliates?"

Dina's eyes flash with persistence. "When hasn't Cheyenne Radcliffe retaliated?"

I sigh, frustration bubbling up. "I just don't understand. Why does she have it out for me?"

Dina leans in, her expression softening. "Because you've always gotten what she wanted."

I blink at her. "What does she want?"

Dina doesn't hesitate. "Patrick, for one. And a writing career she couldn't tear down from behind her keyboard."

"Yeah, I guess that makes sense," I murmur, the realization settling in.

"Speaking of my brother," Dina says in a singsong voice, waggling her eyebrows even though they're half-hidden under her hat. "I hear you two are spending Christmas together?"

I shift in my seat. "About that…"

"You don't need my permission," Dina cuts in, waving her hand dismissively. "We're all grown-ups now. Besides, I have faith that history won't repeat itself."

I let out a slow breath. "You really think so?"

Dina gives me a knowing smile. "That's why you went back in time, right? To make sure you didn't mess up the present."

"No pressure or anything," I mumble.

Dina chuckles softly. "Are we talking about the past, or your first second date on Christmas?"

I bite my lip, eyes wide. "Both."

I can't believe I asked Patrick to spend Christmas with me. Bold move, June. What if we realize we don't have anything in common anymore? Or worse, what if there are long, awkward silences and I have no idea what to say or do?

"Stop spiraling," Dina chides, catching the look on my face. "He's the same Patrick he's always been, and you? You've grown so much. If anything, you're even more amazing now. There's no way he won't fall for you all over again."

But the thing is, it's a ton of pressure. He never let go of me. He bought my books, followed my career... He never really moved on. And if I'm not the person he's built up in his mind—if I'm not this ideal version of me he's been holding onto—then what?

"I don't want to disappoint him," I admit. "He's been holding on for so long."

Dina nods thoughtfully. "You're right, it is a lot of pressure."

"What if we don't fit together anymore?" I say softly, my heart heavy with the fear of all the ways this could go wrong.

She wraps an arm around my shoulders, her curls bouncing beneath her hat. "You'll never know if you don't try."

"I don't want to hurt him again," I whisper, the words catching in my throat.

"No one does." Her gaze softens. "But that's the risk we all take."

I run a hand through my hair, my stomach churning with nerves. "He has kids now. A whole life. Meanwhile, I've just been... surviving. It's intimidating."

Dina tilts her head, studying me. "And you don't think you're intimidating? You're on the bestseller's list, June. You chased your dreams and made them real. Patrick had to adjust his dreams, bend them into shapes he didn't expect. You've been steadfast in yours. That's intimidating, too—just in a different way."

"I never thought of it that way," I reveal, giving a small shrug. Just as I'm about to say more, her grip tightens on my arm.

"She's here," Dina warns urgently, her eyes fixed on the door. "What's the plan?"

"We watch and wait," I whisper back, my gaze locking onto Cheyenne Radcliffe as she strides into the room. She's every bit the image of success in her sharp power suit, her wavy gold hair perfectly styled, and her lips painted a striking red.

"Welcome, everyone," Cheyenne calls out, her voice commanding the space as her heels click sharply against the tile floor. "Give me just a moment to grab a coffee, and we'll get started."

We stay hidden in the back, watching as she glides through the room, her confidence radiating with every step. It's strange seeing her like this—poised, polished, every bit the successful blogger she's built herself up to be. But beneath all that gloss, I know there's so much more to her story. And today, I'm ready to confront it.

The meeting drags on, Cheyenne dominating the conversation with her critical dissection of their current book—a rom-com by an indie author who's a TakTok sensation. She picks apart each chapter, scrutinizing every paragraph with a relentless, almost gleeful cruelty. The realization hits me: Cheyenne has turned tearing down authors into her entire brand. It's unsettling to watch.

"She never stops talking, does she?" Dina laments, leaning closer.

I roll my eyes behind my sunglasses. "I can't believe people actually invite her to speak at these things."

"Right? And people pay for subscriptions to get access to exclusive parts of her blog," Dina divulges, her disbelief clear.

"Oh, wait," I say just loud enough for her to hear, my eyes catching Cheyenne's movements at the front. "Looks like they're wrapping up."

We both shift forward slightly, watching as Cheyenne takes a phone call and retreats to a corner, clearly not wanting to converse with the book club members.

"Still self-centered," Dina grumbles, stifling a yawn.

"And obnoxiously rude," I add, my patience wearing thin.

"You think we should go over there now?" Dina suggests, sounding unimpressed.

I take a steadying breath. "It's now or never."

We weave through the small crowd, my heart pounding as we approach Cheyenne in the corner. She's glued to her phone, oblivious to the world around her. I clear my throat, but she doesn't even glance up. Instead, she holds out her hand, eyes still on her screen.

"Whatever you want me to sign," she says with an annoyed sigh, "just hand it over. I don't have all day."

I pull off my sunglasses, feeling the heat rise in my cheeks. "I'm not here for an autograph." Her eyes finally snap up to mine, recognition spreading across her face like a flame to gasoline. "I came to ask why you spend your time tearing down authors just to make a profit. Don't you have anything better to do?"

Cheyenne blinks, clearly taken aback, but her expression quickly hardens into one of practiced indifference. The ball's in her court now, and I'm ready for whatever comes next.

"Ah, June Nelson," Cheyenne tsks with an air of superiority. "I wondered when you'd find me."

"You were waiting for me?" I ask, whipping my head back in surprise.

She crosses her arms over her chest, her smirk widening. "You were bound to figure out who I was eventually. I just assumed it'd be sooner than this."

"Why?" I ask, shaking my head, still not understanding.

"Why what?"

"Why have you made it your mission to destroy my writing career?"

Cheyenne's eyes flick between Dina and me before settling on me, a slow smile spreading across her face. "You're a great writer, June. Everyone knows it. You write stories that come from your heart, but that doesn't always mean they translate well to the page. We work in an industry where every piece of work has a shot at bestseller status. There's no formula or guidelines to follow for success. It's about timing, luck, and hard work."

"I'm so confused right now," I groan, feeling the ground shift beneath me.

Cheyenne leans in slightly, her voice soft but edged with confidence. "Look, June, I make a living by being brutally honest about my opinions. You can call me mean, but I'm entitled to say how I feel about a piece of writing. Art is subjective, even books. I never set out to target you specifically. But you don't take risks with your writing. You always play it safe. I mean, other than *Midnight Crown*, have you really written another book that pushes boundaries the way that one did?"

I fold my arms defensively. "People don't want to read what I want to write about. They want... They want something different."

"*Retrospective* is good," Cheyenne concedes, "but it's predictable. It's another easy read full of surface emotions.

You're good at churning out the same romance book with different characters and settings. I'm glad *Retrospective* is doing well, but for your next book? Give it your all, June. Write the story you're afraid to write. What do you have to lose?"

I blink, taken aback. "Are you actually giving me advice?"

"Now I'm the one who's confused," Dina interjects.

Cheyenne rolls her eyes. "I'm saying you're better than the work you put out. Show me that, and you'll get your glowing review."

"Why should I believe you?" My voice wavers, the vulnerability creeping in. "You just spent the last 45 minutes tearing apart a book someone poured their heart into."

"Everyone's standards are different," Cheyenne counters with a shrug. "I'm a picky reader, and that book was just… fine."

I exhale, steeling myself. "Alright. I'll make you a deal."

Cheyenne's eyes glint with amusement. "A deal?"

"I write the book I want to write—I take a risk and push boundaries—and you adjust your impossibly high review standards."

Cheyenne extends her hand, her smile cunning. "Deal."

"Seriously?" Dina squeaks beside me, her eyes wide.

"I want an advanced copy," Cheyenne says, her eyebrow arching in challenge. "And an acknowledgment in the back of the book."

"You're pushing it," I warn, my eyes narrowing.

"It's business, June," she retorts with a sly smile.

"Fine," I say, shaking her hand firmly, sealing the most unexpected deal of my life.

"The bestseller's list suits you, June." Cheyenne clicks her tongue and strides off, her heels echoing against the floor. "See you around."

Dina and I stand there, watching her get into a sleek black SUV that pulls up to the curb. We exchange bewildered looks, both of us still processing what just happened.

"Well, that didn't go how I thought it would." I tilt my head as the SUV drives away.

"It was... surprisingly civil," Dina sighs, shaking her head. "Maybe she actually is rooting for you."

We look at each other, then burst into laughter, the absurdity of it all settling in.

Who would have thought?

CHAPTER THIRTY-ONE
A Christmas Date

I'm late. Of course, I'm late. It's our second first date, and I'm scrambling through New York City traffic that's been driving me nuts for weeks. But as frustrating as it is, there's something undeniably magical about Christmas time in the city—twinkling lights, bustling sidewalks, and that crisp, festive chill in the air.

My phone buzzes in my hand, and I answer without even glancing at the screen. "Hello?"

"JUNE NELSON!" Dina's voice practically explodes through the phone. "You better not be standing Patrick up. Or worse, time-traveling again."

"It's the traffic," I huff, weaving through the crowd. "I'm, like, two minutes away."

"Are you sure?" Dina sounds skeptical, like she's bracing for another one of my infamous delays.

"I'm positive," I assure her, picking up my pace even more. "Wait, how do you know I'm running late?"

"Well, he may have, um," Dina hesitates before continuing, "sent me a text asking if I'd heard from you. I think he was worried you were ghosting him."

"I do have a history of ghosting," I admit, the sting of my past mistakes creeping in.

"That's not who you are anymore," Dina says firmly. "You've got to let go of the guilt for the things you did when you were younger."

"You're right, Deen," I murmur, dodging a street vendor. The distant sounds of carolers and laughter fill the background. "I always thought it would take a miracle to forgive myself, but maybe it's not about forgiveness. Maybe it's just about healing."

"And in healing, you find forgiveness?" Dina adds softly, completing my thought.

"Yeah," I say, smiling a little.

"That's a beautiful thought, June," she replies. "Almost sounds like the plot of your next book."

I roll my eyes even though she can't see me. "You're relentless."

"I take that as a compliment." She laughs.

"I've gotta go," I say, catching sight of my destination. "I'm almost there."

"Have fun, June," Dina tells me. "I love you."

"I love you, too," I reply, feeling my heart skip a beat.

We hang up, and I spot Patrick pacing at the corner of 49th, his figure illuminated by the city's glow. I quicken my steps, nerves and excitement coursing through me. Here goes nothing.

"I'm sorry," I blurt out the second I'm in front of Patrick, breathless from my rush. "Traffic was insane."

He smiles, a mix of relief and a touch of anticipation glimmering in his eyes. "No worries."

I swallow, nerves bubbling up again. "You look great." And he does—dark wash jeans, a black leather jacket, and a scarf loosely wrapped around his neck. He looks like a dream I've been holding onto, finally stepping into reality.

"So do you," he says, his gaze lingering a moment longer than necessary.

I fidget slightly, my camel-colored coat suddenly feeling too warm. "Thanks."

As we walk toward the rink, Patrick nudges me gently. "Have you ever skated here before?"

I shake my head. "No, but I did come for the Christmas tree lighting a few years back. My agent, Sissy, insisted we get here at lunchtime just to snag a decent spot."

Patrick chuckles, his elbow brushing mine, sending a fiery spark through me. "Not something you'd rush to do again?"

I laugh softly. "Probably not. But with the right people," I glance at him and shrug, "maybe I'd reconsider."

His laugh is warm, wrapping around me like a cozy blanket on a cold night.

"I've got the tickets," I say, pulling them from my bag as we reach the bustling entrance of the rink.

Patrick takes them, his eyes widening slightly. "You got premium tickets? June, these are so expensive. You didn't have to do that."

I shrug, a small smile playing at my lips. Sissy got them for me. A gift from my very elated publisher. "I missed a lot of Christmases with you. A lot of moments we should have had. This is just my way of making up for it."

He pauses, turning to look at me with a soft expression, like he's trying to figure out if I'm real or not. "You don't have to make up for anything. I'm not expecting you to."

"I know," I say, my smile growing. "But I think I'm doing it for myself."

Patrick nods, a slow smile spreading across his face. "Okay."

"Okay?" I tilt my head, feeling a little more at ease.

"If this is for you, then okay," he agrees, his eyes never leaving mine.

"Okay." This time, I say it with a new kind of certainty. "Let's go."

We grab our rental skates, stash our stuff in a locker, and step out onto the ice. The whole rink sparkles under the glow of the massive Christmas tree, and as we glide onto the ice, it feels like the magic of the city has wrapped itself around us, a perfect backdrop for our second chance.

As we continue to skate, Patrick reaches for my hand, and even through the layers of our gloves, I feel the warmth of his touch. The city around us blurs in glowing hues of purples, blues, and creams, and everything feels both familiar and new. We don't talk much, but every time Patrick laughs, it's like a gentle reminder that forgiveness really is about healing—about letting go of who you were when you were just trying to figure things out.

I was only 21 when I walked away from Patrick in that bar, just a kid who thought she knew what the world looked like. Since then, my life has been small and quiet, but it's been mine. I've chased dreams, stumbled through the wrong relationships, and learned a lot about myself along the way. I could spend forever regretting those choices, or I could embrace the fact that every twist and turn brought me right back here—to Patrick. And this time, I'm not the same girl who ran away. I'm older, a little wiser, and I understand the value of getting it wrong so you can finally get it right.

And Patrick? He's had his own journey. He's lived a full life, busy and complicated, but he's still standing here with me.

"You look deep in thought," Patrick says as we glide along the ice. His voice pulls me back to the moment, and I squeeze his hand a little tighter.

"Just thinking about everything we've been through to get here," I admit.

He nods, his grip steady and reassuring. "Yeah, I get that."

"Would you change anything?" I ask, curious about what's been on his mind.

Patrick takes a moment, his eyes reflecting the glow of the lights around us. "I don't think so. Would you?"

I chew on the inside of my cheek, considering my answer. "Maybe I would've been a little kinder to myself."

"I get that," he muses. "Life's tough enough without us making it harder on ourselves."

I can't help but smile at him, adoration spreading through my chest. "Look at you, all sage and wise."

He laughs, a playful glint in his eyes. "Must be the Aquarius in me."

I throw my head back and laugh with him. "You're really going to credit your whole personality to the stars?"

He shrugs with a teasing grin. "You don't think the universe had a hand in bringing us back together?"

For a moment, I almost forget how to breathe. If it weren't for that unexpected trip back in time, who knows if we'd be here now, skating under the twinkling lights of Rockefeller Center. "Maybe just a little," I say, letting the hope linger between us. "By the way, thank you for finding Sissy for me. Without her, I never would have become the writer I am today."

"You're welcome, June," he says, appreciation shining in his gorgeous eyes.

We fall into a comfortable silence again, our gloved fingers intertwined as we glide across the ice. Snow flurries start to drift down, soft and gentle, and I glance up, a laugh bubbling out of me.

"It's snowing," I say, feeling a lightness in my chest.

Patrick glances up too, a smile tugging at the corners of his mouth. "It is. What do you say we get out of here and find something to eat?"

I nod. "I don't know how you feel about lasagna on Christmas, but I've got a frozen one in my freezer."

"Perfect." Patrick grins, his smile lighting up the moment.

We return our skates, gather our things, and, by some miracle, manage to hail a cab in the snowy chaos. The drive to my apartment is slow and sweet, the city lights sparkling against the falling snow. Patrick slips off his glove and takes my hand in the backseat, his touch sending sparks through me. We share a quiet smile, and I can't help but tuck a strand of hair behind my ear, feeling a flutter of excitement.

When we arrive, Patrick pays the driver, and we make our way up to my apartment on the second floor. The snow is coming down in thick, fluffy flakes now, and I don't think the city has ever looked so magical.

"Bathroom's down the hall," I say as I toss my coat over the back of the couch. "I'll get dinner started."

Patrick disappears down the hall, and I exhale, releasing a breath I didn't realize I'd been holding. I can hardly believe he's here, in my home, about to share dinner with me. It feels surreal, like something out of a dream—or maybe a miracle. I wasn't sure I believed in miracles before that stop sign smacked me in the face, but now? Now, I'm starting to think they might be real.

"How long have you lived in the city?" Patrick asks as I slide the lasagna into the oven.

"I moved here after college graduation," I say, leaning back against the counter. "So... 12 years."

"Do you ever miss home?"

I cross my arms over my chest, considering his question. "Sometimes."

Patrick pulls out a chair and sits down, his gaze steady on me. "Do you ever wonder who you'd be today if you never left?"

I shake my head. "No. I was suffocating there." I notice his expression shift, so I quickly add, "Because of my dad and Lily. Mostly Lily."

"Dina said you patched things up with her."

I laugh softly, a little amazed by the thought. "Yeah. Turns out she's not so bad after all."

Patrick nods, his voice gentle. "We all have heavy things to carry. Lily wasn't immune to that."

"No," I agree. "She wasn't."

Patrick leans back, changing the subject. "If you'd asked me a month ago what I'd be doing for Christmas, I never would have guessed I'd be here."

I swallow, feeling the weight of his words. "Can I ask you something about the other night?"

"Sure," Patrick replies, leaning forward, his navy eyes catching the soft light in the room.

"You, uh, seemed like you weren't interested in..." I gesture vaguely between us. "You and me."

He clicks his tongue thoughtfully. "I was just caught off guard."

"Oh," I murmur, the quietness of my voice reflecting the uncertainty in my heart.

"For a long time, I hoped we'd run into each other again," he confesses. "But as the years went by and we didn't, I tried to push that hope away. Then, when I saw you sitting there, it felt like someone punched me in the gut."

"I'm sorry," I apologize, feeling a little guilty.

"I didn't know what to say or how to act," he admits, his tone almost shy. "But I never gave up hope that one day, we might find our way back to each other."

My heart races, thudding in my chest like hooves on hard earth. "I think I always hoped for that too."

"My life is very, uh, complicated," Patrick says, hesitation lacing every word.

"I gathered as much," I reply, meeting his gaze.

"My girls are so young," he explains, the weight of his responsibilities clear in every word. "And they need me."

"I know," I say with a gentle smile, the thought of him as a devoted father warming my heart.

"I haven't dated since my divorce two years ago."

"You've been busy raising kids," I remind him, understanding the sacrifices he's made.

He nods, but his expression remains serious. "I just remember how hurt you were when your dad married Lily so soon after your mom left."

"I was," I tell him, the memory still tender. "But you know, my dad said something to me once about that." I pause, recalling the words he said to me while I was in the past. *I fell in love again, and I didn't want you to think that just because someone leaves us, we stop loving. We don't. We have to keep going, keep believing in love. We don't shut down just because something didn't work out.* "I thought he was crazy for moving on so fast, but the truth is that we only have so much time. It goes fast. Love, it waits for no one. So, we should grab it with both hands when it does come around."

"You sound like a writer," Patrick says with a wistful smile.

"I am one," I respond playfully. "And you know, you shouldn't let the things I went through affect how you live your life. My circumstances were different. My mom left, and I didn't have much contact with her. That was hard as a teenager."

"You're right." Patrick sighs, the tension in his shoulders easing just a little.

I reach across the table, placing my hand gently on top of his. "I'm not going anywhere. I know I haven't always kept my promises in the past, but I'm not that same girl anymore. However long it takes, whatever you need to do, I'm going to be here."

"We'll go slow then," he agrees, though a frown tugs at the corners of his mouth.

"Why do you look so disappointed?" I ask, teasing him gently.

"Because I really want to ask you to marry me right now." His voice is filled with both hope and nerves.

My heart skips a beat, the words clogging my throat in the best way. "R-really?"

"Yeah," he says, a bit more sure of himself, though the nervousness is still there.

"Before you ask," I say, trying to contain the grin threatening to stretch across my face, "you should probably taste my cooking first. It's not great. And a lifetime of frozen lasagna is about all I can offer."

He laughs, and the sound is like a balm to my soul, healing something that's been cracked and broken for far too long. "I'd eat lasagna every day of my life if it meant I got to spend it with you."

My eyes well up with tears as I stare at the man I never stopped loving, the man who's always been the love of my life.

"It's settled, then," I say with a cheeky grin. "Lasagna every day, forever."

Patrick rises from his seat and moves toward me. As I stand to meet him, his fingers gently thread through my hair, and after 13 long years, he kisses me again—just like we were never apart.

CHAPTER THIRTY-TWO
The One Where We're All Together

The room is warm and filled with the soft glow of fairy lights strung around Dina's living room. We're nestled together on her oversized sectional, the perfect spot to end the year and begin a new chapter. Dina, Bob, the kids, Patrick, and I—all together, just as she wanted.

The kids are curled up in blankets, their eyes heavy with sleep as the clock inches closer to midnight. Dina is holding Bob Junior, who's already drifted off, his tiny hand clutching her mother's sweater. Bob has an arm around Dina, his other hand resting on the back of the couch as if protecting his family from the world. And Hank the Tank is sprawled out in front of the fireplace, snoring loudly.

Patrick sits next to me, his presence both comforting and exhilarating. He's been quiet tonight, lost in thought after his call with his daughters earlier. I could see the strain it took on him, the ache of missing them when they're so far away in London. But I know they'll be okay. They have Patrick, and he's the kind of father who loves with his whole heart. Even from across an ocean, he'll make sure they know that.

I glance around the room, feeling a swell of emotion in my chest. This—this is what I've been searching for all along. A place to belong, a sense of peace, and the knowledge that I'm finally enough. It's taken me so long to realize that I don't need anyone else to validate my worth. Not my mother, not anyone. I am enough, just as I am.

Veronica Nelson may have given me life, but the person I've become—that's all me. The courage to face the world, to love fiercely, and to forgive myself—that's mine. I'm no longer the girl who left Patrick behind, scared of what might happen if I stayed. I'm the woman who's ready to embrace the future, knowing that I'm stronger than I ever believed.

The countdown begins, and the room fills with faint laughter and the sounds of the TV announcing the final seconds of the year. I reach for Patrick's hand, and he squeezes it, his thumb brushing gently over my knuckles. It's a simple touch, but it speaks volumes—of second chances, of new beginnings, and of the love that has always been there, waiting for the right time.

"Ten, nine, eight..." Voices around us chant, and I find myself holding my breath.

As the countdown reaches its end, I look over at Patrick, his eyes meeting mine with that familiar twinkle that makes my heart skip a beat.

"Three, two, one... Happy New Year!"

The room erupts in hushed cheers, and I turn to Patrick just as the first fireworks light up the night sky outside the window. He leans in, his lips brushing mine in a kiss that feels like belonging, respect, trust, and *home*. It's soft and sweet, full of promise for the future.

When we pull back, he rests his forehead against mine, his breath warm against my skin. "This year," he whispers, "is going to be our year."

I smile, feeling the truth of his words deep in my heart. "Yeah," I whisper back, "it is."

The fireworks continue outside, but in this moment, all I can focus on is Patrick, Dina's laughter in the background, and the overwhelming sense that I'm exactly where I'm meant to be.

For the first time in a long time, I know I'm enough. And that's the best way to start a new year.

Patrick and I help Dina and Bob carry the kids upstairs to their beds.

As I hold little Clara, she gives me a sleepy smile and mumbles, "Junie, you make my mom happy."

I return her smile and reply softly, "She makes me happy, too."

"Why were you kissing Uncle Patrick?" Clara asks, her tiny voice demanding an answer even as her eyes droop.

I chuckle, brushing a stray curl from her forehead. "Because I love him."

"Gross." Clara scrunches up her nose, the gentle glow of her ballerina night light illuminating her sweet expression.

I tuck her in, pulling the covers snug around her. "I'll see you in the morning, okay?"

"Bye, Junie," she murmurs before rolling over and closing her eyes.

As I step into the hallway, I run into Dina, and we share a quiet laugh. Then, without warning, she wraps me in a tight hug, and I feel all the years we spent apart—heavy and hard—melt away like snow under the warmth of the sun.

"I've missed you," Dina utters softly, holding me close. "Really missed you."

"I'm sorry it took me so long to get here," I reply, each word thick with emotion.

Dina pulls back just enough to look me in the eye. "You were worth the wait."

"Thank you for keeping my time-travel secret," I tell her, the weight of gratitude evident in my words.

She smiles, a mischievous twinkle in her eye. "I want to show you something."

Taking my hand, she leads me into her and Bob's bedroom. With a flick of the switch, the room is bathed in golden light, and she points to a shelf next to the bed. All my books are lined up, neatly displayed.

Tears well up in my eyes. "You have a bookshelf full of my books."

Dina nods, her smile tender. "I've read every one at least a dozen times."

"You didn't have to," I say, touched by the gesture.

"It helped make the time go by a little faster," she confesses.

"I'm glad." I sigh, feeling the gravity of all we've shared.

"So," she laughs softly, "why did you go back in time? Did you ever figure it out?"

I take a deep breath, searching for the right words. "I think I'm still figuring it out, but I know one of the main reasons was to see myself, my dad, Lily, you and Patrick in a different light. To repair all the broken relationships. To find out that I always had a mom. It just wasn't the one I thought it was. I needed to hear my dad say one more time that I've always been enough just as I am. I thought I had to be different or chase things that everyone else was chasing. But he always told me I was enough, and I finally believe it."

Dina tilts her head, her eyes filled with understanding. "Did you find anything out there while you were wandering that made the journey a little easier?"

I exhale slowly. "Not really. Maybe just Sissy."

"Oh, June," Dina says, her voice full of affection. "I'm glad you finally came home to us."

"Me, too," I respond, knowing that I'm exactly where I'm meant to be.

I leave Dina as Bob walks into the room, giving me a wink before I quietly slip down the stairs. The house is warm and peaceful, the kind of quiet that wraps around you like the arms of someone you love.

Patrick is waiting on the couch, and when he sees me, he stands. I walk over to him, my heart melting as he pulls me close.

"You know," he begins with a smile, "you've never looked more beautiful to me than you do right now."

I chuckle lightly, brushing my fingers across his face. "You have to stop saying things like that."

He hesitates for a moment, worry flickering in his eyes. "I know it's only been a week, but when I look at you, all I can see is my future."

His words make my heart squeeze in my chest. "I'm sorry for all the years we wasted."

Patrick gently tucks a strand of hair behind my ear. "The truth is, we both had a lot of growing up to do."

"We did," I agree, feeling the loss of those years.

"And some of us didn't need a trip to the past to figure that out," Patrick says, a teasing smile tugging at the corners of his lips.

My mouth falls open in surprise. "What?"

"You really thought I wouldn't piece it together?" he asks, a playful glint in his eyes. "Dina's never been great at keeping her voice down, especially during late-night phone calls. Old June? Isn't that what she called you? And when you asked me about the future on our way to Plainer's the day after Dina's 17th birthday, and casually dropped the word 'dabble,' it was pretty clear something was up."

I laugh in disbelief, suddenly feeling whole. "Dina and I really need to work on our subtlety, don't we?"

Patrick's eyes sparkle as he looks at me. "I've always paid attention to the little things about you. At first, I wasn't sure what to believe, but when you walked into that pub after 13 years apart, something just clicked. The way you looked at me... It was exactly like those weeks before Christmas my senior year. I knew then that something extraordinary had happened, something that had changed you. But whatever it was, it brought you back to me, and that's all that matters."

"I... don't really know what to say," I admit, still trying to wrap my head around the fact that he knew all along. "I can't believe you figured it out."

He chuckles. "It was 17 years ago, and you never spoke to me until that day. Not a word—well, not a coherent one, anyway," he adds with a laugh. "Then, out of nowhere, you were suddenly forming entire sentences."

"You knew," I repeat, shaking my head in disbelief.

"Dina's not the only one who can keep a secret," he says, his tone soft and reassuring.

"I know that now," I reply, feeling an overwhelming sense of gratitude and relief.

Patrick looks at me, his expression serious. "I know you probably never heard it enough when we were younger, but you're perfect just the way you are. You're perfect for the people who know you and love you. I watched you struggle with that while we were together. I should have said something, but I didn't know how to say it in a way that you would hear me."

"Thank you for saying it now," I whisper, touched by his words.

Patrick shrugs lightly. "Thank you for hearing it now."

I lean in and kiss him, the moment feeling like a dream I never want to wake up from. Reluctantly, we pull apart, whisper good night to one another, and then I head down the hall to Bob's office, where the trundle bed is set up for me. Patrick stays on the couch, the promise of coffee and breakfast together in the morning to look forward to.

As I fall into bed, I take a deep, sobering breath. A month ago, my life was falling apart at the seams. Now? Now it's everything I've ever dreamed of. Everything I've been waiting for. Everything I know I deserve after years of feeling unworthy.

I've learned a lot of lessons, made a lot of mistakes, but I'm rewriting the ending because it's never too late. It's never too late for a plot twist or a second chance.

Sometimes, the hardest story to write is your own. But you should write it anyway. Because you might just find that you were always enough. And you always will be for the right people.

Epilogue

Dear Mom,

I'm not sure if I'll ever send this, but my therapist says it's a good idea to write it down anyway—something about finding closure or at least a piece of it.

I'm doing well, really. I just finished my latest book. It's still untitled because I'm not quite sure what to call it yet. It's a personal one, a story about us—about two people bound by blood and name, but little else. I used to wish that weren't true, that we could be two people who went through something hard together and then reconnected. I wish forgiveness flowed between us like a gentle stream over river rocks. But instead, there's been darkness. And somehow, I've learned to make peace with that.

I could tell you that you failed me, but we're all only human. I'm not a mother yet, so I can't understand all of its unique challenges, but I know it was hard for you. I know you struggled to love me and to love yourself.

No one knows this, but Patrick and I are trying for a baby, and I plan on being the kind of mother I always needed when I was younger. The kind of mother who stays no matter how hard things get.

Patrick and I are doing good. After our wedding last month, we bought the house across the street from Dina and Bob. Turns out, sometimes you do get to eat meals with your best friend every day, even in adulthood. You'd love Patrick's girls, Stella and Rory. They're perfect, just like him.

I'm still figuring out how to be a stepmother, but I've got the best guide in the world—Lily. We've had our moments, but now we share a quiet, gentle forgiveness, something serene and peaceful. She's even started dating again after we talked about moving on. Bud Nelson was quite a man, and he's not easy to get over. I don't know how you did it. Then again, maybe you never slowed down long enough to realize what you lost when you left.

It's been a while since I've called. My first instinct is to apologize because I've always felt it was my job to fix things. But I'm learning that I don't have to apologize for how I spend my time. I don't have to mend things I didn't break. And I certainly don't owe anyone an explanation for how I choose to heal the pieces of my heart. So, I haven't called in a while. My life is full now, with people who love me, people who want to answer my calls.

When you left, it opened the door to the hardest part of my life. My therapist says you might have your own trauma that you're running from, and that I should keep that in mind as I write this. If you have your own pain, I hope you find the strength to face it one day. I hope you learn to love yourself enough to create a life that feels good on the inside, not just one that looks good on the outside.

As for forgiveness, I think it's important that you know—I forgive you for leaving. I forgive you for the hurt, for breaking Dad's heart. Somehow, your leaving was the best thing that could have happened to us. It made us stronger. It made me stronger.

I'll be traveling again soon after my latest book is released. Sissy Barnes, my agent, has helped me navigate my newfound success. Turns out, I really did have it in me to become a bestseller. Just took me a little while to figure it all out.

My publisher gave me a nice advance, which is how Patrick and I managed to buy the house across from Dina and Bob. My life... It's perfect, Mom. And I have you to thank for some of that.

I love you. Even if you don't love me back, or don't know how to, I love you. And I love the journey I've been on ever since you said goodbye. But now it's time for me to say goodbye. Goodbye to years of waiting for you to call me back. Goodbye to the memories you didn't want to share. Goodbye to the past. To everything it was, and everything it wasn't.

Love,
June
(Your daughter, in case you forgot)

About the Author

Jessi Hansen grew up in sunny San Diego County before falling head-over-heels in love with an Oklahoma boy.

After moving halfway across the country to be with him, she quickly adapted to small town life. Now, she spends her days chasing children, chickens, and the occasional tornado.

When she's not microwaving her cup of coffee for the umpteenth time, reading stories to her children or watching her husband operate heavy machinery (swoon), Jessi is crafting stories about sassy, sensitive heroines and their complex male counterparts. Family, friendship and feel-good endings are her specialty.

You can find more stories by Jessi at
authorjh.com

Find Jessi on social media!
Goodreads – Jessi Hansen
Instagram – authorjessihansen
Tik Tok – authorjessihansen

More Books By Jessi Hansen

The Firsts Series
Firsts Are Always Messy
Sloppy Seconds
Third Time's A Charm
Ava's Choice
Managing Mia
Love Taylor
Inspiring Izzy

The Kit Clark Series
Lede
Beat

Fused Fates Series
Fire
Fury

Standalones
Give Yourself Away
The Summer of Wild
This Ain't My Town

www.ingramcontent.com/pod-product-compliance
Lightning Source LLC
LaVergne TN
LVHW041907070526
838199LV00051BA/2533